Green Kills

Green Kills

Avi Domoshevizki

Green Kills/ Avi Domoshevizki

This book is a work of fiction. Any resemblance to actual events or persons, living or dead, is entirely coincidental.

Translated from Hebrew by Yaron Regev
Editor of the Hebrew edition: Amnon Jackont
Copyediting of the English edition: Julie MacKenzie
of Free Range Editorial

ISBN-10: 151469896X
ISBN-13: 978-1514698969

Contact: avidomoshevizki@gmail.com

To my Dear Parents

Where large sums of money are concerned, it is advisable to trust nobody.

(Agatha Christie)

The true mystery of the world is the visible, not the invisible.

(Oscar Wilde)

Prologue

New York, September 6, 2012, 8:30 AM

Overly fancy offices had always filled Ronnie with a sense of unease. He was a man of deeds, not of appearances. The reception area of the venture capital fund he had entered cried out, "There's money here, and lots of it." Above the receptionist's desk hung a painting from Matisse's dancer series, and Ronnie had no doubt it was an original. He couldn't shake the feeling that the receptionist was chosen because of her skinny ballerina look as well.

The phone in his pocket vibrated. He fished it out and read: I'll bet you whatever you want that she's hot. He didn't have to see the sender's name. It was Gadi. Ever since Ronnie had moved to the United States, the two of them had felt like separated twins. They spoke on the phone daily, shared the details of their lives with one another, and mainly missed each other terribly.

The receptionist fixed a pair of green, questioning eyes on him.

"My name is Ronnie Saar. I'm here to see David Lammar."

"Follow me, please." She smiled as if she'd been waiting all morning for his arrival.

He followed her perfect rear end to a conference room with clear glass walls proudly meant to declare: "Transparency and business integrity are the name of the game." Ronnie knew from experience that the declaration was completely unfounded.

"David, the managing partner, will join you in a moment," she remarked with the professional indifference of a flight attendant. "Would you like something to drink? Something cold, perhaps? Coffee?"

"A glass of water please."

"Perrier or Evian?"

"It doesn't matter. Whatever you like best."

"I prefer Evian."

"Evian will be perfect," Ronnie hurried to answer, careful to maintain his companion's level of seriousness.

The young woman leaned forward, keeping her long legs stretched. With robotic efficiency, she took out a bottle of Evian water from an office refrigerator hidden within a cabinet. She removed the bottle cap with a swift unscrewing motion and poured Ronnie half a glass. The half empty bottle was placed to his left, in the center of a copper foil coaster embossed with the logo of one of the fund's portfolio companies.

"He'll be here soon," she promised and tiptoed out while tugging at the hem of her pencil skirt.

Ronnie took a sip of the water. He couldn't taste any difference between the fancy bottled water and regular tap water and smiled with irony as he recalled how, during his military service, the mere knowledge of available water would bring about indescribable pleasure. Then he fished the telephone from his pocket once more and sent Gadi a message: Hot indeed. But like many other things in this office, completely fake. He left the phone next to him and, as was his custom, allowed his eyes to wander about and investigate, etching in his mind each and every detail in the room.

The company's logo, an image of a four-armed woman at its center with the name of the fund displayed above her head: Visions Partners LLC, was engraved on the glass wall in front of him. He liked the symbolic usage of Lakshmi, the Hindu goddess of wealth and prosperity. It had a touch of sophistication, as well as a wink and a nod to the vast Indian market. Plaques and trophies — tombstones, as the bankers are proud to call them — of every imaginable shape and color sat on low mahogany chests against the glass walls. Each proudly displayed the name of a company belonging to the fund and the amount invested in it. Additional plaques boasted the names of other companies and the amounts at which they had been sold. Ronnie had a memento just like that at home, somewhere in the attic. It had been given to him by the bankers who had led the sale of his company to Johnson & Johnson two years ago. They'd earned more than eight million dollars from the sale, while Ronnie had received a Plexiglas trophy engraved with the name of his company, the buyer's name, and a quite inconceivable number beneath them — four hundred and eighty million dollars. It was the day on which his life had changed. From a penniless kibbutz member who lived off of scholarships and often settled for one meal a day — he instantly became a millionaire who never needed to be worried about having livelihood challenges again.

Ronnie shifted his gaze to the Matisse dance painting beyond the glass partition.

"I see the painting has piqued your interest," he heard a voice to his right say. "My rivals accuse me of a tendency for ostentation. Those who know me better realize that I simply have a weak spot for beautiful things."

Ronnie rose from his seat.

"David Lammar." The man extended his hand.

"Ronnie Saar. Pleased to meet you." The handshake was firm and lasted about three seconds, enough time to create the impression of personal attention, yet not ingratiating or sticky.

David sat by Ronnie's side and angled his chair toward him. "As you would imagine, we've researched you quite a bit, and I have to admit we were very impressed by what we found. What we weren't able to find was just as impressive. I understand you served in a secret Israeli army unit, and you're still on reserve duty even though you live in the United States. Is that correct?"

"I don't see how this has anything to do with the matter I've come here to discuss," answered Ronnie, attempting to subdue the resistance rising in him toward this intrusion. "Yes, I served in the Israeli army and yes, I still do my duty for my country by serving my quota of reserve days. But since then I've also finished a PhD in biological engineering at MIT and founded a successful company that was acquired by J&J. I think that's what I have to sell, not one mysterious story or another from thc time I was eighteen."

"You're right," David said with a forced smile. "I just want to make sure you weren't a professional assassin or something of that nature."

Ronnie didn't answer.

"OK, let's drop the subject," David said, drawing out his words and using the time to prepare the next topic of conversation. "We in the fund believe that your area of specialty, the medical market, will become the next big thing in the coming years. We've decided to recruit in advance a top-notch team, experts in this particular field, in order to strategically strengthen our next fund."

"Your next fund?" Ronnie was surprised.

"Yes, we've been running our second fund for the last two years. A year or two from today we plan on starting to raise funds for our third one." David went silent and following a brief pause added, "I hope you realize everything we're discussing must remain in this room. Consider yourself having signed a nondisclosure agreement."

Ronnie nodded his agreement.

"As you can see," David said, gesturing toward the tombstones commemorating deals, "we've had quite a few successes. So far, we've earned our first fund's investors five times their initial investments,[1] and we've still to exhaust the profit potential. The fund's portfolio contains at least five additional promising companies that may in themselves double or triple the profits returned to investors." David smiled, allowing the impressive information to sink in. "Regarding the second fund, I can tell you that in our last annual meeting with the fund's investors, which took place about a month ago, we hinted to them that based on information we now have, the second fund may outshine the performance of the first one." He casually poured himself some water from the bottle standing in front of Ronnie and drank slowly.

"The third fund, which, as I've already mentioned, we'll begin to raise money for in about two years, will be in a league of its own. This time we intend to raise eight hundred million dollars. This requires, of course, a different level of organizational preparation," his voice rose with restrained enthusiasm, "and this is why you're here, with me. If you prepared yourself for a job interview, I'll have to disappoint you. There'll be no interview. We simply want you. Assuming we can agree on the terms, you can start tomorrow."

David paused, indicating with a gesture that it was Ronnie's turn to speak. He knew exactly what he was

---

[1] The money raised by venture capital funds is invested by them in start-up companies in return for holdings (shares) in these companies. When a start-up company is sold or goes public on the stock market, the money earned is forwarded to investors until all the monies invested in the fund are returned. For each additional dollar earned, the fund investors receive eighty cents and the fund, twenty cents.

about to hear. Ninety-eight percent of the interviewees, no matter how brilliant, slapped infantile smiles on their faces and thanked him with banal responses such as, "I promise I won't let you down."

But Ronnie remained calm and matter-of-fact. "Thank you for the trust you and the other partners are placing in me, but before I can respond to the offer, it's important for me to know more about the course of the career I can expect while working for the fund."

"A good point." David hid his embarrassment behind a compliment. "You'll start as a senior associate[2] in the current fund. If you prove yourself in the course of the next two years, you'll be promoted to the position of partner in the next fund. You do realize, of course, this is an unusually fast promotion in our field. On the other hand, if you aren't good enough — perhaps 'good' is not the right word to use, 'brilliant and committed' may better describe our requirements — then less than two years from now our ways shall part. We've had three senior associates in the first fund, all Harvard graduates. None of them are still with us today. They were very good, I must admit, but not exceptionally excellent. It's all or nothing. That's our philosophy. All or nothing," he repeated quietly.

---

[2] A senior associate normally works alongside a veteran or senior partner (or several such partners) and assists in locating and analyzing investment opportunities. In the major funds, service in such a position is limited to a period of two to four years, following which the junior partner is promoted, if he has proven himself, or is fired.

"Indeed a fast promotion track, and thank you for presenting the less attractive route," Ronnie replied evenly. "How would you like to proceed?"

"Do you have interviews with other funds?" asked David.

"Three more. I've done my second interview at two of them and was invited for a final meeting at both. With the third one I've passed a human resources interview and was invited to meet the senior partners."

"Which funds, if I may ask?"

"I'd rather not provide that information. None of the funds have made me an offer, and perhaps won't do so in the future, therefore I see no point in sharing their names at this stage," answered Ronnie calmly, looking at David's manicured hands, which he felt had delved too deeply into his life.

"Discretion is an important quality in our industry," David muttered, half mockingly. "What I'm about to offer you was agreed upon by all the partners.[3] We don't believe in dragging our feet. As I stated, we've done our homework and researched you; now all that remains is to finalize the terms." He glanced at his watch, and with perfect timing the door opened and an Asian-looking man peeped inside and announced, "David, the call starts in two minutes." Ronnie recognized him from the photos on the fund's website — Henry Chen, the second senior partner in

---

[3] Decisions in the fund are always taken by vote, with the aspiration being that crucial decisions, such as recruiting or investments in companies, will be made unanimously.

the fund and the one who'd established it along with David.

David rose from his seat. "Excuse me for a moment, I need to make a short telephone call to the managing partner of the Fidelity fund. We're closing a joint investment round with him in one of our portfolio companies. This will take five minutes tops. OK?" He did not wait for a reply and left the room.

Ronnie followed David's chubby figure walking quickly beyond the glass wall, and wondered if they were trying to hint they knew about the interview he had with Fidelity the day before. He was flattered by the wooing gestures but decided that unless an especially tempting offer was presented when the meeting resumed he would avoid providing an immediate answer.

He left his seat, went to the hidden refrigerator from which the receptionist had taken the Evian, and fished out another one. Through the transparent wall, he could see a displeased expression developing on her face. He sent her a smile, indicating with exaggerated stage-acting movements that David had drunk the water intended for him. She returned a smile.

David kept his word. Precisely five minutes later, Ronnie saw his plump belly making its way back to the conference room. As if they'd never stopped their conversation, he said, "At this stage, we're willing to offer you two percent of the second fund's profits, in spite of the fact it is already in a progressive stage of its life cycle. I assume you realize this number will likely translate into ten million dollars or more for your share. Obviously, should you become a partner in the next fund, your share in that fund would be significantly higher. I believe there's no need to stress to you that this is an exceptionally generous offer."

Ronnie wondered why David and his partners were so determined to have him in their midst. "This is indeed a generous offer," he agreed with a flat voice.

"Additionally, you will receive a three hundred and sixty thousand dollar annual salary. A number that makes it rather easy to calculate the monthly salary. Needless to say, once you're a partner, your salary will also be significantly upgraded."

David stopped talking and leveled his gaze at Ronnie, awaiting his reply.

"It's way more than I expected your initial offer to be and a little more than what I thought I'd actually get, following a long and laborious negotiation process," Ronnie admitted. "I appreciate your offer very much, but before I'm able to accept it, I'd like to meet with the rest of the staff members. I believe I'll work here for a long while, and they'll be the people I'll spend most of my time with. Would you like to set up another time for these meetings?"

"I'd have been surprised if you hadn't asked for such meetings," said David, and a little smile fluttered on his lips. He took a piece of paper from his pocket and handed it to Ronnie. "This is the timetable for your meetings today with Henry Chen, the partner with whom I built the fund, with George Epidorus, the partner leading of the telecom investments, and with Stephen Doshen, the partner responsible for our software investments. At the same time, I'll ask human resources to draft the contract, and if my partners are to your liking, I believe we'll be able to sign before the end of the day." David set down the paper, extended his hand to Ronnie, and following a brief shake, left the room without adding a single word.

Chapter 1

A grim view of Manhattan was visible through the glass wall in Ronnie's 29th floor office on Sixth Avenue. The weather had persisted in its gloominess for a week. The dark skies refused to yield rain but at the same time were determined to prevent any sunbeams from illuminating the crowded avenue below. His experiences since he had begun his employment with the fund had served to awaken a slight sense of dreariness in him as well. For almost six months he'd been suffocating in this prison house of capitalism: two tables, two chairs, two cabinets installed under two enclosed bookstands and two slaves, willingly locked up in a single room — slaves daily pitted against each other by their masters.

Ronnie turned his back on the city and shifted his gaze to Roy Hilbert III, with whom he shared the office. Like every person who had ever laid eyes on Roy, Ronnie determined that Hilbert's parents must have had a great relationship with the almighty —the man possessed perfect genes. Roy boasted an impressive mane of blond hair, parted with mathematical accuracy right in the middle of his forehead. Ronnie was willing to bet that fixing his hairdo deprived his office mate of at least half an hour of sleep each morning. His straight, noble nose was set with irksome precision between a pair of blue eyes, and he possessed a Kirk Douglas-like furrowed chin. Roy fussed over his attire with the same air of seriousness with which he added the title "the third" to his name each time he introduced himself. His meticulously pressed shirts matched in color the endless variety of chinos, which, he never failed to mention, had been special-ordered from Italy. But, just like every natural element presuming perfection, Roy had a weakness, well known by everyone but himself: He was completely humorless. *He's so full of himself, there's no room left inside for a sense of humor,* Ronnie had recognized the problem as early as the first week of their acquaintance.

Roy, a Harvard MBA *summa cum laude*, was hired by the fund as a senior associate a week before Ronnie. As far as he was concerned, Ronnie was a dangerous competitor in the race for partnership. Since their first meeting, Roy had been uncertain whether he hated Ronnie or was simply afraid of him. He wasn't the only one who felt that way. Two other senior associates, who occupied the adjacent room suffering identical slavery-like conditions, shared exactly the same feelings. All three of them were intimidated by Ronnie but were no less afraid of each other.

"Roy," Ronnie addressed his neighbor with concealed humor, "do you feel like grabbing lunch together?"

"I have to finish an important research job for David," answered Roy with a mixture of seriousness and self-importance. "I'm really sorry. I can't let him down after all the trust he's placed in me." And without waiting for Ronnie's reaction, Roy plunged back into the depths of his computer.

Amazing how he's able to come up with a new excuse every day, thought Ronnie. *One day he'll run out of excuses and I'll have to suffer his presence during lunch as well.* He glanced at his watch for the fourth time in the last half hour. *Why am I drowning in boredom when I have such a challenging and fascinating job?*

The past few months were different than anything he'd been accustomed to. In all the places in which he had worked, he'd learned to value teamwork as the most important principle, but in this office a dog-eat-dog attitude prevailed. His dissatisfaction was further fueled by the fact that the partners — who'd fussed over him till the moment he had signed the contract — were now completely ignoring him. As far as they were concerned, he'd become an email address to which assignments could be sent, assignments that were always urgent and crucial to the existence of this or that project. He had never heard a single compliment from them, but more than once they had delivered scathing reprimands because his work was disappointingly overdue, while keeping their imaginary deadlines to themselves. He knew that many of the ideas he had presented were approved and executed, but he'd received no credit for them. In their eyes, he was nothing but "a servant of four masters."

He took another peek at his watch. It was one thirty-two, a minute had passed since the last time he'd checked. Eight thirty PM, Israel time, he translated to himself. If he knew his workaholic friend Gadi well enough, he would still be in the office in the middle of an endless meeting with one of his demanding customers. *Well, that's his problem*, he thought and pressed the speed-dial button.

The reply on the other end of the line came immediately and in Hebrew. "The putz in front of you is already driving you nuts?"

"Gadi, your last name is Abutbul. Moroccan Jews don't use Yiddish swear words. Say 'little shit' or 'piece of trash,' but not 'putz.' Coming from you, the word sounds too dignified." Ronnie had his first laugh of the day.

"Tell me, why don't you leave that fund of yours already?" Gadi became serious. "You're bored to death there. Every day you're calling me ten minutes earlier than the day before. With my 'easy going and understanding' customers, a month from now I'll be forced to start looking for a new job."

"I've been asking myself the same question every single day. I love what I'm doing, which is apparently enough to overcome the exasperation of working with all these lifeless people in the fund. But considering the way the senior partners are treating me, there's a good chance they'll be the ones making the decision for me."

"So go and work for another fund. You may earn less, but between you and me, you don't need the money."

"Gadi, thanks for your concern. Really. But that's the way it is with all funds. Unfortunately, where big money is involved, there's a lot of competition. And when there's competition, Americans will stop at nothing in order to win."

"So just come back to Israel," Gadi gave him the usual reply.

"What's happening with you?" Ronnie changed the subject, ignoring Roy's furious glances about being distracted from his sacred work.

"All's usual, you know. Providing services for insurance companies investigating theft and robbery, helping the police find their way in the depths of the master criminals' world, and investigating the miserable affairs of the wives of the rich and the famous. I closed two such cases yesterday. My mother would have had to work half a lifetime to earn the amounts they added to my bank account. Those rich people paid without blinking." The ghosts of childhood pains turned Gadi's voice hoarse.

Ronnie felt a pang of yearning. He missed the honesty, directness, candor and mutual trust he and Gadi shared.

"So, when are you coming for a visit in Israel?" Gadi didn't let go. "You know, your parents really miss you. Good thing your sister stayed here...me too," Gadi addressed a sore spot.

"I don't see myself coming back anytime soon, and please don't bring this up every conversation we have. I feel shitty enough about it as it is," Ronnie mumbled in a melancholy voice.

"Ashkcnazi Jcws should say 'likc drcck,' not 'shitty.' How'd you put it? Coming from you, the word sounds too...dignified."

"Gadi, I love you," Ronnie said and laughed, "but I gotta go before the putz has a stroke."

"Let him have one. Yalla, bye. Hang in there. And remember, when you're promoted to partner, the putz will work for you, then you'll be able to abuse him as much as you like." Gadi hung up without waiting for a reply.

Ronnie picked up his coat from the coatrack and left without saying a word. He was aware that it would have been much more decent to have the conversation with Gadi outside the room so as not to interrupt Roy's work, but there was no way in the world he would've given up one of his only pleasures in the office.

Three months earlier, he had discovered a small Middle Eastern restaurant that sold falafel and shawarma. It reminded him of the wonderful falafel he used to eat in the small stand that had opened a short time before his last visit to the kibbutz where he was raised. When he entered the dim, crowded restaurant, he was happy to see that his favorite corner table, right next to the phone booth, was available. He mouthed the words "the usual" as he motioned to the Lebanese counterman and pointed his finger toward his customary table. The man smiled and nodded his approval. Ronnie sat down and, as usual, turned his back to the other diners, detaching himself from the commotion. He turned on his iPad and became engrossed in reading the latest news from Israel.

"Our Hezbollah is giving you problems?" asked the Lebanese, while placing a plate of shawarma, finely diced Arab salad, humus and a bottle of Coke Zero on the table.

"Not that I'm aware of. Perhaps they're resting. But if I were a gambling man, I would say they won't stay quiet for long," answered Ronnie and gave the Lebanese man a friendly clap on the shoulder.

"Unfortunately, brother, you're right. With them, it's always a matter of time before they go off their rockers and start looking for someone to kill." The counterman smiled bitterly and went back to serving a new wave of hungry customers.

Life is always surprising, thought Ronnie. *I have a better relationship with a Lebanese stranger than with any of my coworkers.* Behind his back, the phone booth door opened then immediately closed. *I didn't know people even used them anymore!* Ronnie thought nothing more of it and became caught up in the sports section.

"Put ten thousand on Lucky Runner in the fourth, ten thousand on Black Beauty in the eighth and twenty thousand on Royal Lightning in the last race," an instruction was heard from within the booth. The speaker lowered his voice, but each whisper could be heard through the wooden walls. After a brief respite the man added in an entreating tone, "You'll get everything you're owed by the end of the week. You know I'm never late with my payments."

The unintended invasion of another person's privacy embarrassed Ronnie, but what had made the situation even more embarrassing was the feeling he recognized the man's voice. The phone booth door opened and the man stepped outside. Ronnie instinctively turned his head back and found himself staring at Henry, who froze as they made eye contact. Ronnie was the first to regain his composure and sent Henry a reassuring smile, doing his best not to betray, even with a hint, that he had heard the conversation. Henry came to his senses, flashed a theatrical smile back at Ronnie, and left the restaurant without saying a word. *Perhaps this fund is not so boring after all,* thought Ronnie, troubled. *If the second most powerful man in the fund is a gambler who can hardly pay his debts, what did it say about the way in which the partners were managing their investors' money?*

Chapter 2

Liah roamed about JFK's arrival terminal and waited for the Swissair passengers to emerge from behind the opaque sliding doors. Even though she was only five foot four, fifteen years of ballet lessons had imbued her with an upright, gliding gait, as if her feet were hardly touching the floor. It gave her an air of dignified mystery, further augmented by her high cheekbones and dark eyes. A slight, almost imperceptible, squint in one of those eyes gave them a dreamy, perhaps even seductive, look.

Liah met Ronnie when he was a guest lecturer at Columbia University's medical school, where she was a student. Six months later, she moved into his Manhattan apartment, where they'd been for the past two and a half years. Ronnie had been attracted by her unique appearance but was quickly enraptured by the charms of her quick wits. He often told her he'd never met such an intelligent, yet unassuming person. Even when he discussed subjects related to his own profession, she surprised him with her exceptional insights and her ability to simplify complex situations and define them in a single clear sentence.

The door opened with a whistle of compressed air. Two businessmen emerged, mummified in suits and ties. Ronnie was right behind them, dressed in a pair of jeans and a sweatshirt, his eyes scouting the terminal, seeking her.

Liah ran forward, jumped on him, and covered his face with kisses. Ronnie kept on advancing toward the exit, while she was still hanging from his neck. When they were outside, he whispered to her, "Cut it out, the whole world's watching us."

"I don't care! I'm so happy you're back from reserve duty."

Ronnie's body stiffened. His stay in Israel had made him forget what had happened the day he'd left New York. Humidity hung in the air, he recalled, and left its mark on the multitudes that crowded the street. The day had not yet begun, and everyone already appeared to be on edge as he headed toward Seventh Avenue. After five minutes of walking, he stopped next to a coffee cart with a long and sweaty line in front of it. He waited for his turn. A bagel was the last thing he wanted. He was interested in seeing if the fiftyish-looking man who was reading a newspaper on the other end of the sidewalk was actually following him.

The man folded his newspaper and continued on his way up the street. Ronnie's eyes followed him through his sunglasses. The man stopped in front of a display window in which the coffee cart line was reflected. A moment later, he took out a cell phone, made a brief call, and walked on without looking back.

Ronnie collected the bagel he had ordered and turned on his heel. He almost didn't notice the girl pacing in front of him. It was only the slight expression of interest that crossed her face as he passed by that betrayed her and let him know she was continuing the surveillance of the tail he'd spotted. The ones who followed him didn't seem professional enough to belong to a three-letter law enforcement agency. Still, Ronnie wondered if the United States government was aware of the affairs he was involved with. A feeling of guilt momentarily washed over him. Was it something about his behavior that had brought this about? He took a bite of the tasteless bagel, and then tossed it into the nearest trash can. He strode toward the nearest Starbucks, on 27th Street, while turning off his cell phone. He walked inside, glanced back and discovered his follower remained at the other end of the street, watching the entrance door. Ronnie walked slowly into the heart of the coffee shop, and once he was certain he was concealed by the people around him, quickly went out a side door. He found himself on Sixth Avenue and immediately jumped into a taxi idling at the traffic light. When it drove past 27th Street, he saw his tail still standing and looking at the door he'd entered.

"Are you even listening to me?" he heard Liah's voice scolding him.

"Yes." All at once, he was back at the JFK arrival terminal, back to Liah who, for the past few minutes, just wouldn't stop talking. "You said you weren't really worried about me." That was all he could remember. "That's not showing a great deal of love," he added.

"It shows something else: that I knew exactly where you were."

He became tense. "How?" he asked, attempting to maintain a level tone.

"Remember my friend Ruthie? The one I've been chatting with on Facebook every day?"

"What does she have to do with this?"

"Yesterday, she looked at some of the photos I posted from our weekend in Maine. Her mother happened to see them and said she knows you from her restaurant. Ruthie said it couldn't be, and that anyway, you live in the US. But her mother insisted you'd been eating at her restaurant for a week. She added that she may be old, but she still has an eye for good-looking guys."

"Well, so what does it all mean?" asked Ronnie impatiently.

"The Ness Ziona Institute for Biological Research personnel regularly take their meals at her place. That's what it means." She laughed and continued, "And if that's where you're doing your reserve duty, then I'm not worried."

It's *always the little details that bring you down,* thought Ronnie as they entered the car.

Chapter 3

New York, October 14, 2013, 9:30 AM

Monday had begun just like any other Monday. The weekly staff meeting was brief and devoid of any upheavals, the mountains of sushi, ordered by Evelyn, David's personal assistant, were devoured to the last piece. But, during the final discussions, the partners, especially David and Henry, seemed preoccupied and restless.

"OK. We're done for today," David said, closing out the meeting. "Ronnie, stay with us in the room please."

Ronnie went back to his chair, following with his eyes the junior staff members leaving the room.

"Close the door behind you, please," Henry asked the last one to leave, who obeyed while sending Ronnie a worried look. A midday one-on-one conversation with all the partners was highly unusual and would normally herald ill tidings. Ronnie recalled Roy, who had been summoned to such a conversation just two weeks before, following which he'd been fired. An hour after the conversation had finished, all that remained of his old officemate were two marker pens and a yellow notepad. As far as Ronnie knew, even though they'd never told him, the partners were satisfied with his work. Even so, he wasn't able to get over the feeling he'd soon be watching his own funeral procession.

"We'll be right with you," Henry said offhandedly, as he and his fellow partners examined a two-page document David had just handed them, demonstratively ignoring Ronnie's discomfort. But if they thought they were pressuring him, they were wrong. The wait actually allowed Ronnie to relax. *I might as well keep a level head, they'll soon tell me why they wanted me to stay*, he thought and sprawled comfortably in his chair, took a deep breath, and waited. *If they only knew about all the times I've had to wait two, sometimes even three sleepless days to perform a single action that might have cost me my life...*

"It won't be another minute, Ronnie," it was David's turn to mumble without raising his head from the document, "we just need to finalize a few minor details related to another issue." Ronnie kept quiet. He assumed David was not really awaiting his approval.

Ten minutes later, it appeared the senior partners had reached a decision. All the paperwork was gathered and piled up next to David. David lifted the bundle again and lightly tapped it against the gleaming surface of the table. The papers were soon organized into a single cube-like shape. When his mind was finally at ease with the order he'd instilled in the paperwork, David raised his head and looked at Ronnie. "Thank you for your patience, and please excuse us for the wait. We wanted to speak with you at the end of last week, but since you were away on a business trip, we thought it appropriate to await your return so we could have a face-to-face conversation."

David grew silent, aware that Ronnie remembered the fate of his former roommate. Curiosity took hold, but Ronnie was able to maintain a neutral expression. David waited another moment, exchanging glances with his partners, then carried on, "It's been almost a year since you joined us, and we thought you deserve to know our opinion about you and your performance in the fund. Perhaps we've been a little miserly with our compliments, but I'm sure it will come as no surprise to you if I tell you most of what we have to say is very positive. Your analytical skills are exceptional, and your ability to recognize new market trends has often provided us a significant advantage over competing funds. Your handling of crisis situations has been excellent as well. Nevertheless, we still have two major question marks about you; the first one is whether you'll be capable of working with complete independence, without a senior partner by your side." David was silent again, awaiting a response, even though the question had been phrased as though it'd been directed to the partners.

Ronnie slowly shifted his gaze from one partner to another, trying to conjecture the hidden meaning of what had just been said, but more than that, to guess the words that hadn't been. "For the past year, I've shared my opinions with my partners, not because I'm unable to reach decisions on my own or incapable of innovative thinking. I've done it because that's what the term 'partnership' means to me. When I was hired, David was very proud of the due diligence you conducted on me. I'm sure you discovered that as a CEO, I led quite a few groundbreaking processes and reached quite a few difficult decisions on my own. It's much easier to reach such decisions on your own than to convince and harness an entire organization to follow your lead. As a CEO, I had no choice and needed to act that way. Here, I felt I had a different choice to make and therefore shared all my thoughts with you. If I had to start over, I'd still take the same approach." Ronnie grew silent and waited.

"I assume you had to make some difficult decisions during your military service as well," said David with a teasing smile.

"As I made perfectly clear a year ago during my job interview, my military service is not an issue I am willing to discuss." Ronnie clenched his teeth and said no more. He concentrated on pouring water into his glass and waited. Scolding David in front of his partners was dangerous, but he knew his destiny had been determined before the meeting had even begun. Whatever he said now would hardly change the decision about his future in the fund.

"Now you're setting limits for me as well," David reacted, his manicured fingers drumming the table and betraying his anger.

"Not really. I'm simply explaining my position. I expect you to see my loyalty to a different organization, dealing with other matters, as a good indication of my loyalty to our company. Had I betrayed the country that raised me, a country where all my family still lives, a country whose secrets I'm sworn to protect — all because of my wish to work for the fund — how could I expect you to trust me with the fund's professional secrets?"

The door opened without warning, and Evelyn entered the room carrying a fresh tray laden with sushi.

David picked up a piece of salmon and shoved it in his mouth. While chewing, he said, "You've raised an interesting point, Ronnie. Loyalty. For me, loyalty goes hand in hand with telling the truth. Do you feel the same?"

"Of course, along with other important qualities." The predatory, catlike expression on David's face made Ronnie realize he was about to be hit with the reason for this unexpected interview.

"So, how do you explain the following fact: Two months ago, you did a few days of reserve duty, so you said, something that no other Israeli residing in the United States is doing. What's even worse, we've found no indication that you left the US during that period. The Israeli army is conducting maneuvers and training on US soil?" David chuckled with obvious contempt.

Ronnie remembered the surveillance team he was able to shake off the day he'd left for reserve duty. "As I said before, I have no intention of getting into this subject. I find your scrutiny of my personal activities to be insulting and intrusive. Whether or not you mean to fire me today, I'll see that you get copies of my Swissair round-trip ticket to Israel by tomorrow. I'd like to stop the conversation now. I need to decide whether I'm willing to continue to work for a company that doesn't respect my privacy." Ronnic pushed his chair back, while giving David an angry stare, and turned to leave the room.

"Ronnie, come back please." Henry tried a soothing voice. "There's no need for you to bring copies of your flight tickets. I believe you."

"If you believe me, why did you send people to follow me?"

Henry shrugged.

Ronnie stayed his grip on the door handle. Every nerve in his body was screaming, "Leave!" but curiosity to see what David was aiming at and the knowledge he could always quit tipped the scales. It was in such moments he felt happy about the "drop dead" money he had as a result of the successful sale of his company. The incredible amount of money he had earned allowed him to send David to hell whenever he felt the partner stepped over the limit. He returned to the table and sat down.

"I suggest that we continue," Henry added, placing his hand on David's arm in an attempt to calm him. David left the table, used the espresso machine behind him to fill up a cup of coffee, foamed the milk slowly, and then gently added it to the mug. When he'd finished, he drained the liquid into his mouth with a single gulp and sat back, wiping his mouth with a soft cream colored napkin printed with the company logo.

"Take some sushi," he blurted, as if he'd remembered something important he needed to say.

"Thanks, but I'm not hungry," answered Ronnie. He was beginning to get fed up with David's games.

"We've decided to promote you to a partner position right now," said David, his voice surprisingly upbeat as if they'd not exchanged harsh words just moments ago. "As soon as the next fund becomes active, you'll serve as the partner in charge of investing in companies related to the medical field. In the meantime, we've decided to let you sit on one of our existing portfolio companies' board of directors. That way, we'll be able to see how you operate as an independent partner. It'll also buy Henry some valuable time to round up investors for the third fund." David was silent for a moment, perhaps to emphasize his next sentence. "We've never promoted a senior associate to partner so quickly. I'd like to believe you won't let us down."

"Thanks for your trust," Ronnie answered dryly. "Which company are we talking about?"

"TDO Pharmaceuticals. You should be familiar with it from our weekly meetings, but Henry will pass the baton to you in an orderly manner." David attempted a smile. Ronnie didn't kid himself, he knew the incident between them would not be soon forgotten.

"You couldn't have picked a better company," said Ronnie. Gratitude tempered his words for the first time since the meeting had begun. "Henry, are you sure you're willing to give it up?"

David hurried to respond before Henry was able to utter a word, "So, I understand you're accepting our partnership offer. Great. Regarding your question, I want you to realize Henry was far from pleased with this move. This is a development that was forced on us. For your own good, don't let us down."

Ronnie decided not to let the doubts and threats concealed in David's words to hinder his happiness.

"At the moment, only a slight cosmetic change to your salary will be made," added David. "We'll discuss the terms of your employment in the new fund after it is closed based on the amounts we manage to raise. We have been more than fair to you thus far, and I hope you trust us to continue to be so in the future. Now, take the rest of the day off and spoil Liah, your girlfriend, she probably doesn't even remember what you look like. We'll start the transition period tomorrow. Goodbye."

The final sentence surprised Ronnie, who'd never spoken with David about his private life and hadn't even imagined the partner was aware of Liah's existence. He gave David a questioning look which was answered by a slight, but victorious, smile.

Chapter 4

Ronnie's shoulders filled up the bedroom door frame. He leaned on the doorjamb and looked at Liah. Two and a half years of living together had done nothing to diminish his attraction to her. She was sleeping on her back, hands sprawled above her head carelessly, and Ronnie longed to snuggle beside her and cover her tranquil face with kisses.

"What happened?" She stirred and mumbled, "What time is it? I had the night shift yesterday. I just couldn't wake up this morning when the alarm clock went off. I hope I didn't break it when I hammered it with the pillow."

"Eleven forty-five." Ronnie leaned toward her, gently ruffling her hair and kissing her lips.

She sat up in panic. "What are you doing here in the middle of the day? Did something happen?" She leaned forward, exposing her breasts, which had burst free from her undershirt. "Stop giving me horny looks. What happened?"

"I've been promoted to partner. David decided to send me home to be with you on this happy day," he announced and immediately regretted admitting the idea of spending the rest of the day with Liah wasn't his own.

Liah lowered her eyes, leaned back, and fixed the pillow behind her silently. This wasn't the reaction Ronnie had expected. His favorite, battered Ralph Lauren jacket suddenly felt burdensome. He took it off and allowed it to slip to the floor. Then he drew Liah to him, holding her head between his hands while his lips gently brushed her forehead. Liah stretched her arms behind his back silently, holding him close. They sat that way for a while, until Ronnie felt her grasp weakening. He placed his hands on her shoulders, pushing her away from him a bit; the front of his pressed shirt was damp with tears.

"What's the matter, sweetheart?"

"I'm very happy for you, but…" She gasped for air.

But what? he thought, afraid to ask out loud.

Liah wiped another tear with the back of her hand, sniffled and said, "I'm really happy. Honestly. I know how much you wanted this promotion, and I know you deserve it. But still, I hardly see you as it is. Now there's a good chance I won't see you at all. I love you, and I want to live with you as your partner in every aspect of your life. What I have today is the hope of having an intimate relationship and the knowledge that you love me. But what I don't have is a sense of togetherness, and I'm afraid I'll have even less of it from now on." She leaned toward him and wrapped her arms around him once more, caressing his muscular shoulders. "I love you," she whispered in a choked voice.

Ronnie gently removed her hands, got to his feet, and said, "I'll be right back." When he returned five minutes later, he held a tray with two cups of coffee and fruit salad with yogurt, Liah's favorite breakfast when she needed pampering. She suffered from Crohn's disease and needed to eat before taking the medication that kept her symptoms at bay.

He set the tray on the bed next to her and took his own coffee mug, cupping it in his hands, his eyes not moving away from Liah's tormented face. An awkward silence lay in the room. Liah stirred the fruit salad aimlessly with her spoon. The coffee felt tasteless in Ronnie's mouth. He placed his mug on the small chest of drawers next to the bed, sat beside her, gently held her chin and said, "You're right, I'm very competitive and highly committed to my goals I'll probably be up to my neck in work very soon and won't stop to think about what it might be doing to our relationship. Perhaps 'won't stop to think' is not the right way to describe it — I think about it all the time — but I'm also hoping you'll understand and allow me to continue down this path, in spite of the price you're paying for it. I promise to spend more time alone with you every week. I promise I'll keep it that way after we get married."

Liah's eyes brightened to light brown. She blushed. "How did marriage pop into this conversation?"

Ronnie kissed the tip of her nose and said, "From the moment I met you, I knew I wanted to spend the rest of my life with you. I didn't know if you felt the same way, though. I bought you a ring eight months ago, but I was afraid you wouldn't agree to marry me so I postponed my proposal. This morning, while coming back home from the office, I planned my proposal down to the tiniest detail. I wanted to propose to you in a candlelight dinner, at the Bouley on Duane Street. I managed to get us a corner table for nine o'clock and then proceeded to insult the chef by asking if they have dishes without spices or citrus peels. But just now, while I was in the kitchen, I reached the conclusion that Israeli instant coffee, fresh fruit salad and the light of our reading lamp are romantic enough, and decided not to wait any longer." He got down on his knees next to the bed, moved the tray aside and took out a small blue box from his pocket. Then he opened the cover and placed the box on the soft down comforter covering Liah's legs.

"Liah Sheinbaum, will you marry me?" he asked and sent her a loving gaze.

Liah looked at the ring through the veil of tears in her eyes. This was the moment she'd hoped for from the day she had met Ronnie. It was also the moment she had feared most. She knew she had to confess, but the fear of losing him petrified her.

Ronnie's smile was replaced with a concerned look.

"Ronnie," she stuttered in a whisper. The temptation of surrendering to this unexpected happiness overcame her. She pushed back her doubts and concerns, raised her head, and smiled at him with shining eyes. Ronnie's heart threatened to burst in his chest.

"Ronnie Saar...there's nothing in the world I'd like more than to be your wife."

Ronnie squeezed her to him with a hug then covered her entire body with kisses. He leaned her gently against the pillow, bent toward her, and said, "Liah and Ronnie Sheinbaum Saar. It has such a nice ring to it." He gave her lips a light kiss. "Sounds like the beginning of a story about four best friends," he added and erupted in laughter that released all the tension of last few minutes.

"We'll drop the Sheinbaum," Liah managed to say, before yielding to his hands, which gently removed the undershirt from her body.

Chapter 5

Ronnie opened his eyes slowly. The dim morning light cast a pale glow on Liah's face. She was snuggled up next to him, still fast asleep. He touched her gently, and she hummed and tossed to the other side. Ronnie crawled out of bed and just like he had every morning for the past two weeks, cursed the broken central heating system, which the landlord was in no rush to repair. After quickly brushing his teeth, he dressed in a heavy tracksuit, put on his running shoes, and hurried to his daily appointment with a six-mile circuit.

He ran down the stairs, skipping two steps at a time, and went out into the freezing air. The overnight rainstorm had washed the city clean, and its high-rise buildings gleamed gloriously, but when he lowered his eyes, he discovered the sidewalk was covered with a tattered rug of yesterday's newspapers. He sped up to his usual running pace, allowing his body to celebrate the relaxation of his muscles and his mind to prepare itself for the challenges of the coming day. He set his inner clock to finish the six-mile course within forty-five minutes. The echo of his Asics drumming on the pavement was disturbed by the rattling engines of the few taxis whose drivers still hoped to pick up one last passenger before ending their exhausting night shift. Ronnie kept on running without tiring, completely absorbed in the latest songs from his favorite Israeli musician, Yehuda Poliker, playing in his white earbuds. About three quarters of an hour later, he turned back to 18th Street and went into the deli next to his apartment.

"The usual, sir?" the Indian owner greeted him.

"Of course, Kumar. You didn't prepare the package in advance?" Ronnie teased and put a twenty-dollar bill on the counter.

"Change is on the way." Kumar smiled and handed him a paper bag with two baguette sandwiches, stuffed with the best the deli had to offer, and two plastic containers filled with freshly cut fruit salad.

Ronnie raised his hand in appreciation and collected the paper bag. "Have a nice day," he said and same as every morning, headed out without waiting for the change.

In his apartment, he showered, ate the fruit salad standing up, got dressed, and tucked one of the sandwiches in his bag, knowing he probably wouldn't have time to go out for lunch. He sneaked another glance at the bedroom, only to discover Liah hadn't moved an inch since he'd left, then collected his coat and quietly closed the door.

He reached his office at ten minutes past seven.

"Good morning," he said and smiled at the receptionist.

"Good morning, Ronnie," came the reply, accompanied by the lowered glance of someone who wasn't sure whether or not she should continue to address the fund's newest rising star by his first name. "I was really happy to hear about your promotion."

"Thanks, Valerie, I really appreciate it." Ronnie summoned the warmest smile he could come up with on that chilly New York morning.

The receptionist responded with a timid smile then immediately added in a matter-of-fact tone, "David asked me to let you know that starting today your office will be located in the partners area, next to Stephen's."

"Thanks." Ronnie managed to conceal his surprise and turned toward the kitchenette, where he knew he'd find steaming coffee Valerie took care to brew every morning. With a cup of coffee in his hand and his laptop bag slung across his shoulder, Ronnie headed toward his new office. The bronze plaque engraved with his name made him stop in his tracks. To his surprise, he actually felt excited. He turned the key, which had been left for him in the lock, and slowly pushed the door open.

The room revealed to him was very similar to those of all the other partners. The large red mahogany desk and the low, matching African walnut filing cabinets, lining two of the walls, were brand new. He slowly approached his chair and examined his new desk. On the right hand corner, there were ten boxes of business cards, all bearing his name. The title "Partner" was written beneath. On the other end, a docking station for his Mac had been installed, and in front of it was a large, impressive Apple monitor. The remaining surface of the desk was covered by four thick blue ring binders. On top of the binders rested an envelope, propped up on its open flap. Ronnie sat down, took the handwritten letter out of the envelope, and began to read:

Welcome. On the desk, you'll find four ring binders containing all the information about the company. Additionally, Evelyn has sent you an email with a code which will allow you to access all company documents on the fund's server, as well as an additional code that will open the partners-only libraries. Feel free to come to me with any questions.

Good luck, Henry.

On the file cabinet to the left of his chair rested a miniature vase with a single white rose. An additional envelope was resting against it. *It must be national envelope day*, he thought and went over to read the letter. A wide smile spread on his face as he opened the envelope and found a sheet of pink notepaper inside, scrawled with Evelyn's handwriting: *Good luck, Ray*. A smiley face graced the bottom of the page.

Ray was the name Evelyn had given him, and no one would dare to defy Evelyn. She was David's personal assistant, a woman in her late forties, single or divorced — no one knew and no one was courageous enough to ask. The evil gossips of the office said that she was married to her work and chose to live her own life through David's. Her permanently serious expression, her conservative clothing and graying hair, always gathered into a knot at the back of her head, reminded David of his childhood Bible teacher. Her red glasses, the only trace of color on her makeup-free face, were the only hint that a woman was hidden somewhere behind the restrained visage. The appreciation, verging on admiration, that David felt toward her demonstrated that appearances could be misleading and that behind the outwardly dreary appearance, a strong, brilliant, and determined person was ebbing and flowing, someone who would stop at nothing to complete her missions.

During one of their conversations in the coffee corner, Evelyn had offhandedly mentioned she held two degrees from Columbia University. There wasn't even a hint of vanity in her voice. She had simply reacted to a remark by Ronnie about Liah's demanding studies at the same university.

The only logical explanation Ronnie could think of to explain such a brilliant woman ending up as an office manager was that David paid her an insanely high salary. He felt very fortunate to have Evelyn taking him under her wing and helping him fit in. She had christened him with the name "Ray" about a month after he'd started working for the company. "Why Ray?" he'd asked, puzzled, and she had gravely replied that something in his rough demeanor reminded her of Ray Donovan from the cable TV show.

"Did you know Liev Schreiber, who plays Ray, is also Jewish?" she had whispered with mock seriousness. Ever since that day, she always addressed him as Ray when they were by themselves, and they turned it into their private joke.

Ronnie had never attempted to take advantage of his relationship with Evelyn to gain any favors or cut corners, and she appreciated it. In another of their kitchenette conversations, she provided him, without being asked, an explanation for the special treatment she gave him. "You Israelis are very straightforward. You're the only ones I can joke around with about personal issues. If I tried that kind of humor with one of the American partners, it would probably end up either with me losing my job or him desperately wooing me. I really don't know which of the two scares me the most. Besides, you really do look like Ray Donovan." She sent him a theatrical wink and chuckled. It was the first time he'd seen her laughing, and the first time he'd noticed just how attractive she really was.

Ronnie assumed Evelyn had personally handled the decoration and furnishing of his office. Now he thought she might also have been involved with the secret of his promotion, long before he had any knowledge of it. What else could explain how she'd managed to select and purchase new, matching furniture for his office in a single day? He also suspected David's gesture, sending him home to spend the day with Liah, had actually been Evelyn's idea.

Ronnie connected his computer to the docking station, and the screen in front of him woke to life. He sent a brief email to Evelyn, thanking her for her help. While sending it, he noticed she'd already changed the business title in his electronic signature from "Senior Associate" to "Partner." *Nothing could stop Evelyn*, the thought passed through his mind. He knew that as the information technology manager for the fund, one of the many titles and responsibilities she held, she had access to all the employees' passwords, but he'd never imagined she would use it unless an emergency situation was involved. He emitted a sigh Liah used to call "Ronnie's Polish sigh of frustration" and plunged into the piles of information Henry had left on his desk.

Time flew by quickly. Now and then, one of the fund employees entered his office to wish him good luck in his new position. He gave them each a polite thank you smile and immediately got back to work, avoiding unnecessary conversations. When he finally raised his eyes from the last document, it was already eight o'clock in the evening. A yellow notepad was in front of him, scribbled with dozens of points he'd decided to look into in greater detail. In spite of the late hour, he decided to call Christian Lumner, TDO's CEO. Lumner picked up the call after a single ring.

"Hi Christian, it's Ronnie Saar. Got a minute for me?"

"I'm in the middle of a meeting, but hold on a moment, please," answered Lumner, and before Ronnie could reply, he heard him say to the people in the room, "I need to take this call."

The sound of chairs being pushed back and the footsteps of those leaving the room made Ronnie feel embarrassed. He had had no intention of disrupting the CEO's meeting. It was the first time he had felt the power inherent in his new position.

"Yes, I'm with you." Christian was back on the phone.

"You didn't need to stop the meeting. We could have spoken later, or even tomorrow."

"Everyone is already out," Christian replied coolly, "how can I help you?"

"I've read the material Henry gave me, and I have a lot of questions. I plan to meet with Henry tomorrow, and later on I'd like to meet with you, too. I wanted to know when you'd be available."

"Anytime you'd like, tomorrow or the next day. In three days, I'm supposed to travel to meet some investors, unless you advise me differently, of course."

"Why would I advise you differently?" Ronnie wondered.

No reply came from the other end of the line.

"How about I take an early morning flight on Thursday and meet you at ten in your office. I'd be delighted if you would clear most of your morning schedule for me. OK?"

"OK," Christian answered dryly, "send me the flight details, and I'll have a driver pick you up at the airport."

"No need. I'll rent a car and get there by myself," Ronnie hurried to respond.

"Whatever you like…will there be anything else?"

"No."

"Then I'll see you Thursday," Lumner ended abruptly and hung up.

Ronnie remained seated in his chair, looking at the silent phone. Christian's demeanor was resentful, and Ronnie couldn't help but wonder why. Nothing in the material he'd just finished reading had predicted, directly or indirectly, what had just taken place during the conversation. *What else was stirring below the surface?* Ronnie pondered. He reached for the four ring binders and began to read them anew.

Chapter 6

Boston, October 16, 2013, 7:30 AM

The early flight to Logan Airport in Boston was without incident. Ronnie travelled light and didn't have any suitcases to pick up. He headed straight to the Hertz car rental shuttle. After a short and silent journey, the shuttle stopped in the rental lot. He glanced at the large "Gold Plus members" electronic panel and saw his name and next to it the number 566. Two minutes later he sat in the Prius he'd booked, typed the address of TDO's Waltham offices into the GPS, and took off toward the Ted Williams Tunnel. A single tear of rain sought its way down his windshield, paving the way for millions of its siblings, bursting with a crazed drumming on the roof of his car. He still had more than two hours before the meeting and was hoping he'd have enough time for breakfast at the Embassy Suites hotel, located, according to Henry, not far from TDO's offices.

The memory of yesterday's appointment with Henry filled him with discomfort. Henry had come to the door to greet him and congratulated him on the quick promotion. Ronnie couldn't help but be impressed by his black, burning eyes, which utterly contrasted with his pleasant features. Even though Ronnie hated it when people made generalizations about Israelis, his interactions with Henry couldn't help but bring to mind the advice he'd received some years ago from his marketing manager, who had lived in Beijing for ten years: "The moment you think you know what the Chinese person facing you is about to do, is the moment you lose the battle against him."

"How's your new office?" Henry asked him politely as his secretary entered the room, holding two cups of coffee. She set them on the table, which was covered by a silk map decorated with Chinese paintings.

"Double shot, no sugar and light on the foamed milk," she said to Ronnie and flashed a professional smile at him before exiting the room.

Ronnie, who made it a habit to religiously keep his private life to himself, felt his privacy had been breached for the third time in only two days.

"Shall we begin?" Henry asked, not really waiting for Ronnie's answer.

Ronnie opened his computer. The file with all the questions he'd prepared was already flashing on the screen. "Allow me to be frank with you," he opened, "I went over all the material in the binders and read all the relevant information collected in the fund's database. I can't shake the feeling everything seems too good to be true. From my experience as a CEO, I know every company has its ups and downs, and here, for the first time in my life, I come across a company which functions exceptionally well throughout the years, systematically meets all its goals, and demonstrates an extremely high growth potential. In my experience, the life of a company is composed of a collection of potential crises lurking around every corner. And yet here, all the board reports are optimistic, none of them speak of any problems, and all of the CEO's requests are always unanimously approved. It's a utopian world, and I don't really believe in utopias."

"What are you really trying to ask?" Henry straightened in his chair, fully alert.

"Either I was lucky enough to receive a perfect company or — and I find this second option to be more reasonable — the CEO is not being completely transparent in his reports or even worse, he 'artificially improves' the actual business results. You have a lot more experience than I do. As someone who's worked with the company from day one, I'd appreciate your opinion on the subject."

Henry gave him a cold smile, brushed an imaginary grain of dust from the sleeve of his striped jacket, and said with marked sarcasm, "You have some difficult questions as well?"

Ronnie realized he'd stepped on a hornet's nest. "That all depends on the answer to my first question," he said grimly, letting Henry realize he was not about to drop the subject.

"Christian and I have been working together closely ever since the company was established. I hope he didn't conceal anything from me. On the other hand, I have to note that personally, I don't find things to be as rosy as you describe them, even though I agree with your general conclusion that TDO is a remarkable company both in its performance and in its potential. As you've probably realized after reading the financials, the company, which is about to finish — and based on all indications, very successfully   the clinical trials, is about to run out of cash, and Christian is working around the clock trying to raise additional funding. As stated, the company is about to finish the trial phase soon, but has not begun the sales stage yet. Without the boost of additional cash, the company will go bust. To my regret, and to Christian's, I had to inform him that as we've already invested twenty-five million dollars in TDO and as the rules of the fund forbid us from investing more than ten percent of the total capital we manage in a single company, we will not be able to continue to invest in this next funding round." He went silent for a moment, his fury-filled eyes boring into Ronnie's. "And if you're trying to ask me whether I'm aware of any other issues in the company, the answer is 'no.' Otherwise, as you well know, I would have detailed them in the reports I've submitted to you and all the other partners."

"Christian sounded anxious when I spoke with him on the phone." Ronnie met Henry's eyes.

"He has no reason to be stressed. He just needs to do what he's been told, and everything will turn out fine," Henry fired back. "Naturally, he's disappointed that we've stopped the cash flow, and he has to make an effort to find alternative sources of funding. I introduced him to eight different funds I've known for many years and explained to him in great detail what he must do. This is also the subject I planned to discuss at length with you today. I must admit I'm surprised Christian sounded upset. I'll have a word with him."

"Please don't. If you do that, he'll think I'm running to cry on your shoulder every time I'm bothered by his tone of voice, and I'll lose his respect and trust in my abilities even before we start working together."

"Right. Then I won't speak with him. Will there be anything else?" Henry suddenly sounded eager to finish their meeting, even though it was scheduled to continue till noon. Ronnie chose to ignore it.

"Let's get back to the subject of development. I have to admit I've never encountered a company that managed to develop a product and keep its original timetable without any unexpected delays. This would hold true for any company, let alone one that develops cutting-edge medicine. Based on the reports presented to the board of directors, it appears that TDO is the only pharmaceutical company ever that encountered no issues whatsoever during the development process. I wonder if that's truly the situation or perhaps the CEO interfered here as well and retroactively changed the company goals so they would match the actual results. In any event, the results are so impressive that the company shouldn't have any problem raising more funds."

Henry hesitated for a moment and then said, "Agreed. So let's move on."

The tension evaporated and the conversation continued in a friendly manner. Henry updated him with the list of investors he had introduced to Lumner and the joint history each had with the fund, answered all of Ronnie's questions with equanimity, and did not stop complimenting him on the excellent job he'd managed to do after a single day of research. And yet, Ronnie couldn't shake the feeling something dark and sinister was lurking beneath the surface of this efficiency and mutual kindness.

Perhaps I'm being overly suspicious, he thought, just as his navigation system alerted him he was approaching the highway exit, *I felt exactly the same way when I proposed to Liah. Maybe I'm just being paranoid, thinking all the wonderful things happening to me are merely a deception.*

The road sign marking the exit to Waltham appeared on his right, along with the navigation system's persistent instruction to use it. Once he'd passed the sharp curve up the road and driven across the bridge leading to the high tech park in which TDO was located, he noticed the hotel sign. He turned right at the traffic light and glided down the road, happy to discover an empty parking spot right next to the hotel entrance.

As soon as he entered, he spotted the restaurant door to his right. Ronnie shook the raindrops off his coat, stepped into the crowded room, and sat in the furthermost left corner, at a table overlooking a backyard filled with greenery. He decided to enjoy his meal and not to allow his trepidation about the appointment ruin his breakfast.

Chapter 7

Boston, October 16, 2013, 10:00 AM

How long has he been standing there? Ronnie wondered when he found Lumner standing next to the office door, waiting for him. He hurried to get inside and shook Christian's hand with both of his, noticing the CEO's barely concealed repulsion to the friendly gesture.

"Thanks for waiting, there really wasn't any need to do that."

"I just happened to pass by and saw you coming. Follow me, please. The conference room is available for our exclusive use for the entire day." Ronnie sensed impatience underlying Christian's words. He followed him into the large conference room and sat at the center of the table. Christian continued to the front of the room without saying a word and connected his laptop to the projector. He appeared to Ronnie the perfect image of a successful Fortune 500 CEO sent by central casting. His erect, muscular body was at least six feet tall, he was wearing gray tailored pants with fine beige stripes and a white starched shirt whose closed collar was decorated with the company tie. His tanned face was framed by a perfectly manicured hairstyle, made more distinguished by swirls of early gray.

"I prefer to conduct an open conversation at this stage," said Ronnie. He moved closer to Christian, who recoiled a bit before regaining his composure. Christian closed the laptop and said, "You're the boss. Whatever you want. What would you like to hear?"

"Look, I've spent far more years as CEO of a company similar to the one you're running than as a venture capitalist." Ronnie smiled, trying to break the ice. "I admire CEOs and understand firsthand the complexities you deal with on a daily basis. That's why I have no intention of establishing an adversarial relationship. I'm here to help, and I'd be delighted to establish a relationship based on mutual trust. OK?"

Lumner nodded, but his body language continued to indicate distress. Even though he didn't really need more caffeine, Ronnie poured himself another cup of coffee. Christian sealed up in his disturbing silence and waited. Ronnie leaned back, clasped his hands behind his neck and asked, "What's bothering you, Christian? If it's that Henry had to leave the TDO board, I can assure you I'll do the best I can to step into his large shoes. As disappointing as it may be, I can't be Henry, I can only be myself. I can only hope it'll be good enough for you."

A bitter smile surfaced on Lumner's face, "That's hardly the reason for the stressful situation I'm in. I apologize if I gave you the impression I'm displeased by your emergence in the company. I'm all for building mutual trust. Unfortunately, I've been burned by trusting people in the past. All I ask is that you give me some time to place my confidence in you. Ask whatever you'd like, and I promise to answer in detail and with complete transparency."

"OK. Why don't you start with the status of the fund-raising?" opened Ronnie.

"I hope it goes well. As I mentioned, I'm flying to the West Coast this evening to conduct meetings with two funds that received all the company's business and legal documents two months ago. If there's enough time, I'll also visit the offices of a Canadian fund in Palo Alto that's trying to jump on the bandwagon at the last minute. I know from our clients that at least one fund, Accord Ventures Partners, is advancing with their due diligence. They've already conducted intensive calls asking detailed questions about our product. According to the leading partner at Accord, there are several open questions remaining that they would like to discuss with me face-to-face, before they decide if and how much they would like to invest in the company."

"Do you have any guesses as to what those questions might be?" Ronnie felt the conversation was finally getting on the right track.

"I asked, but they refused to say. I assume they want to understand what risks the development process holds and how much trust I have in the product."

"I don't get it" — Ronnie raised an eyebrow — "we're already in clinical trials. I assumed the development risks were behind us and unless, God forbid, any unexpected surprises pop up, we have a complete product in our hands."

Christian rolled his pen between his fingers, magician-like. He performed this little trick several times, and just as Ronnie was about to repeat his question, Lumner woke up and said, "A few problems emerged during the development process about a year ago. In two separate cases, an entire production lot proved to be defective, and we couldn't determine why. At the moment, we are unable to guarantee that mass production of each manufacturing batch will yield the exact same results, which is naturally a fact that disturbs potential investors."

Ronnie felt the blood draining from his face. He had never heard about the incident. Not during the fund's staff meetings, nor from Henry's mouth. There were no records of it in any of the files Henry had given him. "This is the first I'm hearing of this. I'd appreciate it if you'd update me with all the details. Now that I'm on the board of directors, I'm legally responsible for any complications that might arise as a result of defective medicine erroneously finding its way to the market."

While speaking, Ronnie began to realize the severity of the situation he'd found himself in. Until now, he could have claimed he was unaware that some of the medicine produced was defective; from this moment on, he could not ignore the malfunction that had occurred and its possible implications. The sincerity he had encouraged Lumner to demonstrate had sucked him all at once into a legal complication that could end badly unless managed correctly.

"I assume you'd like to hear everything you can about the product," Christian opened and when Ronnie nodded his agreement, he continued. "The blood-brain barrier, or BBB, is a permeability barrier that separates the circulating blood from the brain extracellular fluid. The purpose of the blood-brain barrier is to protect the brain tissue from infection or antibodies and to maintain the composition of the liquid that contains the neurons, in order to protect neurotransmitter activity in the body. Today, all research in the industry is concentrated on trying to find ways to 'cheat' the BBB system so it will allow medicine to access the brain, especially in cases of brain tumors or severe inflammation. We approached the problem from a different angle. Painkillers and anesthetics aren't blocked by the BBB system — therefore, each anesthetic shot directly influences the brain and the functioning of the patient. At TDO, we've developed anesthetics and painkillers with certain ingredients that the BBB system would normally block. The medicine may have infinite uses and a vast business potential. From painkillers that will not dull the mental clarity of the user, to the ability to conduct operations during which the body will be anesthetized, but the patient will remain fully awake and able to cooperate with the surgeons. The potential annual market size is estimated in the trillions of dollars."

Christian paused for a moment, and when he saw Ronnie nodding in understanding, continued, "During the development stage, we produced six batches of the medication. Unfortunately, the results were not identical in each round. Fortunately, we have an excellent quality control system and discovered the problem very quickly. Once we investigated the reasons, the damaged series were destroyed in their entirety."

"Reasons? What do you mean?"

"Out of six manufacturing rounds, four were perfect, in one the medicine wasn't effective enough, and the last one showed signs of toxicity."

"Toxicity?"

"There was a production malfunction, or more precisely, a human error. We've improved the procedures, and the deviation has not occurred since."

"How come there's no mention of it in your summaries for the board of directors?" Ronnie snapped.

"Henry insisted that any mention of the problem be removed from the summaries," Christian answered without hesitation.

"So how come the new investors know about it?" Ronnie wondered, a concerned look in his eyes.

"*I* told them about it," Christian answered. He had the appearance of a condemned man awaiting the guillotine's blade to end his suffering.

"*You?*"

"I wasn't willing to go on record and lie in the documents I sent to the various funds. I was unable to continue with Henry's plan. You can fire me now, if you'd like." There was a tone of defiance in his voice.

Indeed, I stepped on a hornet's nest when I spoke with Henry, Ronnie thought. "We need to trust each other. We're allowed to disagree, but I need to know from now on you won't do anything behind my back, and mutual decisions will be executed exactly as agreed upon. Can you promise me that?"

"Yes," Christian answered feebly.

"A smart investor on my board of directors when I was CEO once told me that he can't stand the feeling he constantly needs an ear-eye doctor."

Lumner gave Ronnie a questioning look.

"A doctor that'll cure the frustrating feeling that what you hear is not exactly what you see."

A smile settled on Christian's face and he said, "A wise man indeed."

"OK, let's move on, then. I'll need to update Henry about our conversation."

"You do what you think is right, but if I were you, I wouldn't."

"Why not?"

"Well…" Christian squirmed, "Now we're running the company, not Henri. It doesn't sound to me as good practice to involve him in every single thing."

Ronnie decided to ignore the unconvincing answer. "OK, but answer me one more question. If it were up to you, would you continue to conduct additional tests, or do you think there is a risk toxic medication might find its way into the trials?"

"That's a theoretical question. It's not up to me. I presented my recommendations to the board, and the decision that was eventually reached was to carry on. Based on all the analysis conducted so far, it was also the right decision, whether I supported it or not. Besides, if we stop the experiment now, you know we won't be able to raise money and the company will close its doors. I'll have wasted seven years of my life, and you'll lose twenty-five million dollars of your capital. In a perfect world, we might have reached a different decision. In the real world however, we were forced to be pragmatic."

"You haven't answered my question, Christian."

"Yes, I have. You may choose to ignore the answer, but I gave you my reply."

"If your son or daughter needed an operation tomorrow, would you approve their participation in the trials?"

"Yes."

"You don't sound too convinced."

"The answer is yes, but if you need more information, I suggest you speak with an advisor we employ. He's a well-known authority in the industry. His name is Dr. Jörgen Zimmerhof and his offices are in New Jersey. I'll send him an email right now, asking him to meet you as early as tomorrow. He also thinks continuing the experiments with the medication that has already been manufactured and checked many times is completely safe."

Utter silence now lay in the room.

"All right. I'd love to get all paperwork involving the case." Ronnie regained his composure.

"I'll see that you get everything, even though we have no official summaries," answered Christian. When he saw the confusion on Ronnie's face he added, "As I mentioned, that was the instruction we received from your predecessor."

"And Henry didn't give you an explanation for it?"

"You must know a different Henry than the one I'm familiar with," said Lumner bitterly. "Henry doesn't think any of his instructions should be explained. He expects them to be carried out in full or else..."

"Or else what?"

"Will there be anything else?"

"Or else what, Christian?"

"You seem like a decent guy, it would be a shame for you to get into trouble after only three days in your new job and lose it. Let's drop the subject."

A knock on the door made them both jump. A short man whose belly protruded through a missing button on his shirt came inside and turned to Christian, "I'm sorry for the interruption, but can I have a moment of your time?" Lumner apologized to Ronnie and exited the room.

Ronnie remained by himself, his mind a tumble of insane thoughts. *Could I have been so wrong in my understanding of the situation? Could I have been assigned to this job to serve as a scapegoat if and when the need arises?*

A short time later, the CEO returned to the room accompanied by the chubby man. Christian's mood seemed much improved. "Meet Jim Belafonte, the company's chief technology officer," he announced. "He's the man who helps me hang on to my sanity under all this pressure. Jim is the company's most important asset. Currently, he's taking care of the next stage of the trials: surgeries which will be conducted independently by doctors, without the participation of company personnel. According to FDA regulations, you and I need to approve the continuation of the experiment. I've already signed the paperwork, I'd like you to sign it as well." He presented the documents to Ronnie, who looked at them as if they were drenched with poison.

Ronnie was silent, allowing Jim to understand he should leave the room.

The door closed, but Christian remained standing.

"Sit down, please," said Ronnie.

Lumner sat unwillingly, and without being asked, said, "I understand your concern, but I don't think there's any danger here. The medicine vials that will be used in the surgeries are the last two taken from a lot already vetted in the last six rounds. The damaged batches were destroyed, and we haven't produced a new batch. Furthermore, all the bottles have been carefully examined. Jim and I personally approved each bottle and signed its label. The only difference between the current clinical trials and the previous successful ones is that a company representative will not be present in the operating room. Anyhow, in our previous trials the doctors didn't really need our help."

Ronnie took the pen. His hand hovered hesitantly above the document.

"You have to sign; otherwise, you'll be giving our company the kiss of death. I can't fly to the West Coast and tell the funds that would like to invest in us that our newest board member is uncertain about the safety of the company's flagship product so we've had to stop the experiments. I just can't." Christian looked at Ronnie pleadingly.

"I've learned from experience that if you think you're wrong — there's a good chance you're really wrong," Ronnie chose his words carefully, "and I really don't want to be wrong in this case."

"Neither do I. I wouldn't sign it and risk human lives if I had even the slightest suspicion that the medicine is dangerous. Not for any fortune in the world." The CEO suddenly seemed very determined in his recommendation.

"OK, I trust you." Ronnie allowed his hand to drop onto the page, and feeling coerced, added his signature next to Christian's.

"Thanks, Ronnie," Christian said, sounding relieved. "Let's go outside and take a walk in the grove behind the buildings. The rain has stopped and the air is clear. I'll show you the Celtics' practice arena. If they're practicing now, it could be an interesting experience. And since you're not interested in an official presentation, we can continue our conversation out there."

A serene atmosphere prevailed across the pathways that crisscrossed the tangled grove. They walked silently, the thick atmosphere that had prevailed in the conference room just moments earlier now forgotten. The place reminded Ronnie of the historic Ficus Boulevard in the Israeli kibbutz Givat Brenner; he felt a pang of yearning in his heart.

"Perhaps I'm being paranoid," Christian broke the silence, "but lately, I have the feeling that I'm being followed. I've also been receiving strange letters from someone who knows the company inside out. I don't know if it's industrial espionage or a frustrated employee. I'm telling you this to prove I'm counting on you. I haven't told Henry. Not that I have any proof he's involved, but I find it hard to trust him. The surprise on your face when you heard about the manufacturing problems we encountered convinced me you're not involved with any related plot. Yesterday, I spoke with two people from the company you founded, and they said they would risk their lives for you. So here, I'm risking mine as well." They continued their walk silently, approaching the Celtics' practice arena, when suddenly, Christian whispered sharply, "Don't turn your head, but I've seen the man at the end of the pathway six times over the past two weeks. What are the odds I'd see the same person so many times in the course of just a few days?"

Ronnie peeked at the man from the corner of his eye. "Perhaps he just moved to the area and spends time in the same places you do; perhaps you share common interests and tastes."

"You don't really believe that," Christian murmured and turned back. "We'll give the Celtics a pass, if you don't mind. I don't feel like wandering here anymore."

Chapter 8

New York, October 17, 2013, 5:00 PM

The previous day's events had left Ronnie distraught. Ever since his workday had begun, he'd been unable to concentrate on any of his assignments. From the moment he'd signed the FDA document, approving the continuation of the trial, his destiny had been tied to that of TDO. He analyzed the situation again and again and always reached the same conclusion. He had only two options: sign the documents or resign. The second option was probably the wiser and more cautious, but Ronnie knew his nature wouldn't allow him to avoid the challenge. The meeting with Dr. Jörgen Zimmerhof, from which he'd just returned, reestablished his belief that using the existing medicine posed no real danger, but before he received a written opinion, he knew that the risk he'd taken might come back to haunt him at any given moment. He wondered what Liah might say about all this and dialed her number. He hung up after the first ring. The entire undertaking is top secret, he reminded himself and felt embarrassed by the question which popped into his mind: *Why can't I trust the woman who'll soon be my wife?*

An impatient honk rescued him from his own thoughts. He returned to the right lane, allowing the long line of vehicles that trudged behind him to move on. With his right hand, he called Gadi, who, as usual, answered after a single ring.

"What's happening?"

"A lot. I don't even know where to begin."

"It's your fault. If you'd called yesterday, you would have fewer things to bitch and moan about today. Why didn't you call?"

Ronnie began to relax. "Just because. Lots of things happened and I didn't think you'd be interested."

"Like what?"

"I've been promoted to partner," Ronnie announced dramatically, and immediately added, "and I proposed to Liah and she accepted."

"Without consulting with me first? You can't be serious. This is exactly how you get your life into a mess," Gadi answered, completely ignoring the bit involving partnership.

"Not in this case, definitely not in this case."

"Then you leave me no choice. I'll be taking the first flight tomorrow, and we'll go out to celebrate. It's been almost three years since the last time I paid you a visit. If I understand things correctly, Liah will soon be your new boss, thus I have to establish the rules of the game with her. I hope it goes well, or else..." Gadi laughed.

"Don't be insane and don't waste your money," said Ronnie, but in his heart he prayed that Gadi wouldn't change his mind.

"I'll take business class and send you the invoice. Tomorrow at six-thirty, I'll be picking you up from the office. Get reservations for a fancy, expensive restaurant. You're paying for that as well."

"Honestly, I'm really happy you're coming," answered Ronnie and, for the next half hour, updated Gadi with everything that'd taken place during his meeting with the TDO CEO.

"Awesome. We're going to have a blast. Bye." Gadi finished the call in his usual abrupt manner and hung up the phone.

Ronnie was now all smiles and tranquility. Gadi was his best friend, against all odds, actually. When Ronnie was seventeen, he'd volunteered, like all his classmates, to instruct at-risk youth in the City of Lod. During their opening conversation, the social worker explained to the volunteers that according to her philosophy most of their energies should be invested in trying to save the youths who had not yet begun to lead a life of crime, those who still showed up at school now and then, their occasional attendance indicating a desperate call for help more than any real desire to study.

Ronnie raised his hand and passionately expressed his opinion that the system was choosing the easy way. "It does not matter whether they show up at school, we need to find the ones who have real potential and invest in them so that they can serve as role models, perhaps even provide guidance for other children. I believe this is the right way, and I'd like to contact such a school dropout to prove I'm right."

It was only after his teacher, who was present at the appointment, had intervened and vouched for him that the social worker agreed to cooperate. "But only if I'm convinced you're aware of all the risks and receive written consent from your parents."

The youth the social worker had connected Ronnie with was Gadi, a fifteen-year-old boy who came from one of Lod's roughest areas, Yoseftal Street. His father had disappeared when Gadi was only three years old. His mother had raised him by herself since then, barely able to make a living by doing janitorial work for City Hall and cleaning private houses. All the relevant authorities were in agreement that the child was brilliant, but lacked any will or ability to accept authority. He regularly hung around criminals and hadn't seen the inside of a classroom for quite some time. After much effort and not a few threats, a meeting between the two teenagers had been arranged. It was marked as an utter failure from the very first moment. Gadi demonstrated deep contempt and an unwillingness to communicate with the spoiled kid from the kibbutz. "I don't need any favors from you," he repeated again and again throughout the conversation. Finally, he defiantly left, leaving Ronnie by himself, beaten and frustrated. In a spur-of-the-moment decision, Ronnie decided to follow him, and when he finally found him, kept on walking beside him down the alleyways of Lod without uttering a

single word. After about twenty minutes, Gadi shouted
at him, "What do you want? You're such a leech! Do I
need to beat the crap out of you so you get your ass out
of here?" His body language clearly indicated he was
ready for battle, in spite of the marked differences in
age and size.

Ronnie stopped. "I'm a nerd from the kibbutz. I'm
not looking for a fight, but I can still kick the shit out
of you, if I have to. But maybe, instead of really going
at it, we stand here by the fence and do some arm
wrestling. If you win, I'll turn around and get out of
your life for good. But if I win, you're going to give
me a chance to get to know you better, and for you to
know me. If, after we know each other well, you still
aren't interested in my company, I promise that I
won't insist."

Gadi smiled, sure of his victory. He jumped over
the fence, turned around, and positioned his right
elbow on the concrete rail, ready for battle. Ronnie
stood in front of him, ignoring the sharp stones digging
into his elbow and said, "Just start whenever you're
ready."

Before he could finish the sentence, he felt Gadi
furiously attacking his arm, leaning his entire body
weight against it. Ronnie remained firm and
unmoving. Years of hard physical labor had
strengthened the muscles of his arm. As minutes
passed, Gadi's breath quickened, but he couldn't move
Ronnie's hand even by an inch. Finally, he raised his

eyes, looked at Ronnie, who wasn't even sweating, and panted, "Draw?"

"Draw," Ronnie agreed.

Gadi wiped his hands and said, "That means you didn't win, doesn't it? So I don't have to get to know you. Seeya!"

"You know what, you're probably right. Just do me a favor and take me back to the place where we first met. OK?"

Gadi, who had expected an entirely different reply, turned around, said, "Come on," and began to walk. On the way, Ronnie spoke about the kibbutz and invited him for a visit. Gadi pretended he wasn't listening. When they parted, Ronnie gave him his home telephone number and to his surprise, after some slight hesitation, Gadi agreed to take it and wrote the number on his wrist.

Over the following months, the boys would meet at least twice a week, with Gadi remaining restrained, but not missing a single meeting. One day, Gadi arrived at the kibbutz unannounced and knocked on Ronnie's door. Ronnie's mother, who opened the door, told Gadi that her son was in Tel Aviv and would return that evening. "But," she added, "you're welcome to wait for him. We're just about to go to the kibbutz dining room to have lunch. Why don't you join us?"

Gadi stepped inside hesitantly and remained standing at the center of the room.

"My name is Judith, and this is Moses, Ronnie's father, and that's his sister, Rebecca. Gadi is Ronnie's friend," Judith introduced all the people in the room to him, "and he'll be joining us for lunch."

In the dining room, Gadi filled his tray with enough food to satisfy the hunger of an entire pack of wolves and devoured every last bit. They ate in silence, and once they'd finished, Moses turned to him and said, "I need to head out to the cowshed to fill up the feeding stations. You look like a strong young man. Unless you've got something better to do, I'd be happy if you could give me a hand."

Gadi joined Moses. The afternoon hours passed by quickly, and when they returned home, Ronnie welcomed Gadi. "You smell like cow shit." He was beside himself with pleasure. "Go take a shower, then we'll go meet a few of my friends at the kibbutz club. After that, my mother insists you call your mother and tell her you're sleeping over. She won't hear of you going back to Lod by yourself at night."

"We don't have a telephone," answered Gadi, embarrassed, "but I can try and call the family my mother works for; she babysits their children in the evenings."

After Gadi had showered, and as they walked toward the club, he quickly said with his head downcast, "This is the first time in my life anyone has worried about me."

In the months that followed, Gadi put Ronnie and his family through a series of tests. He deliberately got into fights and was arrested for disorderly conduct, giving Ronnie's parents' names to the police so they would come to bail him out. Each time, they did indeed come, accompanied by Ronnie, and vouched for him without asking any questions. One time, Ronnie took Gadi aside and told him, "Since you're jerking us around and expect us to come here every time, we might as well pay you back. Starting tomorrow, you're going back to school and you're studying seriously. We came here in the kibbutz vehicle; you'll find a schoolbag there filled with all the books you need and new notebooks. It's time for you to take responsibility for your life. By the way, I'm not asking, I'm telling!"

Gadi returned to school and became a good student, although not a very diligent one. With the social worker's approval and his mother's blessing, a year later, Gadi moved to the kibbutz. Two years after Ronnie had enlisted in an elite unit, Gadi joined the army as well. The army had realized the best way to catch criminals was to work with men who'd grown up with them, so Gadi was stationed in the criminal investigation division, where he took an investigator's course, graduated with honors, and became a living legend, closing the highest number of cases in the unit's history. "The criminals don't stand a chance against him," people in the unit said knowingly, "he knows how to think like them, only ten times faster."

When Ronnie was discharged after five years (his mandatory three plus two additional years as a paid, career soldier) and began to study at the Israel Institute of Technology, Gadi enrolled in the Haifa University department of criminology. They both graduated with honors. Even though Gadi was wooed by various security organizations, he eventually decided to open an office of his own, handling private investigations and security services. Ronnie moved to the United States to continue his studies. They both found the distance between them to be difficult, and the occasional visits had done little to satisfy their need to spend time with each other, a need they tried to fill with daily telephone conversations.

The sound of an incoming telephone call disrupted Ronnie's memories. Evelyn's name appeared on the screen. "David wants you to come to his office immediately. He asked me to make it clear that he means now," she said, then whispered, "Henry's in the room as well, they're both waiting for you. It looks very serious."

"Thanks, Evelyn. I'll be right there." He drove the remaining two miles quickly then left his car at the parking lot entrance. As he hurried down the corridor to David's office, he was accompanied by the questioning stares of the employees. David was clearly in a state. He sat with his elbows on the table, his head in his hands. Henry was standing by his side, a distraught expression on his face, his eyes flitting around as if seeking something.

"You wanted to speak with me?" Ronnie opened.

"Christian Lumner was found dead in his hotel room," Henry immediately fired at him. "A suicide note was found next to him in which he begs his loved ones' forgiveness. It didn't contain any explanation for his act."

A wave of pain struck Ronnie. "I met with him just yesterday. There wasn't any indication he could be planning something so extreme. You have any idea what could have made him do this?"

"I'm not interested in the private lives of my CEOs," Henry answered frigidly. "We only need to prepare for the event the police may tie this case to the company or its products. We can't have the company value drop, especially now that we've started to raise money for the fund."

Ronnie couldn't believe his ears. Henry had just been told that one of his portfolio companies' CEOs had taken his own life, and all he cared about was the possible damage to the fund-raising process?

Henry read his thoughts and added, "Don't give me that self-righteous look. Obviously, I'm grieved by this terrible disaster. But we'll have time enough to mourn. At the moment we owe it to ourselves, and even more so to our investors, to do some damage control. The company is yours. When you agreed to take it, it was for good or ill. Sadly for you, and for us, it turned out badly very quickly. But weren't you the one who said a company is always on the verge of the next crisis? David and I expect you to drop everything else and fly to California to take care of this matter so that our fund's name won't get entangled in this unfortunate development. I've asked Evelyn to get you a ticket on the red-eye. Please update me personally with any developments."

"There's no point in my going to California. I don't really know Christian. I've only met him twice, once briefly, here in our offices about a year ago, and a second time during my meeting with him yesterday. If there's anyone who knew him well enough and could testify to his personality and the situation of the company, as well as quash any rumors before they spread, it's you."

"I'm swamped with raising money for our next fund. David and I've discussed this and decided you're the one most suitable for the job. We're counting on you."

David didn't raise his eyes from the table. "We've considered all the options," he mumbled. "I agree this is a compromise, perhaps not a very good compromise, but a necessary one. Please go and do the best you can." His voice died out at once.

Henry stood, indicating that the meeting had come to an end. "Evelyn will give you the tickets and your hotel details. It's the same hotel Christian was found in. That way, you'll be able to speak with the appropriate people and perhaps understand a little better what happened there." He nodded to David and went out of the room without saying another word.

Ronnie felt like a child who'd received an undeserved punishment. David looked at him pleadingly, trying to stifle a sob stuck in his throat. If Henry had seemed unaffected by the tragedy, David appeared completely destroyed, although, to the best of Ronnie's knowledge, he didn't know Christian personally.

Ronnie left the room silently, closed the door behind him, and went to Evelyn to collect his airline tickets and hotel reservation confirmation.

"Sorry," her lips whispered. Her shining eyes betrayed what was in her heart. She handed him an envelope with a limp movement.

Ronnie headed toward the exit. On the way, he speed-dialed Gadi.

"Yes, sir," Gadi answered after a single ring.

"Change of plans. The CEO I told you about was found dead in his room at the Sheraton Sunnyvale." He opened the envelope and took a peek at its contents, "I'm flying from Newark tonight, United flight 1051 taking off at ten thirty-four and landing in San Francisco at one thirty-six. I have a room booked at the Sheraton. I'd be pleased if you could join me."

"Done."

"I'll explain the situation once we meet in Sunnyvale, but at this stage, I want you to act as if you don't know me. Check if I'm being followed or if there's any other suspicious activity you can identify."

"OK. Bye."

Ronnie hung up and called Liah. Just this morning he would have sworn he would never do what he was now about to do.

Chapter 9

"Ronnie, for the hundredth time, explain to me what's going on."

Ronnie lay a comforting hand on Liah's arm and turned his eyes to the front of the plane, examining the faces of the passengers who continued to pour through the entry door. "I'll tell you all about it after we take off." Earlier that evening, he'd called her, told her about Lumner's death, and apologized for having to leave her to go to the West Coast.

"Buy me a ticket as well," she demanded decisively. "There's no way I'm spending the first week of our engagement without you. Should I pack for you, too?"

"Thanks, this is a wonderful idea," he answered. "Just take out the green trolley suitcase from the closet. It's always ready for a short business trip." Next, he called Evelyn and asked her help in buying an additional business class ticket. Fifteen minutes later, he received a text message: I've made reservations for Liah. I saw to it that you're sitting together. You can go straight to the boarding gate. I'm sending the electronic tickets to your phones.

Thanks, he texted back a concise message, and a few seconds later typed an additional one: You're the best. Well done, it's great to know I can always count on you. He signed it "Ray" and pressed the send button.

"We are about to close the doors and will be ready for takeoff soon. Please take your seats, bring your seat backs to the upright position, and fasten your seatbelts," the laconic message was heard on the plane's PA system.

"And?" Liah asked again, "You thought I wouldn't notice Gadi boarding the plane and you two ignoring each other? Your best friend in the world is on the plane and suddenly you two don't know each other? What are you, little children?"

"Gadi's on the plane?" he whispered, an amused expression on his face. "Where?" He turned to look down the aisle with theatrical exaggeration. When he turned his head back to Liah, he smiled at her fondly and whispered, "Well done, I thought you were occupied with your reading and wouldn't notice."

"Why are you whispering, you idiot? Look around you; you think any of these tailored business class types speak Hebrew? By the way, do you plan on taking Gadi on our honeymoon as well?"

"Aren't you tired of being right all the time?" He stroked her cheek, taking pleasure in the silky feel of her smooth skin against the back of his fingers. "It's so much fun you've decided to join us. I can't tell you how happy I was when you insisted on coming. You gave me the perfect excuse I needed not to sleep with Gadi without him feeling rejected."

"If you plan on continuing to avoid giving me an answer, prepare to suffer," whispered Liah with mock severity and pinched his arm fondly.

The sound of the engines intensified. The plane began to accelerate on the runway and within seconds took off and began to ascend to cruising altitude.

Ronnie pushed his seat back a bit, and as he saw Liah leaning hers back as well, keeping eye contact, he realized the sooner he let her in on the secret, the better.

"When I got back from Boston, I tried to tell you about my meeting with Christian. I don't know if you fell asleep on the first or second sentence, so perhaps I'd better start over."

"I fell asleep on the first. You're not as interesting as you think you are." Liah wrinkled her nose.

For the next hour, Ronnie described to Liah everything he'd gone through since Tuesday, his first day as a full partner in the fund. He did not skip dry descriptions about the financial situation of TDO and found himself analyzing at length the advantages of the medicine the company had developed and the successful trials it had thus far performed. Liah, whose professional curiosity was aroused by the idea of the innovative medicine, asked many difficult questions, until Ronnie was finally forced to mutter humbly, "I'm sorry, Dr. Sheinbaum, I don't have all the answers. Can I continue to describe the financial situation?"

"I beg your pardon, Sherlock, but the scientific part is much more interesting than all your dusty financial and progress reports."

Ronnie continued and told her about his meeting with Lumner in Boston and the strange direction it had taken and did not skip the description of the person they'd encountered while walking in the orchard.

"So that's the reason you brought Gadi all the way from Israel? To watch your back?" Her voice was tense with concern.

"I didn't bring him. He decided to come as soon as he heard we were getting married. He insists on giving the bride his seal of approval before I lead her to the altar."

"And if he doesn't approve?" An unexplained cloud of anxiety settled on Liah's face.

Ronnie felt ill at ease. What was she afraid of? "Gadi's smart. He'll approve." He returned to describing the morning following his appointment with Christian. "Henry and David were waiting for me in David's office. What surprised me the most was that neither of them was interested in hearing, even briefly, about my conversation with Christian. If I were Henry, I'd have been dying of curiosity to know whether his demand to embellish the company reports had been exposed. He must be very sure of himself and perhaps also holding a few aces that could overshadow my discoveries."

The stewardesses began the meal service. They both attacked the food and hungrily devoured everything they were served. "When one is hungry, even airplane food tastes good," Liah mumbled, but it seemed her thoughts drifted elsewhere. The monotonous sound of the engines and their full stomachs lulled them into a drowsy comfort. As soon as they'd finished eating, they both pushed back their seats, impervious to the noise of the clearing of the trays.

Two hours later, they found themselves standing next to a luggage carousel, tiredly gazing at its gaping maw, waiting for it to spit out their first suitcase.

"Excuse me, sir, is this yours?" Ronnie heard Gadi's voice, addressing him in English.

Ronnie turned around and saw Gadi holding a small bundle with two keys hanging from it. Ronnie demonstrably fumbled in his trouser pockets, gave Gadi an embarrassed smile, and said, "Thank you. I must have dropped them when I took my cell phone out of my pocket. Thank you, sir." He took the bundle and stashed it in his pocket without giving it another glance.

Ronnie's and Liah's suitcases arrived in the first batch. "First time in my life I've been lucky," Liah muttered. Gadi had vanished, but Ronnie wasn't worried. He knew his best friend was somewhere within reach, and guessed the key chain he'd received contained a GPS transmitter that allowed Gadi to know his location at any given moment.

The digital clock above the reception desk showed the hour to be three thirty-four AM when they stepped into the hotel lobby. A drowsy desk clerk greeted them. "Welcome to the Sheraton," he said. "Name please?"

"Ronnie Saar. Two people."

"Yes, I see." The desk clerk raised his head and gave Ronnie a curious look, "No checkout date?"

"Please put it down as Monday morning. I'll update you if it changes," answered Ronnie. The desk clerk's curiosity-filled eyes gave him an idea. "I understand there was an unexpected death here yesterday."

"Yes, terrible." The desk clerk was now fully awake, torn between his duty to be discreet, and his desire to speak about the subject that had shaken and horrified the hotel staff.

"Did you know the man who died?" asked Liah.

"Of course." The desk clerk was drawn into the conversation. "I've known Mr. Lumner ever since I started working here. He always used to check in to the hotel in the middle of the night. 'That's how you gain an additional workday.' That's what he always used to say. He always had time for small talk, even when he was very tired. A charming man." Genuine pain clouded his face.

"I always wondered if things like this can be predicted," Ronnie remarked. "Was there anything unusual about his behavior?"

"Not at first. He arrived around one thirty AM, as usual. He took the last United flight from Boston." His voice rose with pride, "He gave me a Boston Celtics hat as a present and made it clear he expected me to wear it the next time he came to the hotel."

"You said, 'not at first.' What did you mean? What happened later?" As usual, it was Liah who directed the conversation to the desired direction.

"Eh…While we were speaking, his phone rang. I remember thinking it was a strange time to be getting calls, even from the West Coast, and certainly from the East Coast. Mr. Lumner answered the call, listened for a moment, then walked away and spoke in whispers. Two, three minutes later, it looked like he was losing his patience. I heard him raise his voice, saying something like, 'There's no way I'll give you…' and then he went back to whispering. He was very upset. He took his key and went up to his room without wishing me a good night. It was very strange."

"Did you tell that to the police?" asked Ronnie.

The desk clerk shrugged. "No one ever came to talk to me."

"I suggest you do," said Ronnie in an authoritative voice. "It's your civic duty."

"Thanks for the advice," the desk clerk's voice turned cold. "Here are your room keys. Breakfast is served from six to eleven. I'm afraid the meal is not included. I'll call the bellboy to help you with your suitcases."

"No need, we'll manage on our own. Good night," said Ronnie. He took the key cards and turned toward the elevators with Liah. Suddenly, an idea came to him and he headed back, pulling Liah after him.

"Did Mr. Lumner receive any other calls or visitors during the night?"

The desk clerk hesitated and shifted his gaze to Liah's face. She answered him with a warm smile. "About half an hour after he had gone up to his room, I transferred a call to him." He yielded to Liah's smile. "Five minutes later, Mr. Lumner called down and asked me not to put any more calls through. He sounded upset or tired. I guess he was tired. By the way, the call was from China. I know that because I was curious about the area code and found out what country it was from."

"Do you have any record of outgoing calls as well?" asked Ronnie.

"Wait a minute. Let me check the copy of his bill," answered the desk clerk, his eyes nervously shifting from side to side. "No, no charges for outgoing calls. But that's not unusual. Nowadays, most people use only their cell phones."

"Thanks. And good night again." Ronnie left a twenty-dollar bill on the counter, grabbed Liah's arm, and turned to the polished steel doors of the elevators. While waiting for the elevator, he saw Gadi out of the corner of his eye, entering the hotel and going toward the reception desk.

Chapter 10

Sunnyvale, October 18, 2013, 8:15 AM

The guest in room 1022 lingered next to the door, carefully examining his reflection in the entryway mirror. He found the image to be pleasing. Five feet eight inches of muscles, oriental features he inherited from his Taiwanese mother, and hair that refused to turn gray, completely blurred the truth he was in his late forties and concealed the many injuries his body had suffered during his long career as a martial artist. He wore a pair of plain jeans and a black, slightly oversized t-shirt with a Nike symbol spread across it. On his feet he wore a pair of blue sneakers, and his watery, cobra eyes were concealed behind dark sunglasses. He moistened his index finger with his tongue and fixed an imaginary errant hair on his right eyebrow, took a last glance in the mirror, and left the room.

The corridor leading to the elevators was deserted. *As always, luck is on my side,* he thought, as the door of the empty elevator opened with a faint whistle. He stepped in and pressed the "Lobby" button, maintaining an emotionless expression as the metal cell began its descent.

He ran the usual list of activities in his mind: telephonic checkout — done, the falsified details were already in the hotel's computer; he'd left nothing behind in the room; and all fingerprints were erased. He knew from experience only careful planning and an almost paranoid caution had kept him alive thus far. The elevator stopped on the eighth floor. A man and a woman in their thirties stepped inside, nodding a good morning greeting to him. The guest answered with an offhand nod of his own and returned his gaze to the floor indicator screen above the door. There wasn't any need. The man was focused on the woman's face, and it was doubtful he would be able to identify him from their meeting in the Waltham orchard.

"Lobby," the mechanical voice announced as the elevator stopped and the door slid silently into the wall. Ronnie gestured with his hand politely, inviting the guest to be the first to exit, smiling back at the thank you nod the stranger sent him.

The guest crossed the lobby without stopping and went out the revolving door into the hotel's private access road, where his rental car was waiting. His hand slid a ten-dollar bill into the palm of the valet, as the latter gave him the car keys.

"You like him more than you like me?" Liah caressed Ronnie's cheek.

"Did you notice he was wearing a Phi Beta Kappa ring? For the life of me, I can't really see him belonging to that elitist honor society."

"At least he's not a sloppy dresser like you. I still want to die every time I see you show up to the fanciest events dressed like a dairy farmer." She kissed his smiling mouth, and her hands lovingly brushed his unruly hair as they walked hand in hand toward the dining room.

Chapter 11

"I have to admit they cleaned the room really well," muttered Gadi. "The little shits wiped out all the evidence." He pulled a chair from a nearby table and sat at Liah and Ronnie's table in the hotel dining room.

"Yes, that's fine, Gadi, you're welcome to join us." Liah smiled at him.

"Late last night, probably because the hotel management pressured them to do so, the police approved cleaning the room your Christian had slept in. After I checked in, I paid the room a little visit. Everything is spotless. It's impossible to reach any conclusions about what actually took place in there."

"Why did you let them know you're interested?" Ronnie wondered. "Why would you want to draw their attention?"

"Who said I asked for permission? I just said I dropped by the room for a visit. I visited several other places in the hotel as well, it was pretty interesting." Gadi smiled mischievously. "Besides, at the very least, the night clerk already knows I'm interested. He knows you're interested as well. At least that's what he told me last night. Do you know how much a desk clerk working for this fancy hotel makes a month? It's a scandal! On the other hand, his measly salary gave the hundred-dollar bill I just happened to have in my pocket pretty good purchasing power. Being a good person, I thought the money should be in the hands of someone to whom it could really make a critical difference." Gadi stopped and winked at them. "Would you believe I'm able to use 'purchasing power' and 'critical' in a single sentence without getting confused? To make a long story short, by mere coincidence, the desk clerk needed to print out a list of all the guests who stayed in the hotel yesterday, including the checkout times of those who'd exhausted the 'Sheraton experience.' He was so excited by my philanthropic display that he accidentally printed two copies. One of them is now in the hands of Benjamin O'Hara, a New York detective I've been cooperating with for many years. I assume we'll know if we have a possible lead by the end of the day." Gadi spread his hands forward, leaned his head back slightly, and gave them a proud look, like a child expecting to be praised for his resourcefulness.

"Who said we're going to investigate what happened?" asked Ronnie with mock anger. "What my company wants is to get out of this without our name being mentioned and move on. Do me a favor and let go of it. It would be a pity if your help drags me into this mess. It's better for me, for the fund I'm working for, and for TDO to remain invisible. OK, Gadi?" Ronnie tried to explain, even though he knew Gadi had now entered his "selective deafness" mode. The moment he had his sights locked on something, curiosity became the only force that drove him, and until he could satisfy it, he would remain locked on target like a cruise missile. His target's destiny would be that of a cruise missile's as well.

"Understood, sir. And you're welcome. Shall we eat something? I'm dying of hunger."

The three of them went over to the buffet, which was laden with numerous dishes.

"Nothing beats the cheeses you get in Israeli hotel breakfasts," mumbled Liah, a hint of longing in her voice. "Who would want to eat beans or miso soup for breakfast?"

The two boys weren't listening. They were busy filling their large plates with food and exchanging meaningful glances, understood only by them. For a moment, they seemed to her like a pair of lovers, and she felt a pang of jealousy. Their eyes scanned the restaurant and its guests, and once they'd finished their coordinated examination, they signaled a confirmation to one another with a mutual wink of an eye. Liah couldn't help but admire the fact they were able to perform these actions while selecting food and conducting small talk about the weather, the flight and other nonsense she knew did not really interest them in the least. "You're acting like two second-rate spies," she said sarcastically, "whispering and sending each other signals. Who do you think is listening to you? That old lady over there who's going to collapse to the floor if she adds one more slice of bread to her plate? Oh, I know, those two young guys over there wearing suits. They're the enemy. Take it easy, boys. We have a long day ahead of us."

"Look, Liyush," Gadi addressed her with a nickname he'd just invented, "you know I'm not prejudiced against anyone, I'm just suspicious of everyone. You can never be too careful. I'm not really afraid of the old lady. I think I have a fair chance of beating her in hand-to-hand combat. The young guys over there are really detectives. Good job. Now let's eat."

The three of them quieted down and concentrated on the plates in front of them.

"Mr. Saar?" Ronnie raised his eyes and saw the two suit wearers standing over the table. One of them quickly flashed a detective's shield clipped to his belt.

"Yes. How can I help you?"

"We'd like you to join us for a brief conversation, after you finish your meal. We can conduct it in the hotel lobby or down at the station, wherever you choose."

"I suppose I know what this is all about, and I'd be delighted to speak with you. How about fifteen minutes from now in the lobby?"

The two young men nodded in agreement and returned to their table, where they continued to follow each of Ronnie's movements. Gadi kept on eating as if all this had nothing to do with him. "Liyush, well done identifying those two," he said into his plate. "You've got yourself one hell of a bride, Ronnie."

"Enough with your nonsense, Gadi," Liah snapped at him. "This is not a game anymore. Ronnie, what do you plan to do?"

"Mainly to listen and try to get some information from them. It's nothing to be excited about. They know I had nothing to do with this."

"Then how did they find you so quickly?" Liah insisted.

"They think like Gadi, only they have more manpower to handle information processing," answered Ronnie with ease, while in his mind he was already busy planning the tactics of his conversation with the detectives. "They must have run a background check on Lumner and my name came up. Once they discovered I was at the hotel, someone in the police decided it could be worthwhile to talk to me. The easiest explanation is that our friend from last night had a word with them and perhaps, to impress the police, decided to play amateur detective as well, and now they think I might know something. Everything is fine. Don't worry."

"If you'd like," Gadi said while chewing, "you can turn the large key in the bundle I gave you last night a hundred and eighty degrees. That way I'll be able to hear your conversation with the policemen. Anyway, the GPS is working and I'll know if they happen to decide to take you down to the police station."

Ronnie took the keys out of his pocket and activated the transmitter according to Gadi's instructions. "Behave yourselves," he said and left the dining room. The two detectives hurried after him.

Gadi gave Liah a long stare. "What?" she asked.

Gadi didn't waste any time. "I didn't believe Ronnie would ever trust a woman again. You know he was in a very serious relationship before you, and she really hurt him?"

"I know. She cheated on him with her ex-boyfriend. We don't have any secrets." Liah's eyes were buried in her coffee mug.

"I've never seen him so in love. Promise me you won't hurt him," Gadi added.

Liah immediately rose from her seat. "Thanks. I need to get back to the room." She gave him a light kiss on the cheek and left without turning her head. Before entering the elevator, she stole a glance at the lobby and saw the two detectives sitting next to one of the tables with Ronnie by their side.

"Thanks for agreeing to speak with us. I'm Detective Quincy and this is Detective Rogers," opened one of them. "As you know, Mr. Christian Lumner was found dead in his hotel room yesterday. He left a brief suicide note which was as mysterious as his death. I understand you're sitting on the board of directors of the company he worked for, and wondered if you had any piece of information you think might shed some light on this incident."

"Just out of curiosity, how did you find out I'm a member of the company's board of directors?" answered Ronnie with a question of his own, keeping his tone light to mask his deep interest in the answer.

"From the company's directors registry. It has your name as the chairman of the board as of October 1st," Quincy answered willingly.

Ronnie felt as if he'd just received a baton blow to the head. As far as he knew, changing the name of the chairman in a company's directors registry was a process that took time and would require his signature on the documents. As he had held the position less than a week, his name, along with his forged signature, must have been submitted even before he'd agreed to accept the job.

"I understand," he muttered, trying to reorganize his thoughts. "Unfortunately, I don't have any information that might explain Christian's suicide. Had I suspected he would perform such an extreme act, I would have alerted the authorities in advance instead of waiting for a disaster to happen."

"You have a slightly unusual accent," Rogers cut him off, wrinkling his forehead with interest.

Ronnie hated comments like that. Occasionally, Americans he'd meet would drop hints that he didn't really belong. At least that's what it felt like. "Yes, I'm Israeli, and even though I've been living in the States for more than ten years, I still have my Israeli accent."

"Do you know why Mr. Lumner was here?"

"He flew here to discuss the possibility of raising money for the company with venture capital funds. Unfortunately, he never got the chance to meet with them. I can't understand why a man with suicidal thoughts would fly from Boston to California only to commit suicide…"

"The hotel desk clerk who checked him in on the night of his arrival claims that Mr. Lumner received a disturbing call in the middle of the night. Do you happen to know anything about that?"

"No, I don't. I suppose the easiest thing would be to look at his phone's incoming call list and see where the call was from."

"At the moment we have no information about the caller's identity," came the answer. "The list of recent calls in the cell phone we found in his room had been erased."

"Why would someone about to commit suicide delete the list of calls from his phone a moment before the act?" Ronnie stopped for a moment, scratched the back of his head, then muttered, "Are you sure this is a suicide?"

"Why do you say that?" Quincy hurried to ask. "Do you know of any enemies who threatened to murder him?"

"Of course not. But the flight to the West Coast, deleting his call log, the call he received in his room in the middle of the night, his request to the desk clerk to hold any calls—"

"How do you know about the call he received in his room?" Rogers barged into his words, sticking to the role of the hardened, crafty investigator.

"Let's give each other a little credit. I assume the desk clerk told you about the conversation I had with him last night. I'm trying to be open and fair with you and expect you to do the same, as much as duty allows you to. Now, with your permission, let me ask again: Are you sure the man committed suicide?"

Quincy and Rogers exchanged a quick glance, and after Rogers nodded in agreement, Quincy offered, "The official police investigation line is that it was a suicide. Our working premise is that Mr. Lumner wanted to spare his wife from finding his body and decided to take his own life far from home. Nevertheless, we're still examining other possibilities. I have to admit, the questions you've raised crossed our minds as well, and we can't shake the feeling it all seems too organized, as if someone staged a neat and tidy suicide by the book. From our experience, that's never the case. We've asked for a court order to get the call list from Verizon, his cellular provider. We'll have the list tomorrow at the latest. I wonder why it was so important to the deceased, or whomever else it was, to erase the information about the telephone calls. Perhaps he had a lover who'd left him and he didn't want us to find out. Who knows?"

Ronnie was startled. The detectives didn't say it outright, but it was clear they had not entirely ruled out the possibility of murder. "Allow me to ask, how did Christian kill himself?"

"With sleeping pills. The chambermaid found him in the morning. The initial blood tests showed he had enough alcohol and benzodiazepines in him to take down an elephant."

"Sleeping pills and alcohol. The question is, where did he get such a large number of sleeping pills in the middle of the night? It's unlikely he'd brought them from home to commit suicide here, of all places. We spent the entire previous day together, then we shared a car to the airport. At no point did he act like someone who was tired of living."

"We've been bothered by the same question. We canvassed the pharmacies in the area that were open during the night, and we found no evidence of sleeping pills being sold. The only explanation for him having so many sleeping pills is that he'd brought them with him. Which is, as we've already agreed, very strange," Quincy summed up.

"I assume you've already told his wife…"

"Yes, she asked for our help with bringing the body back to Boston. Poor thing. They have one-year-old twins," answered Quincy, and for the first time his voice was filled with human emotion.

"Indeed a very sad occurrence." Ronnie got to his feet. "If there's anything else I can help you with, please don't hesitate to ask. Now, if you'll excuse me, I have a few urgent matters to attend to."

"Thanks for your cooperation. If you can think of anything else that might help us, please contact me," said Quincy and handed Ronnie his business card.

"Gladly," answered Ronnie and shook both their hands, already calculating his next move.

Chapter 12

"What's the matter?" Ronnie tensed up as he entered the room and found Liah sitting on the bed, her knees against her chest, arms wrapped around them. "Did Gadi say something stupid?"

"While the reason for being here is absolutely clear to me, deep down, when I decided to join you, I was hoping for a little intimacy. A trip to Sausalito, good food, walking aimlessly at sunset and having lots of sex. This tragedy and the police investigation caught me off guard, emotionally speaking. It's not your fault, but..." Disappointment trickled into her voice.

"I need to organize my thoughts before we'll be able to go out and have some time for ourselves." Ronnie hugged her feet and leaned his head on her knees, yearning for her touch. After a long minute of futile waiting, he went over to his computer. Liah came and stood behind him and glanced at the document he was reading. It contained Christian's list of appointments, as he had emailed it to Ronnie during their meeting. She noticed immediately that only a single appointment had been scheduled for Friday. It was the meeting with McGrady, a senior partner at Accord Ventures. The appointment with him was supposed to run for five hours, and in a remark, Christian had added that McGrady would be joined by the staff that conducted the due diligence on TDO —

as well as with representatives of the consulting firm the fund had hired. The rest of the appointments, three in all, were all squeezed to fit into Monday's schedule.

"Why couldn't Christian arrange his appointments so that he would be home for the weekend?" Liah wondered, although she shouldn't have been surprised considering all the weekends she'd had to spend by herself over the past year.

"Friday's appointment was very important. Accord is the fund that was supposed to lead and invest a considerable amount of money in the current financial round. I think Christian wanted to give them all the time in the world and, if need be, to continue the meetings over the weekend. Perhaps he planned to fly back to his family for the weekend, if no more meetings were necessary. From the conversation I had with him while we drove together to the airport, it was clear his twin sons were the most important things in his life."

"He had twins?" she asked, shocked.

"Yes, they just celebrated their first birthday a month ago. Heartbreaking," his voice became hoarse, "but it also raises a big question mark. What kind of man would let problems at work cause his two small children to become fatherless?"

A silence settled in the room. Suddenly, Liah didn't find the idea of going out to be so appealing. She hugged Ronnie to her, liberating both her thoughts and the tears that began to wash her face.

"I'm sorry," Liah murmured, and Ronnie felt her sweet breath on his cheek. "It was insensitive of me to pressure you to go out. But I really think you need to take a break, even for just a few hours. Perhaps we'll go out to do some jogging? I think it could help us both to clear our heads. And besides, I don't understand what you're chasing now. You've already made it with your own company. You're not lacking the money. So what's driving you?"

"Money is not the issue. Ever since I can remember, it's always been important for me to do what's right and not necessarily what other people think is right and bring to closure every task I undertake in the best possible way. If it's important for you to name this quality, perhaps 'determination' will do it."

"You know, 'determination' is how a person would name his own quality. The rest of the world will simply call it stubbornness. And you, as we well know, are as stubborn as a mule."

"As far as I can recall from my days in the kibbutz, a mule is actually a very nice animal." Ronnie laughed.

"Perhaps on the kibbutz, but have you ever seen a mule in Manhattan?"

"Whatever. As I said before —"

The phone on the table vibrated to indicate a new text message. Come to Pete's Café at 11:45, Gadi instructed. Liah Googled "Pete's Café." After a series of energetic typing outbursts, she pushed back from the table and said, "The coffee shop is about three miles from the hotel. How about we run there? Gadi will probably be able to drive us back, and if he won't — we can always run back as well."

"You're as efficient as you are beautiful." Ronnie smiled lovingly, and they both went to change into their running clothes.

They ran silently, both absorbed in their own thoughts. Ronnie matched the pace of his running to Liah's while stealing concerned glances at her, looking for signs of pain. A half hour after they'd left the hotel, they entered Pete's Café, covered with sweat from head to toe. The coffee shop was crowded with small groups of young people, all trying to shout loud enough to overcome the terrible acoustics. Gadi sat at a corner table, three glasses in front of him. Ronnie and Liah made their way toward him. A moment after they sat down, a young man wearing Bermuda shorts and an undershirt approached them and asked if he could take the remaining chair. Liah smiled at him approvingly and the guy smiled back.

"Leave it here," Gadi snarled at him. The guy raised his hands apologetically and left.

"You couldn't find a louder place for us to meet?" asked Liah. "Or did you choose it so the bad guys won't be able to eavesdrop on our conversation?" she added with half a smile.

"Truth is, I wasn't thinking anything of the sort. But I remembered the last time you visited San Francisco, you told me you loved the iced coffee at the

Pete's there. I took an educated guess that you'd run here and that it'd take you about half an hour. I ordered your favorite coffee about a minute ago. No sugar, of course," he added and pushed the glasses at them.

Liah blew him a theatrical kiss. "You're quite an asset. If Ronnie wasn't in love with me, I wouldn't blame him if he came out of the closet for you."

"Who told you he hadn't done that already before he even met you?" Gadi asked with an emotionless expression.

"What you don't know can't hurt you," said Liah in a surprisingly serious tone.

Gadi gave her an inquisitive stare.

"Are you children quite finished?" asked Ronnie.

"O'Hara processed the information I sent him, and less than an hour ago, he sent me the results." Gadi returned to his report. Liah and Ronnie leaned a bit toward him and looked at him expectantly. "Obviously, he wasn't able to run a background check on all the hotel guests in such a short time, so he chose the easy way. He assumed most of the people who stayed in the hotel had some high-tech background or were working in industries related to the field, so they were all likely to have LinkedIn accounts. Sure enough, a quick checkup that cross-referenced the names, telephone numbers and email addresses they'd left at the hotel when checking in verified this assumption and provided a preliminary explanation for their presence at the hotel. He ran a more thorough background check on the five guests he wasn't able to associate with the industry. Two couples came to visit their children, working for local start-up companies, and two others were construction contractors working on an office building in the city. The only guest who aroused suspicion was one John Brown, about whom no information could be found. The telephone number he'd left is disconnected and the house number of the street address he gave in Chicago, on South Franklin Street, doesn't exist. In a checkup O'Hara conducted, it turned out a man answering to that name had rented a vehicle for two days and paid in cash. The credit card he left as a deposit belongs to a bank account under his name, but it's unclear whether the account has any available funds in it. No less surprising, is that no one at the car rental company can recall what the mysterious John Brown looked like. Even our curious desk clerk seems to have come down with a case of temporary amnesia, and no wage increase could cause him to remember any identifying details," Gadi finished and leaned back, a troubled look in his eyes.

"Even if we assume he was involved" — Liah hesitated — "what form could his involvement take? They found a suicide note on the table, there were no signs of violence in the room, and Christian's stomach was stuffed with sleeping pills."

"I have no idea," Gadi admitted. Liah shifted her eyes to Ronnie, who answered her by raising his eyebrows in aggravation. He too tried to find a solution to the question, which hadn't stopped bothering him since he'd spoken with the two detectives. "I suppose we can't share our findings with the police. After all, there's no way we can explain how the guest list fell into our hands."

"Right, but don't let it bother you. I'm willing to bet they're working on the same list right now and will soon reach the same conclusion."

"How can you be sure of it?" Ronnie wondered.

"They're in the middle of doing just that. When O'Hara's men spoke with the couple who came to visit their son, the man was angry because he'd wasted his time detailing the reason for his stay in the hotel just a few minutes before. Even the excuse they gave him about confusion caused by a change of shifts couldn't calm him down. On the contrary. O'Hara said he'd charge me for all the time his man had to spend listening to a long, tiresome lecture about the importance of handing over the baton in an organized way. I feel sorry for his son." Gadi smiled.

"I still don't have an answer for Liah's question nor for the question of who would have an interest in killing Lumner and why," Ronnie mused aloud.

"So, I have something to work on. I believe I'll know the identity of our mysterious stranger by the end of the day." Gadi winked at Liah and turned toward the door. "I suppose you'll manage to run all the way back as well. Don't run too fast, you don't want to get the old man too tired."

"Wait a second, Gadi..." Ronnie wanted an explanation of his friend's plans, but Gadi left the coffee shop without adding another word.

"Do you have any idea where he's going?" Liah wondered.

"No, but I'm sure he has. Gadi is not one to make false promises. I'm always amazed by his ability to manage. Did you know he's not only fluent in English but in Spanish as well? And that he received most of his foreign language education by watching American movies and Latin American soap operas."

They sipped the rest of their coffee then headed out of the coffee shop and began their run back to the hotel.

The guy wearing the Bermuda shorts left his seat, and while going toward the table where the three had just sat, pressed the dial button on his cell phone. He went to the chair Ronnie had sat in, detached a miniature listening device from it and briefly reported to the person he'd called, "They spoke in a language I couldn't understand. I'm sending you the audio file."

Chapter 13

Sunnyvale, October 18, 2013, 12:45 PM

The young man emerged from the coffee shop and walked with his head down, busy with the iPhone in his hand. *He's sending the audio file of the recording to his operator,* Gadi guessed, *and once his operator is finished translating what we've said, he'll realize I'm onto him and then, once he comes crawling out of his hole to look for me, I'll be ready and beat the shit out of him...* Gadi continued to follow the man with his eyes as he turned toward the parking lot and saw him take his car keys from his pocket and press one of the remote control buttons. A shrill beeping came from the center of the lot. The young man smiled contentedly to himself and headed toward the car.

Gadi hurried to his own vehicle, started the engine and began to follow the man's car. After seven minutes of driving down the seemingly endless El Camino Real, the two vehicles glided into the downtown Domain Hotel's parking lot. The young man left his car in the parking lot, got out still busy with the phone in his hand, and turned toward the lobby.

"My God, you're such a rookie," Gadi murmured with a sigh, "let's hope your boss proves to be a bit more challenging." He continued through the parking lot toward the rear parking area on the other side of the building. There, he exited his vehicle, brushed his pants, scanned the area, and when he didn't detect anything suspicious, walked toward the hotel entrance. When he passed next to the young man's vehicle, he bent for a split second and attached a tracking device to the inside of the right wheel fender. Then he turned and walked back toward his car. On the way, he took out his cell phone, activated the tracking application, and made sure the device he'd attached to the young man's vehicle was actually working. Once he was back behind the wheel, he dialed O'Hara.

"O'Hara Investigations."

"O'Hara, please."

"Who may I say is calling?"

"Gadi."

"Gadi who?"

"Just get me O'Hara immediately or start looking for another job."

The line went silent. Gadi punched the steering wheel in frustration. A moment before he hung up, a baritone voice was heard, "Gadi, you son of a bitch, if you talk to my secretary like that one more time, I'll never work with you again. Is that clear?"

"Clear. Crystal clear. Now talk to me. What's going on?" Gadi snapped impatiently.

"Our guy left Sunnyvale and took a flight to Boston, still using the same identity. He was supposed to land at Logan about an hour ago, but I couldn't find any evidence indicating he'd rented a vehicle under his name. Perhaps he changed identities after he landed, or maybe purchasing a ticket to Boston was only a diversion, and he flew to a different city under another name. What would you like me to do?"

"Try to look for him in Waltham hotels. It's a shot in the dark, but what do we have to lose? Update me if it's my lucky day. I'm flying to Waltham now, and if the bastard tries to get into the TDO offices, I'll catch him. One of his men is here in the Domain Hotel. I've attached a tracking device to his car. I'm sending you the transmitter identification code. Have one of your people follow him. OK?"

"Gadi, who's paying for all this?"

"As far as you're concerned, I am. Bye," he said, disconnected the call, and dialed Ronnie.

"Yes, Gadi."

"Did Lumner tell you about any weird things happening in his office? Perhaps he felt someone was following him?"

"Yes. He also wanted us to go out of the building to conduct a private conversation. Why?"

"We may have gotten lucky. We'll talk later," answered Gadi and hung up, leaving Ronnie frustrated by the fact he did not detail or explain his conclusions.

Liah, who had just come out of the shower, noticed Ronnie's contemplative expression and asked, "What's the matter?"

Ronnie updated her with the details of the conversation.

"I can't shake the feeling he knows more than he's telling us. The way he left the coffee shop so quickly. His promise to discover the identity of the mystery man from the hotel, and now this. I don't know whether I should be happy or sorry for bringing him into this situation," Ronnie said, sighing.

"I'm bothered by something else," Liah began hesitantly. "Gadi has never kept any secrets from you. If he's doing that now, it means he thinks we'll be safer that way. Perhaps we should just drop it. It's really not our job to catch a killer, even if he did murder the CEO of the company you're the chairman of. Perhaps it would be safer to convince Gadi to come with us to the police, give the two detectives we met this morning all the information you both have and go back to New York?" Liah gave Ronnie a pleading look.

"I never thought anyone would be able to construct a sentence containing the words 'perhaps it would be safer' and 'go back to New York' and make it sound reasonable. But you may be right. I'll talk to Gadi soon and then we'll decide."

He dropped to one of the sofas so preoccupied that he wasn't even aroused by the sight of Liah's body, revealed through an opening in her bathrobe.

Chapter 14

Chicago, October 18, 2013, 5:25 PM

The wind blew so violently it seemed to penetrate the window frame on the Sears Tower's twelfth floor. The large man moved to sit on the other side of his impressive desk. The telephone rang. He stretched across the desk, struggling with his flaccid belly, reached his hand out, and picked up the receiver.

"Hello."

"Robert?"

"What do you want?" Robert groaned when he identified the voice.

"The mission you instructed me to perform has been carried out."

"What have you done? How could such a supposedly simple action end up as such a disaster?"

"You asked for results — you got them." Anger brought out the traces of an Asian accent in the voice of his interlocutor. "We told you the man's resistance would be removed; that's exactly what happened. What's the problem?"

"We wanted you to pressure him, convince him with some talking, perhaps threaten him a bit, but killing him…?"

"It's a pity you never told me that. I have a recording of our conversation. Would you like me to play it for you? Perhaps then you'll be able to explain when exactly you limited the scope of my action."

There was silence on the other end of the line, finally broken when the Chinese man continued with a cold voice, "And I expect, as we've agreed, to have two hundred thousand dollars deposited in my account by Monday morning."

"You'll get the money," Robert hurried to say, "but what the hell did you tell him that made him take his own life?"

"Are you sure you want to know? Besides, who said he committed suicide? By the way, next week, you'll get an additional call from me with new instructions."

"W...w...what? What sort of instructions?" Robert mumbled, staring at the phone after he realized the call had been disconnected, an acidic taste crawling up his throat. He called back, but to his surprise, his call was answered by a cellular company automated message: "We're sorry, you have reached a number that has been disconnected or is no longer in service." He tried a few more times but to no avail. All his attempts were met by the same irritating message.

I'm in over my head in a vicious mess. The shocking realization overwhelmed him as he loosened his tie and attempted in vain to undo the top button of his shirt with trembling hands.

Chapter 15

San Francisco International Airport, October 21, 2013, 6:30 AM

The sun sent its first rays, trying to warm the morning air, in vain. Liah and Ronnie stood wrapped around each other in front of the United Airlines terminal.

"I hope I'm able to catch the night flight back. I'll be back home same time tomorrow at the latest," he whispered in Liah's ear, while trying to release himself from her hold on his body. His action only served to achieve the opposite result. Liah tightened her grip, refusing to let go. Concern for Ronnie paralyzed her.

"Don't worry. I promise not to do anything stupid. All I plan on doing today is to meet with McGrady from Accord Ventures to try and keep the prospect of their investing in TDO alive. If I have time, I'll try to meet with the rest of the funds. No macho stuff, I promise."

"But Ronnie ..." Liah began, when a police officer the size of a small hut and armed like Robocop emerged to their right and interrupted.

"Sir, please move your vehicle. This is a no-parking zone," he barked at them without trying to conceal his dislike of the hundreds of tearful farewells he had to witness on a daily basis.

"Yes, sir," answered Ronnie, gently disentangling himself from Liah. He lovingly caressed her cheek and blew her a final farewell kiss. His eyes continued to follow her as she moved through the gigantic revolving door and was swallowed into the terminal.

It was eight thirty AM when he drove his car onto the famous Sand Hill Road, the holiest of holies of private equity and venture funds in the United States, the dwelling place of more than a trillion dollars. Fifteen minutes later, the efficient hostess of the Madera led him to a table for two at the rear of the restaurant, placed the menu on his table, smiled, and left, hurrying to admit the next of the customers crowding the entrance.

"Coffee?" A waitress emerged from nowhere.

"Gladly. And I would like to order a Louisiana lump crab meat frittata, whole wheat toast, and orange juice."

"Thank you, sir. Your order will be coming out in about seven minutes."

Ronnie leaned back and began to run possible scenarios for the upcoming meeting in his head. *Whatever happens, it's important to keep Accord Ventures in the game. If they decide to get out of the investment race, TDO will remain without cash and will be doomed to close. It's obvious they understand the delicate situation the company's in, so they'll try to pressure us to lower our valuation...* The phone in his pocket gave a single vibration, announcing a new incoming message. Ronnie examined the screen. The message was sent from an unlisted number: You will soon get a low purchase offer for TDO. Expect pressure from unexpected sources. Please do not share this message with anyone. Additional information will be sent later on.

Ronnie read and reread the message several times. Finally, he regained his composure and forwarded it to Gadi, adding at the end: Gadi, try and see if you can trace the sender of this message.

The reply came immediately: Done.

I'll never understand how he's able to reply so fast, Ronnie thought, *it seems like he spends his entire life texting and talking on the phone.*

The phone vibrated again, this time a ring accompanied the vibrations.

"Ronnie, it's David. When are you coming back to the office?"

"Probably tomorrow. I'm meeting with Accord Ventures today."

"What for? We need to sell the company as quickly as possible, even at a loss. A new investment, especially following Christian's death, will take months. Leave everything and come back to the office. Henry and I would like to have a word with you."

"Since I'm already here, it seems logical to meet with McGrady from Accord."

"You're wasting valuable time."

"I'm not so sure about that. It'll take time to find a buyer, and Accord is already at the end of the process."

"Ronnie, the TDO investors think otherwise. I believe we can get an acquisition offer faster than you think. This is also Henry's opinion."

"If you know something I don't, now's the time to update me. If you don't, I intend to conduct the appointment as scheduled."

An angry silence settled in. Ronnie patiently waited, until he heard, "I think you're making a serious mistake, but do what you see fit. Goodbye." The call ended abruptly.

The bitter taste of an approaching failure filled Ronnie's mouth. He replayed David's strange instructions in his mind, the impatience in the managing partner's voice, and the text message he'd received. It was all obscure. Frightening would be more accurate. He felt new variables had entered the complex equation of his life, variables that might soon turn it upside down.

Chapter 16

"I'm still shocked by the terrible news," McGrady opened the conversation right after they'd taken their seats in the conference room. "I can't understand what could have caused an accomplished person such as Christian to end his own life. If I'm not mistaken, he was married and had young children…" Ronnie nodded, but McGrady didn't wait for a response and continued sluggishly, "I spoke with him on Thursday, sometime in the late afternoon, just as he'd boarded his plane. I apologized for not calling earlier and gave him our decision regarding the TDO investment. Even though he didn't like what I had to say, he accepted it in a professional manner."

Ronnie was suddenly overwhelmed by the same irritation that had become an inseparable part of him in the past few days. *Every time I speak with someone about Christian, I get some additional piece of information I didn't even know existed,* he thought, straining to maintain his self-control. "I'm sorry, Mr. McGrady, but —"

"Roger. Please call me Roger," McGrady cut him off.

"OK, Roger. Allow me to be frank with you. I don't know anything about the conversation you're referring to. It would be helpful if you could fill me in on the details."

"Yes, of course, Ronnie," answered Roger, slipping Ronnie's name into the sentence in an attempt to give his words a more personal touch. "On Thursday, we called a meeting of the fund's investment committee to discuss the possible investment in TDO. It's no secret we've put a lot of work into evaluating the company and estimating its potential. My conclusion, as someone who spearheaded the deal, and the conclusion of the entire staff was unequivocal: TDO has a bright future ahead of it and investing in the company can potentially yield our fund substantial profits. That's why I entered the discussion with a strong recommendation to invest in the company. I even intended to propose that we provide the entire amount required for this current investment round ourselves. Christian knew in advance this would be our recommendation. I was so convinced the investment committee meeting would only be a matter of following procedure and that the investment would be approved quickly, that ten days ago I flew out to Boston to participate in a TDO internal strategic discussion. My goal was to speed up the pace of my integration on the company's board. Christian was so full of life and energetic during that strategy session. I find it hard to believe he killed himself just a few days later."

"And what happened during the investment committee meeting?"

"At first it appeared to proceed as expected. I presented my partners with all the parameters that I thought defined the investment as a successful one, and when I finished, I could recognize the agreement on their faces. However, in the discussion that followed the presentation, two problematic points were brought up. One was the inability of the company to warrant that no inherent problems were concealed in the production process, and the second was a recommendation to wait until the two independent operations, scheduled for the coming week, were performed. The partners thought it would be best not to rush into an investment before these two potential risks were addressed and resolved to our satisfaction. When everyone had finished speaking, I realized I wouldn't be able to approve the investment at that particular meeting, and the discussion would resume only once we had positive data concerning the two sticking points that had emerged. As I mentioned, I updated Christian with the details of the investment committee decision only when he was already on the plane, on his way to meet me. Until that point, he must have believed his meeting with me would end up with us providing him with a term sheet." Roger went quiet, an expression of genuine sorrow appearing on his face.

"How did Christian take it?" asked Ronnie, trying to gain time to enable him to digest the news.

Roger thought for a moment, and when he finally answered, some wonder was woven into his voice. "Of course he was disappointed, but he immediately pulled it together and said he was already heading to the West Coast anyway. He wanted me to take some time to have a face-to-face meeting with him. He said he had some additional information that might change the partners' opinion. Of course I agreed to meet with him. I thought after four months of working together I owed him at least that, but I was also intrigued to hear what he had to say. I have to admit when we spoke, he sounded convinced the information he had was substantial enough to change the fund's decision."

"Did you try to get that information from him?"

"Of course" — Roger smiled — "but Christian, even though he sounded very relaxed, insisted on delivering it face-to-face and not over the phone. We set up a meeting for Friday morning. I could hear the flight attendant in the background, asking him to turn off the phone because they were about to take off."

Ronnie sat silently, digesting the information.

"I'm sorry I didn't ask you before, but would you like some coffee?" Roger suddenly woke up. "I feel like I need a strong espresso to recover."

"Gladly." Ronnie rose, and together they stepped out of the conference room and headed toward the kitchen. Five people were crowded around the espresso machine, and judging by their ages, Ronnie guessed two of them were partners and three were junior employees.

"This is Ronnie Saar, the new TDO chairman," said Roger. He then introduced two of the junior guys, mentioning they were members of the TDO due diligence team. One after the other, they approached him and expressed their sorrow over Christian's death.

Ronnie couldn't help but be impressed by the genuine sorrow that prevailed in the place, a feeling that regretfully wasn't shared by his associates back at Vision Partners. Before they left the kitchen, Ronnie turned to them and said, "I really appreciate your genuine condolences, thank you," and left the room feeling their stares on his back.

He followed Roger back to the conference room. "I understand your position," Ronnie said the moment they sat down, "but in order for me to understand precisely where we stand, please allow me to ask you a few focused questions."

"By all means." Roger spread his hands invitingly.

"Assuming the two surgeries are satisfactory and we demonstrate our ability to manufacture a couple of new and successful lots of the medicine, would you still be interested in investing?"

"In principle, yes. Of course, the decision will now heavily depend on the experience and capabilities of the new CEO."

"And if we decide together the identity of the new CEO, will that lower the level of uncertainty you're currently feeling?" Ronnie persisted.

"I believe so, but as you probably know, I'll need the approval of the investment committee in any event."

"If, under the conditions I just suggested, you promise to recommend the investment, then I'm happy. I can't expect any more than that at this stage."

"I promise."

"Excellent. I'll pass along any name that comes up as a good CEO candidate for your initial approval. In the meantime, we'll keep in touch. Are we agreed on that?"

"Agreed," Roger confirmed.

"I really appreciate the level of openness with which you've conducted this conversation."

They shook hands, and Roger accompanied Ronnie to the exit, where he patted him on the shoulder and said, "I don't envy you the task ahead of you. Good luck."

"Challenges are the spice that gives life its flavor." Ronnie smiled and for the first time understood the meaning of the reputed Chinese curse, "May you live in interesting times." Not even the purple blossoms woven in the trees surrounding the parking lot could cheer him up and shake the disturbing feeling he would soon get into the Guinness Book of Records as the chairman having the shortest tenure before his company went bust.

He got into his Prius and drove to the airport. It was time he shook up David and Henry and heard everything they knew and had not shared with him yet.

Chapter 17

"Who gave you permission to pry into my private life?" Liah exploded.

"I didn't ask for permission. I'm asking you again: When were you going to tell him?"

"That's none of your business. Once I settle things, I'll tell him."

"Nonsense. You haven't been able to settle what you refer to as 'things' for the past four years. What makes you think you'll be able to do that now?"

"I'll do it. After he realized I'd disappeared to the United States, he sent me a message through my parents that he's willing to compromise. I believe I'll be able to make him let me go for a reasonable price. Perhaps even soon."

"I've known people like him. Chances are slim. Bitches like him will never sign a document the other party is willing to sign. They spend their lives thinking they can always get more." Gadi raised his voice, "How on earth did you get involved with such a loser? You, of all people? The living embodiment of reason and calculated logic."

"I didn't know he was like that." For the first time, the rage on Liah's face was replaced by anguish. "I don't know what to do. I don't want to lose Ronnie. Don't tell him anything. Promise me. Please promise me."

"He'll kill me if I tell him. But he'll also kill me if he finds out I knew and didn't tell him. I guess that makes me dead, whatever happens."

"What do we do?" she asked heavily, her eyes straying.

Gadi's voice became surprisingly warm. "You're the best thing that ever happened to him. With you, he managed to erase the scars he bore and get back to being a normal person. I won't let the demons of his past to return to haunt him. I'll help you."

"How?" asked Liah fearfully. She knew that soon, very soon, she would need to deal with the problem whose consequences frightened her so. But more than that, she was afraid to think about what Gadi meant when he'd promised her his help.

Chapter 18

The sonofabitch is a professional, Ronnie read the message sent to him the previous evening before he'd taken off for New York, call me.

Gadi answered on the first ring and began reporting without wasting time. "While you were having a good time with Liah over the weekend, I was working. One of O'Hara's employees went to the TDO offices during the weekend impersonating a detective, you know, false IDs and everything, only to hear from one of the vice presidents, Jim, who was working in the lab over the weekend: 'Aren't you guys talking to each other? Another detective just left the offices ten minutes ago.' In the search my man conducted in the company offices, no listening devices or cameras were found. This Jim was busy supervising some sort of freaking process in the laboratory and allowed our guy to walk around the building by himself. I guess the previous fake detective did the same thing, which left him all the time in the world to erase any evidence of his past deeds. Unfortunately, we couldn't get a description of the impostor. The son of a bitch was completely invisible. That nerd Jim answered all my guy's questions with the same irritating answer: Average. Height — average, hair color — something between black and brown, sort of average, etc. He may be a genius in science, but when it comes to real life he is literally blind. The long and short of it, it's a dead end."

"Perhaps it's not a dead end. At least now we know someone is trying to hide something. If we discover who or what they were trying to hide, perhaps we can get back on track. By the way, where are you right now?"

"It doesn't matter," answered Gadi, "you'd kill me if you knew." And without allowing Ronnie to reply, continued, "On Friday, I sent one of O'Hara's men to the West Coast to take care of another matter for me, and I urgently flew to perform a critical task for my most important client. Now I need to disappear for a few days, but O'Hara's men will continue to operate for you...and before I forget — I need to update you about two more things: My man in Boston said that an unmarked car with two passengers who had 'detective' written all over them arrived just as he left the parking lot. If the police took the time to send detectives to the company on the weekend, they must be onto something important. There are two possibilities here: Either they've reached the same conclusion I have about the mysterious man from the hotel, perhaps even suspect that he's involved in Christian's death, or during the investigation of Christian's death, they've reached the conclusion it's somehow related to his work at TDO and hoped to find evidence in the company offices that might explain the suicide. Investigating over the weekend, it means they must be under some kind of pressure. It may be worth your while to sniff for information with your two West Coast detective friends. And one more thing," he continued passionately, "last night, O'Hara managed to finally get information regarding the message sent to you while you were in Menlo Park. It came from a prepaid mobile phone. It means the sender is either someone who can't afford the monthly payment plan, or — and this is more logical — someone who wants to remain anonymous. All I know at the moment is that the call came from the East Coast. Other than that," Gadi fired off, "you'd better close the audio transmitter on your key chain before you get home. I sampled some of your conversations and it was occasionally embarrassing. We'll keep in touch. Bye."

So much like Gadi, the thought passed through Ronnie's head, just as he saw his suitcase emerging from beyond the bend of the conveyor belt.

The drive back home went without incident. He did have to hear fifty minutes of a telephone conversation the driver conducted in some sort of African language, but it was better than having a polite conversation with a philosophical taxi driver.

"Liah?" he called when he got into the apartment, filled with longing. The silence that greeted him sent a sharp pang of fear into his stomach. Ronnie set his suitcase on the floor and hurried toward the bedroom. The illuminated clock next to the bed made him realize what time it was — three AM. He took off his clothes and stepped into the shower, allowing the water to wash the past day's experiences off him. When he got into bed, he gently embraced Liah's warm body and seconds later was sucked into a deep and dreamless sleep.

Other than Kumar's annoyance, the next morning's run was also uneventful. The shop owner carried on at Ronnie for not letting him know ahead of time that he was back in New York. Now his usual breakfast was not ready! Ronnie listened to the reproachful speech with a smile, knowing that Kumar was secretly proud of the fancied sense of ownership he had over his customer.

When he got back to the apartment, he was surprised to discover Liah still sleeping. He looked at her for a long time then bent to kiss her. At the last moment, he gave up and left the bedroom.

When the sound of his footsteps had subsided, Liah opened her eyes slowly and, without raising her head, searched the room. She knew she wouldn't be able to continue to ignore Ronnie for long but kept on lying still, the thoughts running through her head intensifying her distress. The clinking sound of dishes being washed emanated from the kitchen. As opposed to everything she'd earlier planned on doing, she tossed the blanket aside, ran to the kitchen, and jumped on Ronnie, kissing him wildly.

"Forgive me for not brushing my teeth yet, but I was afraid you'd already left. Wait, don't go anywhere." She ran to the bathroom, where she stood in front of the mirror, feeling paralysis taking over her body again. She washed her face, brushed her teeth, and washed her face again with freezing water. Finally, she took another look in the mirror, nodded to herself with encouragement and went out. When she reached the kitchen, she found Ronnie sitting with his iPad and reading news from Israel.

"Amazing," he told her without raising his head, "not a dull moment in our small country. You finally don't hear about the Palestinians for a few days, and the economy is somehow being stabilized, so now crime raises its ugly head. No value for human life anymore. People just kill a man on the street for some drug money. This is the third time this week that the ultra-orthodox from Bnei Brak have been attacked and robbed, and the police are doing absolutely nothing about it."

"You have enough concerns of your own without worrying about a robbery that went bad in Israel."

"It drives me crazy. They murdered some poor man named Shlomo Klein who studied in the yeshiva and barely had enough to eat. Someone stabbed him in the heart, stole his wallet, and ran away. How much money could a yeshiva student have? It's terrible to lose one's life over a few pennies…"

The silence that settled in the kitchen caused Ronnie to raise his head. Liah was standing in front of him, face ashen. He went to her quickly, took her arm and carefully sat her in the nearest chair.

"What's wrong?" he asked with concern.

She was silent for a long time that seemed like an eternity to him and finally looked at him with sad eyes and said in a choked voice, "I don't know. I guess I've been working too hard. I felt very tired yesterday, now I suddenly have a dizzy spell. I think I'll go back to bed. No reason to worry, honey. Go to work. I'll call you if I need you. Just keep your phone available all the time."

Ronnie hesitated. "Perhaps we should go to the hospital. Fatigue and a general feeling of illness are the first signs of a coming Crohn's outbreak. You're the doctor; I don't really need to tell you that."

Liah looked at him tiredly, nodded her head and said, "It's all good. Really. It's all good."

Ronnie held her arm and supported her on her way to bed. He covered her with a blanket, brought the makeup bench closer to the bed, and placed on it the breakfast he'd prepared. After she promised him again she would call him at the first signs of another dizzy spell, he left the house and drove to work.

The moment she heard the door closing, the tears that were locked up within her burst out. "What have you done, Gadi? What have you done?"

Chapter 19

New York, October 22, 2013, 8:30 AM

The polite nod that welcomed Ronnie at the reception desk, the tense silence that surrounded him as he made his way to his office, and the people who avoided his eyes as he greeted them with a "Good morning" all served to awaken a feeling of impending doom within him. He turned to David's office. When he met Evelyn's gaze, he realized that something was indeed about to happen. Something bad that had to do with him. Something that, for some obscure reason, everyone knew about — everyone but him. Without asking for permission, he opened David's door and went inside. "This 'wife is the last to know' attitude doesn't suit me at all," he declared to David's scowling face. "I expect to be the first to know about matters relating to me and not the last."

"Sit down, please, Ronnie. I'd expect a bit more maturity from you."

Ronnie somehow managed to restrain himself from tightening his hands around the plump senior partner's neck and remained standing with his eyes blazing. "Let's keep my education for another time. Talk, or I'll be leaving my resignation letter on your desk. Then I'll go to the authorities and share all the suspicions that have been running through my head since I returned to New York. So decide what you want to do and be quick about it."

Ronnie looked at David, who gazed right back at him without blinking. "Sit down, Ronnie," he instructed again quietly.

Ronnie turned on his heel and silently headed toward the door. As he grasped the handle, he heard David's measured voice, "The last two clinical trials with the TDO medicine have failed."

Ronnie turned around slowly and returned to the desk without lowering his eyes from David's.

"What do you mean when you say the clinical trials have failed?"

"The patients died. Both of them. The police are already involved and so is the FDA. We learned about it only last evening, when you were already on the plane. I didn't think you'd be insulted that I allowed you to get a good night's sleep and decided to tell you about it in the morning, once you reached the office."

"I'm the one who signed the authorization to conduct the clinical trials," said Ronnie with a hoarse voice.

"I know. You had no way of knowing something like this might happen. After all, eleven trials have been successfully conducted, and if I understood correctly, the same medicine used for the previous six trials was also used for the last two."

"How do you know that the medicine from the same production lot was used for the current clinical trials? I never reported what Christian and I had approved for these operations."

"Someone from the FDA was looking for you yesterday. When I told him you were on a flight, he asked to speak with me and told me everything that'd happened. I immediately updated Henry and he told me it was the same medicine. Otherwise, I wouldn't have known. I'm not involved with what's going on in the company." David emphasized his words in a way that made it perfectly clear which one of them was sunk up to his neck in this new problem and which one of them would keep his hands clean, no matter what happened.

"So you're saying they're looking for me because I am the one who signed the clinical trials approval for the company?"

"Yes, and also because you're the chairman."

Ronnie remained seated and looked thoughtful.

"Is there anything else, Ronnie? Anything I can help you with?" David's concern sounded genuine.

"Yes. Can you explain to me how my name appears on the company's directors registry as the TDO chairman? I haven't signed any related documents yet. I've been serving as chairman for about a week. At the end of last week, I discovered — or more precisely, the police discovered — that I'm listed as the TDO chairman as of the beginning of the month."

A cloud of concern passed over David's face. "I really don't know. This is very strange. Hold on a moment," he mumbled and called Evelyn into the room.

"Evelyn, what's the status on the paperwork for changing the name of the TDO chairman I asked you to prepare with the company attorneys?"

"It's been waiting on my desk since the end of last week," answered Evelyn with typical efficiency. "When I asked the lawyers to prepare the documents, they laughed and said they'd already been prepared. As soon as I hung up the phone, the documents were waiting in my email. I wanted Ronnie to get back so I could have him sign them. Should I bring them now?"

"Look, Evelyn —" David began to answer when Ronnie cut him off and said, "There's no need. I'll collect the paperwork on my way out. Thank you, Evelyn. That'll be all."

When Evelyn exited the room, David gave Ronnie an embarrassed look. "Please explain," he asked.

"Look, David, I gave this matter a lot of thought, before deciding to ask you this question. Bottom line, even though I must admit you have an irritating and condescending way of speaking to me, I've decided you're not a bad person, and you're probably not involved in all the recent TDO complications. But that doesn't change the fact a lot of strange goings-on have been taking place below the surface. The documents that the company's legal advisor received and were signed by me before I even agreed to accept the job, Christian's death, and now, the death of patients in operations that were supposed to go smoothly. One dead patient would be bad enough, but two? Something doesn't smell right, and I intend to find out who's responsible. I need to ask you to keep the forgery of my signature secret, until we know who we can and can't trust. I can't ignore the fact Henry has a lot to gain by having me listed as the chairman instead of him. I insist that we keep him in the dark about any action we take. This is also how we should act with all the staff in the fund, from the most senior partner to the most junior employee. Perhaps it's a bit paranoid, but it's better to be paranoid than end up under a tombstone. Agreed?"

"I'd stake my life on Henry," David exploded. "He would never do anything that might hurt me or the fund."

"What about me? Would you swear that he'd never do anything that would sacrifice me in order to save his entire world? Did you know he instructed Christian to falsify reports and clinical trial results so he'd be able to raise money? I pray you didn't." Ronnie stared at David's shocked face. "I need to know you're with me on this, or I'm going straight to the authorities. I believe they'll realize very quickly I'm not involved."

David seemed devastated. Ronnie assumed the thought that Henry, his good friend with whom he'd founded the fund, might have performed criminal acts was difficult for him to digest. If Ronnie was right, even about a small part of his suspicions, their partnership and possibly the fund itself were about to end.

David lowered his head submissively and asked, "And what do you intend to do in the meantime? Burn Henry at the stake?"

"I don't intend to do anything for the time being. I don't have any proof that Henry's behind this, and until I do I have no intention of involving him or anyone else. At the moment, what's more important than finding suspects is to clear the fund and myself of any involvement. If you agree with me, I'm willing to take the risk upon myself and not turn to the authorities at this stage."

"Thank you. I really appreciate your loyalty to the fund. I want you to know, as far as I'm concerned, this kind of sacrifice is not taken for granted. I give you my word and promise to keep this between us. Thank you."

Ronnie stood up, left without adding a word, collected the documents from Evelyn, and headed to his office. He closed the door behind him and called Gadi. Strangely, his call went straight to voicemail. "Where are you, Gadi? Call me when you're available," he left a laconic message and disconnected. It was the first time Gadi hadn't answered after a single ring. *I guess he's on a flight*, Ronnie tried to explain the strange phenomenon.

He dropped to his chair and turned on the computer when the phone in his hand suddenly vibrated: This is not about you. The future of many other people is at stake. Try to understand what happened in the last operations.

Ronnie was rereading the message when suddenly the door opened and Henry barged in. The senior partner stopped in front of him, his fists leaning on the desk, knuckles whitened with the effort, his body leaning forward, and his face reddened with anger. "Are you happy now? In times of crisis, time is our most valuable asset, and you've wasted it with investors instead of doing what you were told to — try and sell the company. Why on earth every time I give someone some authority, he's suddenly convinced he has godlike knowledge? Couldn't you just do what you were told?"

Ronnie read the message one more time.

"Answer when I'm talking to you. You've ruined a company I spent the past seven years building. Answer me!!!"

"I don't know of any acquisition offer," said Ronnie coldly, "and if you have any information about the subject, you should have passed it on to me. If I'd had different data, I might have acted differently. By the way, that was the last time you raise your voice to me. Get the hell out of my office and come back when you're willing to speak in a civilized manner."

"You're gambling with something that doesn't belong to you," Henry screeched angrily.

"Well, you're the expert on gambling," Ronnie hissed and sent him a defiant look.

Henry froze for a moment then turned around and left the room.

Chapter 20

Ronnie could not continue to ignore the fear that had begun to take root. Gadi, the only person he could always trust, was gone without a trace. And Liah? Something had changed in her since his marriage proposal, which he'd been sure would make her the happiest person on earth. For the past week, he hadn't been able to understand her behavior. Then there were these messages he'd been getting from an unknown party. Who was the sender? Where did he get his information from? Is he sending his messages in order to help? Or perhaps he was attempting to mislead him. Maybe it was another one of Henry's or one of the other partners' dirty tricks?

He recalled a quote from Asimov: "In life, unlike chess, the game continues after checkmate." *It's time to start taking the initiative*, he decided and straightened up. Filled with motivation, he took out his phone and dialed.

"Good day, Jim speaking."

"Hi Jim, it's Ronnie. I'm curious to hear about the autopsy results for the two people who died on the operating table."

"Hi, Ronnie. Good to hear from you," Jim sounded genuinely pleased. "Unfortunately, no postmortems were performed. The families objected, so the bodies were taken and buried."

"I don't get it. Isn't it standard procedure to perform a postmortem in a case of unexplained death?"

"Absolutely. But in both cases, for religious reasons, the families objected to the autopsy and threatened a lawsuit if it was performed against their will. As far as I know, they signed documents releasing the hospitals from any responsibility and demanded to have their loved ones released for burial."

"I —" Ronnie attempted to understand when Jim cut him off and continued, "What could possibly explain this strange behavior is that the Philadelphia family belongs to the Amish community, and the New York family are Orthodox Jews from Brooklyn. As far as both families are concerned, the deaths of their loved ones were an act of God."

"A strange coincidence, don't you think?"

"Not only is that strange, I also can't think of a reason the patients died. All the previous operations were successful, we used the same medicine that was used in those procedures and even so this tragedy occurred. Of course, we're checking all the processes on our end again, but I have to say so far we haven't discovered any problem and everything seems in order. So either we've been struck by ill fortune, or someone interfered in a criminal way."

"Are there any more vials remaining from this batch, ones we could send to a neutral laboratory to be examined?"

"Unfortunately, no, those were the last of the batch we used for all the clinical trials."

"Are you sure?"

"Yes. I'll send you a photo of all the vials left in the safe. They're all empty and were all used in the previous trials."

"What bothers me even more, is the fact the same disaster took place in two different hospitals, with two different medical staffs, while using the same medicine from a batch that's already been checked," Ronnie summed up quickly. "I'm going to Mount Sinai, where the patient from Brooklyn had surgery. I'll try to fish for information that'll help us understand what's going on. Meanwhile, you keep checking as well, and update me if you find out anything." He disconnected and pressed the receiver against his forehead, the thoughts gushing in his mind. A few long minutes later, he called Gadi and reached only his voicemail again. Ronnie sighed with frustration and rose from his seat.

"Evelyn, I'm going out of the office, and I'm not sure I'll be coming back today. I'll be available on my phone."

"Take care of yourself, Ray," she murmured without raising her eyes from the document she was reading.

Ronnie stopped for a moment and tried to catch her eye. She continued to concentrate on the paperwork on her desk, so he turned and left.

A taxi stopped next to him and spat out a passenger. He slid into the backseat in his stead.

"Mount Sinai," he instructed the driver, took out his phone, and dialed.

"Detective Quincy," a firm voice was heard from the other end of the line.

"Hello, this is Ronnie Saar."

"Hello, Mr. Saar. I'm glad you called. I promised you an update," Quincy replied in a matter-of-fact way. "According to Verizon, only two telephone calls were erased. One call came from an unlisted number in China or Hong Kong, about the time Mr. Lumner arrived at the hotel; the other one was made by Mr. Lumner to his wife, about two thirty AM."

"Strange that he called his wife so late at night."

"Good point. We asked her about the call, and she admitted it was strange, but there was a power outage at her house, and the electric company repairmen were there to fix the problem, so she was awake when the call came in. She made the comment that they must have gotten there so quickly because of the late hour. Because she was busy with them, she couldn't really speak with her husband for long. From what she can recall, all he said was that he missed her. Beyond that, nothing out of the ordinary was said between them during the conversation."

"And the call from China? I understand you've reached a dead end regarding that call as well. Could you explain, please?"

"Unfortunately you are right. Someone invested a lot of work in routing that telephone conversation so its origin would remain confidential," he replied, his frustration clearly showing. "Our experts were unable to trace the origin of the call. It could have been made from China, but it could've originated in the United States as well. I know it's frustrating, but unfortunately there's no way to determine whether the conversation was related to business matters or to the suicide. The postmortem showed the cause of death was indeed a high dose of sleeping pills. No evidence of violence was found on the body. Therefore, even though there are still a lot of unresolved questions surrounding this case, we have no choice but to close it as an unfortunate suicide."

"OK. Thank you for your cooperation. If your conclusions change, I'd appreciate an update."

"Of course. Have a good day, and we expect you to reciprocate." The call was disconnected.

Ronnie tried to call Gadi again. "Please leave a brief message, and I'll get back to you shortly," the voicemail message promised again.

"We're here, sir. Seventeen fifty not including tip, please."

He handed the driver a twenty-dollar bill and made his way to the hospital through worry-filled family members and frantic medical staff.

Chapter 21

New York, October 22, 2013, 1:40 PM

"Yes, Jim," Ronnie answered the call, ignoring the reproachful stares from the other people in the elevator.

"When you get to Mount Sinai, look for Brian Campbell, he's our technical support guy over there. I let him know that you're coming; he'll try to connect you with the right people over there. I'm sending you a text message with his phone number."

"Thanks, Jim."

The elevator door opened, and Ronnie found himself in front of the orthopedics department's reception desk. He dialed the number Jim had sent him and turned his head when he heard "My Way" playing nearby. "Hello, this is Ronnie Saar. I'm in front of the reception desk," he began to say, when he noticed the Sinatra fan raising his head and searching for him. Ronnie waved his hand, disconnected the call, and approached Brian.

"Jim suggested that I wait for you here. How can I help?" Brian extended his hand hesitantly.

Ronnie responded with a brief handshake. "I'm interested in speaking with the surgeon so I can try to better understand what happened in the operation."

"As I've already explained to Jim, no one here will agree to talk to you. Even though Mount Sinai received release forms from the family, the hospital's lawyers won't allow any staff members to speak to outside parties," Brian explained. "Trust me, I've tried to fish for information and failed."

"Where can we find the doctor who performed the operation?" Ronnie insisted.

Brian leaned over the reception desk and exchanged whispers with one of the nurses, who smiled at him fondly. He straightened up and began to walk toward the patient rooms, signaling for Ronnie to follow. "We'll stalk Dr. Bijrani. Right now, he's visiting a patient in room 409," he whispered.

That doesn't sound good... Ronnie remembered what he'd learned during his military service: Bijrani was a common last name for members of the Baloch tribes of Pakistan and Afghanistan, tribes known as Moslem fanatics. Before he was able to reply, he found himself standing in front of a man in his late forties dressed in green surgical scrubs. A name tag was displayed on the right lapel of his lab coat and his face was adorned with a thick black beard, already strewn with white.

"Excuse me, Dr. Bijrani," Brian addressed the doctor, who looked at him curiously.

"Yes, Mr. Campbell? How can I help you? If it's about the operation again, you're wasting your time." The doctor turned to leave.

"Pleased to meet you." Ronnie hurried to intervene. "My name is Ronnie Saar and I'm the chairman of TDO. I'd really appreciate a minute of your time. I understand there're things you can't talk about, and that's fine. I promise to keep the conversation brief."

"It will indeed be brief," the bearded doctor muttered.

"Was there anything in the patient's medical history that could explain what happened?"

The surgeon gave Ronnie a blazing stare and hissed, "When I told you I wouldn't speak with any of you about the medical details of the deceased patient or what happened in the operation, what part of that didn't you understand? But just so you won't get any ridiculous conspiracy theories into your head, I can only tell you the operation was routine, and that the patient was a perfectly healthy man who had the misfortune to undergo surgery at the wrong time. You should check for the problem with your company and not at the hospital."

"What do you mean by his 'misfortune'?" Ronnie hurried to ask. Bijrani walked away, while turning his head and muttering, "You…you always think other people are responsible for your problems." Then he disappeared around the corner.

"What was that all about?" Brian wrinkled his forehead.

He knows I'm Israeli, Ronnie realized but said only, "Just another person who hates the pharmaceutical industry. Excuse me a moment." He dialed a number, listened for a moment, and then returned the telephone to his pocket with undisguised vexation.

"Who else could help us, Brian?"

"Like I told Jim, I tried to talk to the nurses, the doctors, and management. They're all maintaining a bond of silence. Because no autopsy was performed, I believe even they don't really know what went wrong. As far as they're concerned, it's better for this affair to go away and not evolve into a medical malpractice lawsuit. But, Mr. Saar, perhaps there's another way to get answers to the questions you just asked the doctor." Brian lowered his head.

"Which is?"

"Forgive me for saying this —" Brian stuttered when Ronnie cut him off.

"Speak. Just say what's on your mind."

"I suppose you're Jewish." Brian looked at Ronnie, and when he saw Ronnie was unresponsive continued, "As you know, Abraham Berkowitz, the deceased, came from an Orthodox Jewish family from Brooklyn. You Jews have a tradition called shiva. I suggest you take advantage of it and pay the family a visit. Here's their address." Brian turned to the desk, wrote something on a sheet of notepaper and handed it to Ronnie.

Ronnie put the note in his pocket and asked, "Before I leave, could you please tell me more about your involvement in the experiments so far, and whether you saw anything unusual in the last one?"

"Gladly." Brian seemed happy to share details about his work routine with the chairman of the company. "Officially, my job is to consult with the surgeons on how to use the drug we developed at TDO — and also to be present during the operation, in case a problem arises. In practice, because we're a small company, I was also in charge of safeguarding the medicine from the moment it arrived at the hospital to the time it was taken to the operating room."

"Why does the medicine need to be 'safeguarded'?"

"Because we're at the experimental stage that's supervised by the FDA, it's important to track and document the location of the medicine minute by minute, from the moment it's manufactured to the time it's used. One can't always plan the precise moment the medicine will be brought into the operating room, and therefore, we must make sure no third parties have a chance to interfere in the process. The medicine arrives in a sealed container, straight from TDO, and is secured in the safe. The chair of the department of orthopedic surgery has the key to the safe, and I keep the container key. I'm the only one who can open the container in the operating room, an action that breaks the seal impressed on the lock when the medicine was packaged by TDO. That's the procedure I followed in all the operations, including the last one. There wasn't anything unusual about the last container, and I'm willing to testify that other than the five minutes I took for a coffee break, the safe in which the container was stored was under my supervision at all times."

"Could someone have sabotaged the container while you were away?"

"Definitely not. As I said, any attempt to mess with the lock would've broken the seal, which would immediately disqualify the medicine from use. Actually, the procedures do not call for me being with the medicine once it's locked in the safe, but Christian thought one could never be too careful. Unfortunately, that didn't help." Ronnie saw genuine sorrow on Brian's face when he mentioned Christian's name.

"And you're sure the seal was whole? Perhaps you didn't pay attention? After all, I'm sure up till now everything has always gone smoothly, and you didn't have any reason to be suspicious," Ronnie persisted.

"Of course I'm sure. Furthermore, since the first clinical trial, I've been documenting all the processes. I thought one day the documentation would give us a nostalgic way to remember the way the company was run during its first years. I did the same this time. But only up to the moment the container was opened. After that, as you know, I was required to leave the operating room and let Dr. Bijrani perform the operation by himself." Brian took his iPhone out of his pocket, fiddled with it a bit, then smiled when he heard a beeping sound from Ronnie's pocket, announcing an incoming message. "I sent you a photo of the seal before I opened it," he explained. "If you look at the image properties, you'll be able to see the time stamp, which is the same as the time the operation started."

"The bottle appears to be completely intact," Ronnie muttered while enlarging the image. "Could anyone have replaced the medicine in the operating room?"

"I can't see how. The medicine did what it was supposed to, and the patient reacted well almost until the end of the operation. His condition deteriorated only at the end of the process."

"How do you know that?" Ronnie was surprised.

"Because of the length of the operation. At least an hour had passed from the time I left the operating room to the time the emergency medical staff rushed in."

"I'm going to meet with the family now. Let's hope I find something that'll help us shed some light on this mystery. Meanwhile, try to squeeze some more information out of the nurses or the secretaries...I've noticed they're quite attracted to you." Ronnie smiled.

Brian smiled back.

Chapter 22

New York, October 22, 2013, 3:10 PM

Trying to reach you, he read the incoming message from Liah when the phone in his hand rang. "I'm transferring David," Evelyn said sharply, and immediately after that Ronnie heard the fund manager's voice barking at him, "I understand that you won't be coming back to the office today. I wanted to update you with another important TDO-related development."

"Hold on a moment, David. I'm in a very noisy place. Let me find a spot where I'll be able to talk to you." Ronnie scanned the hospital lobby, trying to find a quiet spot for the conversation.

"Just call me when you can." The call was disconnected.

Ronnie took a deep breath and shrugged with slight exasperation. He decided to give up on his plan of taking the subway to Brooklyn and flagged down a taxi. The moment he sat in the yellow cab, he called his office.

"I'm transferring you to David," Evelyn answered after a single ring.

"You asked me whether we had an acquisition offer for the company," David continued as if their call had never been interrupted, "so now we have one. When the company began to encounter financial difficulties, I started to work on an alternate plan, in

case Christian wasn't able to raise the required funds."
He stopped for a moment, allowing his last statement
to sink in. "I've always believed the safest strategy is
to hope for the best, but prepare for the worst." He'd
begun to speak like a pedagogue again. "A month ago,
I contacted a friend from my school days, Robert
Brown, chairman of Mentor Pharmaceuticals, in an
attempt to interest him in acquiring TDO. For the past
two weeks, we've conducted countless conversations
about the subject, conversations in which Christian had
been actively involved as well. To be fair, I need to
mention that Christian objected to the deal. He agreed
to approve it only if he was certain the fund-raising
was so delayed he ran the risk of running out of cash
and not being able to pay the employees' salaries.
Robert, an experienced manager and quite a shark in
his own right, understood Christian's tactics and gave
us a deadline for providing a final answer, after which
the offer would be withdrawn. Unfortunately, the
deadline expired last Friday. Therefore, when you
asked me whether there was a concrete M&A offer
pending, I didn't know what to answer. This morning,
I turned to Robert again and managed to convince him
to renew his offer for an additional week. Robert
agreed but mentioned that in light of recent
developments, the price they'd be willing to pay will
be lower. How much lower? I don't know. I suggest
you speak to him as early as today and try to divine his
intentions. Drop everything, if you need to, and go
straight to meet him. I'm a great believer in face-to-

face conversations. Evelyn will send you all the details."

"And what was the previous offer?"

"Four hundred million dollars."

"No wonder Christian objected. The moment we resolve the problems and go on the market with a stable and reliable product, and I'm sure even your friend is convinced we'll be able to solve the problems eventually, otherwise he wouldn't be willing to pay a single dime for the company, we'll earn more than that amount as early as the second year of revenues. And now you say they're offering even less? I'll talk to him, but the chances I'll agree to the deal are slim."

"We've got two dead patients whose bodies are still warm, a CEO who committed suicide, and you're acting like you're holding the goose that laid the golden eggs." David raised his voice in frustration. "Unless you come to your senses, we'll end up with no company at all. Sometimes you need to know when to let go and make sure that at least the money we've invested doesn't go down the drain."

"I'll talk to the other investors. If they all want to sell at any price, I'll close the deal with Robert. If they don't, I'll take my chances and continue to try and build a company that'll yield us much higher profits in the future."

"You're acting like a lion, king of the financial world, while in actuality, you're nothing but a stubborn mule who won't take advice from anyone," David roared.

"You're not the first to call me a mule, but my stubbornness has brought me all my accomplishments in life."

"And now it'll ruin you, and you'll be dragging us down with you. I'm closer than ever to throwing you out of your job and giving back all responsibilities to Henry, who — unlike you — would've closed the deal in an instant."

"Why don't you do that?" Ronnie reacted coldly. "Although I think neither you nor Henry would especially like to dirty your manicured hands in the mess that's been created. It's much easier to just sit in the office and criticize me —"

"Ronnie…" David began, but Ronnie didn't allow him to speak.

"I thought we agreed to work in full cooperation during our last meeting. I guess I was wrong. Because I'm tired of watching my back for knives thrown at me from my home court, I expect you to reach a decision about me as soon as possible. The moment you know whether you want me in the picture or not, send me an email letting me know I'm fired, or alternatively, an email authorizing me to be the sole member of the fund in charge of the negotiations with Mentor. Either way, I'm not going to do anything until I receive one of the two emails. Goodbye."

Ronnie hung up, leaned back, closed his eyes, and tried to relax, forgetting all about Liah's message.

He found David's sudden urgency to be strange. It was pretty safe to assume a man in his position had undergone more than a few crises throughout his business career and would know how to handle them in a calmer, more professional way. *Something else is hiding behind this behavior*, he thought. *Perhaps it's that we're in the middle of raising money for the fund, and a resounding failure at the wrong time might just ruin it all. On the other hand, one would expect him to understand we must work as a team and not allow pressure to hinder us from making the right decisions. Come to think of it, why doesn't he fire me and take the task of selling the company upon himself, or give Henry that responsibility? What's the risk involved with the position I'm holding? Why are they allowing me to lead the process even though they think the road I'm taking is the wrong one?*

Traffic was moving slowly, and even the taxi driver gave up his maneuvering attempts and allowed the vehicle to crawl with desperation toward the Brooklyn Bridge. The phone rang. Ronnie glanced at the screen. The call came from an unlisted number.

"Ronnie Saar," he answered in an official tone.

"Hello, my name is Sinead Clark, and I'm Robert Brown's personal assistant. Mr. Brown is the CEO of Mentor Pharmaceuticals and he'd like to speak with you. Can I transfer the call?"

"I'm sorry, Sinead, I'm very busy at the moment. When I have a minute, I'll ask Evelyn for your phone number and will gladly get back to Robert."

The surprised secretary grew quiet, then whispered something away from the receiver. "Mr. Brown says the conversation will be brief and asks to speak with you now," she said hesitantly.

"Unfortunately, I'm busy now with other people and need to hang up right now. Please apologize on my behalf. Either David or myself will get back to you shortly." Ronnie couldn't help but smile at the sight of the surprised expression on the taxi driver's face reflected in the mirror. *Either I've just made the mistake of a lifetime, or I've forced David to act. Obviously, it's no coincidence that right after I asked David to send me an email clearly defining my status, Robert gives me a call.* For the first time in days, Ronnie felt back in control. *I've finally managed to rock the boat. Now let's wait and see how everyone reacts...*

The crawling movement of the traffic soon turned into a complete standstill. Ronnie decided to try and call Gadi again. To his surprise, his call was answered after a single ring.

"Ronnie, you're a pain in the ass. Stop calling me so many times. I'll get back to you when I can." Gadi hung up. Ronnie redialed, but reached voicemail again. He stared at the phone, frustrated, when a message bearing Gadi's number came in: What you don't know can't hurt you. Trust me.

Ronnie quickly typed: I need to update you with recent developments. Two patients have died. Christian's case was closed for lack of evidence. I desperately need your help. Call me.

Wow. Looking for a quiet spot and getting back to you. Came the answer and with it, another small grace, the traffic began to flow again.

A moment later, the phone rang. "Talk. What's going on?" Gadi opened, ignoring the need to explain his disappearance.

For the next ten minutes, Ronnie detailed all that'd happened to him since they'd parted ways. He described in great detail his conversation with the police detectives, not forgetting to mention the dead ends they'd reached when they'd checked the origin of the telephone calls Christian had received the night of his death and the call Christian had made to his wife. Then he moved on and told Gadi about the two patients who'd died on the operating table and about the strange coincidence involving both families' refusal for an autopsy.

"Something is rotten here," Gadi remarked in his usual picturesque manner. "It may be a shot in the dark, but I think pretty soon I'll be able to see the whole picture. Give me a day or two to check, and I'll get back to you. Now excuse me, I need to go work for you. Take care of Liah."

"Liah?" Ronnie asked with surprise.

The telephone in his hand went silent. He finally remembered and called Liah, but his call went straight to voicemail.

Chapter 23

As soon as he neared the family's address in Borough Park, he saw hundreds of black-clad mourners filling the street. Ronnie asked the cab driver to stop and got out two blocks from the house. He stepped into a glatt kosher grocery store and said, in response to the curious stare of the shop owner, "Shalom. Perhaps you could tell me where I can buy a yarmulke. I'm on my way to offer my condolences."

"Is the gentleman Jewish?" The bearded man gave him an inquisitive look.

"Yes, from Israel."

"And the gentleman doesn't have a yarmulke?" he asked in a reproachful tone.

"I have one, but I came here as soon as I heard about his passing. Could you please tell me where I can buy one?" Ronnie repeated the question, trying to keep the conversation short.

"Please, take one of mine." The shopkeeper handed him a shiny, black satin yarmulke, still gazing at Ronnie suspiciously. "And the gentleman knows the deceased from where exactly?" The interrogation continued.

"It's a long story. Thanks for the yarmulke. I'll bring it back to you when I leave."

"Keep it, and go to shul when you get back home."
The grocer cancelled Ronnie's suggestion with a wave
of his hand.

Suspicious stares accompanied Ronnie as he
approached the home of the bereaved family. The men
who began to gather for the evening prayer, ceased
their preparations and surrounded Ronnie.

"Can I help you, sir?" one of the younger men
addressed him, blocking his way.

"I came to perform the mitzvah of paying the
mourning family a visit and offering my condolences,"
Ronnie answered in Hebrew then immediately said in
English, "I'd appreciate it if you could direct me to
where the family is sitting shiva."

"Why don't you join us for the evening prayer
first" — a prayer book was shoved into his hands —
"then you're welcome to go into the house." The men
turned back and Ronnie joined them, thankful that he
had made it a habit to visit the synagogue on Rosh
Hashanah and Yom Kippur.

The murmur of prayer filled the street. The sea of
people in black began to move in rhythmic waves, as if
obeying the instructions of an invisible choreographer.
Ronnie looked around him and felt a pang of envy in
his heart. He'd never experienced such a sense of faith,
deep and devoid of doubt. He returned his eyes to the
prayer book, but his thoughts turned to his own
personal prayer. Then the evening prayer was
completed and the street began to empty out.

"Follow me." A black-clothed youth whose side-locks curled all the way down to his shoulders turned to Ronnie then walked with him to a narrow apartment in one of the nearby buildings. A young woman sat on a mattress, surrounded by relatives and friends.

"I'm sorry for your loss. May you never know sorrow again." Ronnie lowered his head.

"Thank you. And who are you, sir?"

"My name is Ronnie Saar and I'm from Israel. The company I'm chairing was involved with the operation during which your husband passed away, may he rest in peace, and because the tragic outcome of the operation bothers me deeply, I wanted to come and pay my condolences."

She stared at him in astonishment.

"It must be a great loss," Ronnie said with genuine sympathy, "such a young man..."

"And healthy as an ox" — a tear rolled down her cheek — "if it wasn't for the accident, he wouldn't have seen a doctor for many more years. His leg broke in four different places in a car accident. It ruined our lives and our livelihood, now it's taken him as well."

"Several operations are normally performed to heal such fractures..."

"Right. The first operation didn't solve all the problems. My Abremale felt very bad for not being able to go to work, that's why we pressured the hospital to schedule an earlier date for the operation. We were so happy when they called us a week ago and let us know there was a time slot available earlier than anticipated. We didn't know how to thank that nice secretary enough. And now he's dead." The widow broke into a fit of crying, and her children echoed her and began to cry as well. "He was such a healthy man…and now God has taken him away." She covered her face with a handkerchief, while her youngest son hugged her tightly.

"I'm sorry to hear that. May the Lord give you comfort," Ronnie mumbled, lowered his head and retreated. He sat in the back of the room for a while, nodding politely to the people coming and going. About half an hour later, he left.

Only when he was far from the mourners' house, did he remove the yarmulke from his head and immediately called Brian. "Do you have the details of our guy at Jefferson Hospital in Philadelphia, where the second operation was performed?" Ronnie spoke as soon as Brian answered the phone.

"Yes. Hold on," came the answer, and the line went silent for a moment. "Are you writing this down?" Brian was back on the line and dictated the telephone number to Ronnie. "His name is Moses Lynne, and I'm sure he'll be happy to help."

"Thanks." Ronnie disconnected the call and dialed the number he'd just received.

"Moses." Ronnie heard a youthful voice.

"Hi, Moses. This is Ronnie Saar, TDO's chairman. Can I ask you to check something for me?"

"I'll be delighted to, Mr. Saar."

"I'm sure you know which patient I'm calling about. Please check when his surgery was scheduled and if the patient had a problematic medical history. Call me back at this number."

"Mr. Saar, I'll check when the surgery was scheduled right away, but regarding the medical file, I'm afraid the hospital is keeping that secret, and all my attempts in recent days to get information were met by a wall of silence. What I can tell you though, is that during the discussion that preceded the operation, we asked the orthopedics department's manager to choose, at least for the current stage of the clinical trials, only patients with no medical history of heart conditions, diabetes, etc. The department chair promised us this was in line with the hospital's best interests. This is a university hospital, and they intended to publish an article about the operation. I believe they kept their word."

"OK. I understand. I'll be waiting for your call. I'd like it if you could do it right away. It's really urgent," Ronnie said while going down the subway stairs. The ride on the number 4 express was uneventful, and when he climbed up the escalator leading to 23rd Street, a new message was already waiting on his phone: I tried to call you, but there wasn't any answer. The knee replacement operation was scheduled about two months ago. Couldn't find anything unusual in the process of scheduling the operation date. Hope this is the answer you were looking for. Moses.

Another dead end. Ronnie glanced at his watch. It was too late to return to the hospital or the office. He turned and began to walk toward his apartment.

He was met with darkness when he opened the door. He shuffled toward the kitchen, took out a Sam Adams bottle from the refrigerator and threw himself on the living room sofa. Then he saw a yellow note pasted on the television screen: *I guess you were right. My Crohn's has raised its ugly head again. I've been taken to Presbyterian Hospital. Love you. Liah.*

He hurried off the sofa, turned around, opened the door, and ran downstairs, praying he'd catch a cab quickly.

Chapter 24

Ronnie opened his eyes, glanced at his watch, and quickly sat up when he saw where the hands were pointing. He couldn't recall the last time he'd slept so late. He'd spent most of the night next to Liah's bed. Last night, when he had reached her hospital room, she seemed like a small pale dot in the middle of a white hospital sheet. She was in a daze from all the medication she'd received, and they hardly spoke. The doctor who arrived after midnight to follow up with her asked to speak with him outside the room.

"We gave her a cortisone shot and some sedatives to relieve the symptoms during the night," he reported. "It's important for us to know whether Liah has undergone stressful events lately. Crohn's is a disease suffered by perfectionists. When something ruins their plans, they react with stress, which in turn awakens the Crohn's demon from its sleep."

"Not as far as I know. The only thing I can think of that may have caused some stress is that I proposed to her nine days ago," mumbled Ronnie.

"I don't think that's the reason, unless, and pardon me for saying so, she's not really interested in getting married. If that's not the case, this may be the first time someone has been hospitalized for being too happy. All right, if you think of anything, please update the medical staff. I suggest you go home and get a good night's sleep. With the amount of narcotics she's been given, I don't think Dr. Sheinbaum will be waking up anytime soon," he summed up.

Ronnie took the doctor's advice and went home. He arrived at two o'clock and spent the rest of the night in his own bed.

He called the hospital and was told no visits were allowed before the afternoon; it didn't matter that Dr. Sheinbaum was a staff member. He hung up, frustrated and dragged himself to the kitchen to make his morning coffee. Not really interested in the dubious pleasure of taking the subway in rush hour, he decided to stay and begin his workday from home. He turned on his computer and discovered an incoming email marked as "urgent" from David. His lips curled into a smile as he opened the email and read it.

"Per your request, attached please find a letter authorizing you to be the fund's sole negotiator of TDO's sale. Below, you'll find Robert's phone number. Now cut it out with your games. Call him immediately and close the deal before he changes his mind."

Ronnie printed the letter, wrote down the telephone number that appeared at the end of the message, closed the computer, shut his eyes, and recalled a sentence his father, an amateur historian, told him Napoleon had once said to his valet: "Dress me slowly because I am in a hurry." Sometimes, you need to take your time. He dressed leisurely and went down to Kumar's deli to collect his paper bag. When he returned, he set the table and put out only half the

contents of the bag. Liah's absence filled him with a
sense of gloom. He slowly sipped the coffee he'd
prepared himself while dialing the telephone number
he'd received, and waited.

"Good morning, Robert Brown's office. Sinead
speaking, how may I help you?"

"This is Ronnie Saar, may I speak with Robert?"

"Just a moment, please."

"Hello, Mr. Saar. You're an extremely busy
person," the authoritative voice of Robert rumbled.

"Hello, Mr. Brown. I apologize for not getting
back to you last night, but there were a few things I
needed to finalize in order to conduct the negotiations
with you in good faith. Let's get to the matter at hand.
I understand from David that Mentor is interested in
acquiring TDO. I'd love to meet with you to discuss
the details, of course. I'm available today and
tomorrow, and I'm willing to fly to Chicago
immediately, assuming your schedule allows it, of
course."

"Unfortunately, I'm not available for an
appointment either today or tomorrow," came the
answer Ronnie had expected.

"I understand. So I suggest our secretaries
coordinate a time that'll be suitable for both of us. Like
I said, I'd be happy to come to your office to save you
some valuable time."

"Before you drag yourself all the way to Chicago,
perhaps we should agree on the terms of the deal,"

Robert continued, not even trying to hide his pleasure at the fact he was now the one holding all the aces.

"Gladly."

"Write this down," Robert commanded. "The offer is valid only till Saturday the twenty-sixth. We're offering to acquire TDO for three hundred million dollars. TDO's shareholders will receive Mentor shares in exchange for theirs. The exchange rate will be based on the value of Mentor's shares on the day the contract is signed. If you agree to the terms, I'll clear some time for us to meet on Friday morning, and of course, I can extend the deadline, based on the progress of the negotiations."

"The offer is clear. Thank you. I understand that in the past you offered four hundred million dollars for the company —"

"Patients die, a CEO kills himself, what did you expect? For the value of the company to rise?" Robert's tone became coarse.

"I'll get back to you with an answer later on today. Have a good day," Ronnie said with a pleasant voice.

"Remember, you've got till Saturday." The call was disconnected.

Things are about to get interesting, Ronnie thought bitterly. He searched his computer for the phone numbers of the three other board members and began to make the round of calls.

"Steve."

"Hi, Steve, this is Ronnie Saar, Henry's replacement as chairman of TDO. We haven't had a chance to meet yet, but I've heard some great things about you."

"Thanks. Sad story with Christian, isn't it? How can I help you?"

"An offer's on the table to purchase the company. They're offering us three hundred million dollars through a share exchange. I don't have the offer in writing, but I believe it's serious. In my opinion, it's an extremely low offer — almost demeaning — and the moment we prove we were not responsible for the recent patient deaths, we'll own a company that's worth over a billion dollars. Anyway, I wanted to hear your opinion, as someone who's been involved with the company longer than I have."

"Sell." The brief answer surprised Ronnie.

"Excuse me?"

"Sell," Steve sounded determined. "When the lawsuits against the company arrive, I prefer to be light-years away from it. Just make sure the contract mentions that the day the purchase is made, we're released from all past debts and all future legal claims."

Ronnie was amazed. "You think there's a chance the company is somehow responsible for the deaths?"

"It doesn't matter what I believe. The moment a lawsuit is filed, we'll be at the mercy of jury members who don't understand the first thing about microbiology or pharmaceutical development processes. You want to gamble on the results? I don't. I'd rather gamble on things there's a chance I'll profit from. The company belongs to my investors, and I have a principle not to gamble with their money. I hope I'm being clear enough."

"Every investment is a gamble, but what sets us apart from gamblers and turns us into good investors are good judgment and the ability to assess the risks as well as the potential upside. In the case of TDO, I believe the chances of success are high," Ronnie attempted to speak convincingly.

"And I don't! Will there be anything else?"

"No. Thank you. I'll let you know about my decision as chairman and the fund's position soon."

"I think I know what the position of your fund is, and I hope you know the wise decision you should take as chairman. I hope you won't force me to summon a shareholders' meeting that'll compel you to make the right decision."

Anger began to churn in Ronnie's stomach as he dialed the second number.

"Hans Schmidt."

"Hi, Hans, this is Ronnie Saar, I'm replacing —"

"Yes, I know who you are. I just received a message from Steve to expect a call from you about selling the company. Allow me to save you the presentation. Sell. At any price. The gamble is too risky here. It's better to earn less than lose all the money," echoed the baritone voice on the other end of the line.

"Hans, they're offering only three hundred million dollars for a company that could easily be worth five times as much. Wouldn't it be worthwhile for us to wait? Isn't that the name of the game in our world? The big success story that'll have your name appear on the annual Midas List of top tech investors?" Ronnie tried to appeal to his interlocutor's ego.

"We all want to be recognized as the best, but the graveyards are full of lousy gamblers. Ronnie, I really think we should sell — even at an unattractive price. The sooner, the better." Hans mellowed down a bit.

"OK. I hear you. With your permission, I'll get back to you once I get the opinions of all the parties involved. Thank you for expressing your opinion in such a clear way. Have a good day."

"You too. I hope to hear from you soon."

Ronnie wasn't surprised that his third call was almost identical to the first two. Sell. We mustn't gamble. The sooner we sell, the better. Same messages and same manner of speech. It wasn't a coincidence that David had waited to send the letter, Ronnie realized, he'd needed that time to get the investors on his side. *Now they know my fund wants to sell. No wonder they'd all used the word "gambling." It was the same word Henry spat in my face just a few days ago. This game is fixed, and I'm the only player on the field not in on it. On the other hand, perhaps I'm wrong and they're right, maybe we should sell.*

Ronnie stood up and began to pace the room, trying to postpone the inevitable. Finally, he dialed Robert, and when the latter answered, said, "OK, Robert, the company's board has agreed to the acquisition. Please send me a detailed offer and set up a time for our meeting."

"You've made the right decision," Robert determined. "I'll send you the documents later today. They've been ready and waiting for three weeks." Ronnie could have sworn he heard him laughing contentedly before hanging up the call.

Chapter 25

The telephone ring startled Ronnie. Brian's name flickered on the screen.

"Yes, Brian."

"I think you should come to the hospital. I may have finally found a breakthrough that'll shed some light on everything that's happened." He wasn't able to conceal his pride.

"It might be easier if you'd just tell me," Ronnie practically barked at him, then immediately regretted his words and added, "My fiancée is in the hospital, and I was about to go visit her. It would be very helpful if you could update me over the phone."

"I'm afraid that's not an option; it's important that you come here," Brian said secretively. "I'll wait for you in the same place we met last time."

"I hope there's a real good reason. I'll be with you in half an hour," Ronnie muttered, slightly put out.

He remained seated, feeling drained, and stared at the silent telephone. Finally, he pulled himself together, collected his bag, and marched toward the subway station so immersed in his own thoughts, he didn't notice the man with the Asian features following him and entering the subway car next to his.

Thirty-five minutes later, he stood, as promised, in front of the reception desk and saw Brian whispering with one of the department doctors. When Brian noticed him, he threw the doctor a remark and she burst out laughing. Then he patted her on the shoulder and approached Ronnie.

"Let's go down to the cafeteria," Brian whispered mysteriously and turned toward the elevators without waiting.

Something has taken the shyness out of Brian, Ronnie thought and followed him silently.

When they reached the cafeteria, Brian led Ronnie to a corner table, sat in front of him and sent him an indecipherable gaze.

"Do me a favor, we're not actors in a spy movie," Ronnie said impatiently.

The sharp words took the wind out of Brian's sails all at once. He lowered his eyes and a blush spread up his neck.

"I'm sorry, Brian." Ronnie placed his hand on Brian's arm. "I really appreciate what you're doing, but I'm under a lot of pressure. I'm sorry for erupting like that. It was uncalled for."

Brian raised his head and quietly said, "No, you're right, I got carried away. Sorry." He looked at Ronnie, and when he saw that he'd calmed down, continued, "As you've noticed, I've managed to establish a pretty good relationship with the staff, especially the female members." The blush rose up from his neck to his face. "After you left the hospital yesterday, I continued with my efforts to try to understand what'd happened and mainly to understand what our friend, the Muslim doctor, had meant by talking about our patient's 'misfortune.' I checked with all the nurses and doctors, but no one would talk. I have to admit I was very frustrated —"

"Brian, let's get to the point," Ronnie interrupted as gently as he could.

"Sorry." Brian smiled with embarrassment. "A short while after I called you, one of the receptionists came to me, her name's Gabriela, and asked how much the information I'm trying to get is worth to me. I was very surprised. I've never had a special relationship with her. You know, she's old..."

Ronnie gave him a hint by raising an eyebrow.

"Yes...I'll keep it short. I asked her what she meant, and she told me her son was just accepted to MIT. He wants to study genetics. He received a partial scholarship, but unless he gets a full scholarship he won't be able to attend. She gave me a questioning look, and I immediately told her our company helps outstanding students, but I'm not in a position to promise her anything. I tried to figure out what information she has, but she was very secretive. Finally, she suggested I bring someone who's authorized to promise her what she needs and went away. That's why it was important for you to come personally." Brian stopped talking and stared at Ronnie.

"Let's go talk to her." Ronnie started to leave his seat.

"She won't talk to you in the hospital." Brian motioned with his eyes for Ronnie to sit back down.

"She finishes her shift in about half an hour and will meet you at 97th Street at the Central Park entrance. I suggest that we go back to the department. She's sitting in the office in the reception area and she'll be able to see you through the glass. Once she's seen you, you'll go wait for her at the scheduled location and let her be the one to initiate contact. Sorry I'm behaving like I'm in a spy movie again, but this is what *she* requested." Brian flashed an apologetic smile.

"Terrific. It looks like I have some time to spare before my cloak and dagger appointment. I think I'll grab a bite to eat. Want to join me, Casanova?"

"I…" Brian hesitated but then joined Ronnie as he shuffled through the food line with his tray.

Ronnie chewed mechanically, his thoughts drifting to Liah and his worries about her health. Brian, on the other hand, wouldn't stop reciting nostalgic and amusing stories from TDO's history. It was clear he cared deeply about the company, just like many other people Ronnie knew who were lucky enough to be part of a start-up's founding team.

"We need to get a move on," Brian suddenly turned serious and they walked back toward orthopedics. They stood next to the reception desk and chatted when suddenly, as if he'd received a sign, Brian shook Ronnie's hand and said, "I'll see you later, then. Goodbye." Ronnie glanced at the three women behind the desk. None of them seemed particularly interested in him.

Even though it was a short walk to the park, Ronnie felt the freezing wind all the way to his bones. *When will I finally learn New York is cold in October?* He was annoyed with himself. He was standing at the entrance to the park rubbing his hands furiously to try and warm himself, when a woman in a blue skirt and gray coat, wearing a pendant with a large silver cross approached him and asked in a low voice, "Mr. Saar?"

He nodded and began to walk after her into the park. After five minutes of marching down the park's pathways, the woman sat on a bench and waited for Ronnie to join her.

"Brian tells me you have some information that might help my firm understand a little better what went wrong with the operation," Ronnie began, straight and to the point.

"I never said I know what happened during the operation. I only said I know about something irregular that has to do with it. But there's another subject we need to discuss before I'll be willing to talk." She stared at Ronnie with a penetrating gaze.

"OK, let's take it from the top. My name is Ronnie Saar and I'm the chairman of TDO. And you are?"

"Gabriela Rodriguez."

"Pleased to meet you, Mrs. Rodriguez. I understand your son was accepted to the MIT graduate biology program, wants to study genetics, but is lacking some funds to pay for school. He received a partial scholarship, so I assume he was an excellent student, right?"

"My Javier finished college at the top of his class."
Gabriela's chest swelled with pride.

"Our company has a small scholarship fund that
supports exceptional students and also provides them
with part-time employment. Regardless of what you
tell me, I promise I'll get him an interview in the
company's offices in the Boston area. If he's as sharp
as you say, I promise you, we'll offer him a
scholarship and open many doors for him. I give you
my word," Ronnie repeated his promise, allowing his
words to be digested.

Gabriela examined him with suspicious eyes, and
after some slight hesitation, asked, "Let me
understand, are you saying that even if I get up and
leave right now, you'll still give my Javier a chance at
a scholarship and see to it that he's interviewed by
your company?"

"That's exactly what I'm saying." Ronnie looked
into her eyes. "But any information you might have
will help us solve our current difficulties so we can
concentrate on all the good things our company can do
for the community. That's why I'm asking for your
help. I promise that everything you tell me will be
confidential and that I'll never expose you as my
source."

"And how will I know you'll keep your word?"
she asked, and in her voice Ronnie could hear years of
disappointment over broken promises.

"I don't know what to tell you. Neither of us really
wants any written documentation of this conversation.

I guess you'll just need to follow your gut feeling and your heart," Ronnie explained softly.

"You've got a weird accent." She changed the subject.

"Yes, I'm from Israel, the Holy Land." He decided it wouldn't hurt to try and play the religious card.

The woman rose from the bench and began to pace up and down the pathway, deliberating how to proceed. Ronnie remained seated. After a few moments that seemed like an eternity, she sat next to him again, clutching her handbag close to her chest. "Until very recently, a girl named Roselyn D'Angelo worked with me in the department. About a week and a half ago, I noticed she'd been acting really weird, like she was afraid of something. When I asked her what was going on and if I could do something to help, she avoided the subject and said she didn't know what I was talking about. From that moment on, she did everything she could to avoid me."

Gabriela paused for a breath, an expression of relief on her face. "A day before the operation that went wrong, Roselyn told us she'd decided to go on a trip to Guatemala or someplace like that and handed in her resignation. I was really sorry to hear that because Roselyn is a hardworking and honest person, one of the good girls. She dedicated her life to taking care of her elderly grandmother. When I asked her who was going to take care of her abuela while she was away, she told me she'd found a home nurse for her. We all wished her the best of luck and asked her to write us about her trip. She promised to update us with Facebook posts and pictures. After the patient died, I accessed the file with the patient information so I could pass it on to the legal department; that's our standard procedure. I discovered Roselyn cancelled an operation for another patient, who'd been scheduled two months ago, and gave his appointment to the new patient. Out of curiosity, I gave the original patient a call. Apparently, he'd been told his operation was postponed because of an unexpected emergency surgery. Needless to say, the tragic operation was never classified as 'urgent.' Out of curiosity, I kept digging and discovered there was only one emergency operation that day, and it was for a man who was injured in a car accident that very same morning, long after the operations were switched. I didn't tell the hospital management about it, because I didn't want to get Roselyn in any trouble…"

Gabriela's eyes wandered nervously to and fro, and Ronnie gently put his hand on her arm to try and soothe her. "Could you send me a copy of the documents proving what you've just told me?"

"No. I've said too much already." Gabriela stood up, and it was apparent she regretted talking to him.

"Sit down, please," Ronnie asked quietly, "and give me your son's information so we can contact him. I promise you everything you've said stays between us. I really appreciate your courage in agreeing to speak with me. You've done the right thing." Ronnie waited until she wrote her son's telephone number then took the note from her hand and left the park. A short time later, an Asian man left a bench at the other end of the path, turned in the opposite direction, and disappeared among the multitudes walking in the park.

Chapter 26

The sound of an incoming call found Ronnie two blocks from Presbyterian Hospital, where Liah had been admitted. The number was unlisted.

"Good afternoon," he answered, quickening his pace, hurrying to see Liah and also to warm himself a bit.

"Mr. Saar?" A resolute masculine voice was heard.

"Yes. Who's asking?"

"This is Special Agent Archibald Bukowski from the FBI. I'd appreciate it if you could come to our office at 26 Federal Plaza. I'll be waiting for you."

"May I ask what this is about? I'm terribly busy at the moment. I'd love to meet with you tomorrow, anytime that would be convenient for you."

"The time that's convenient for me is *right now*. If you don't get here in the next hour, I'll get a warrant for your arrest and you'll have the NYPD and the FBI looking for you. Ask for Special Agent Bukowski when you get here." The phone went silent.

Twenty-five minutes later, Ronnie emerged from the exit of the number 5 subway at the corner of Chambers and Centre and began to march toward Broadway, where he turned right and headed to the FBI building.

"I have an appointment with Special Agent Bukowski," Ronnie addressed the redhead behind the reception desk.

"Name?" She raised her eyes and gave him a bored look.

"Ronnie Saar."

"Please sit down." She pointed a chunky hand toward the black armchairs in the lobby.

Ronnie sat down, closed his eyes and waited, sunk in thought. Fifteen minutes later, he heard the receptionist calling his name, so he approached the reception desk.

"I need your ID, please." She collected his driver's license and gave him a visitor's badge in return. "Please attach the badge to the right side of your jacket and don't take it off while on the premises," she recited. Then she added, "Take the elevator to the tenth floor. Agent Bukowski will be waiting for you."

"Mr. Saar?" A stout man in his fifties was waiting for him when he stepped out of the elevator. He wore a gray suit, his tie hanging loosely from his neck. Ronnie nodded and followed the agent through the maze of corridors. Bukowski opened a door in one of the corridors and waited for Ronnie to step inside. Then he motioned to the only chair on the near side of the desk, which was not stacked with paperwork.

"Thanks for coming so quickly," he began, speaking in a completely different tone than the one he'd used over the phone. "I invited you to have a conversation, and at this point, it's just a conversation.

I am interested to learn everything you know about the case at Mount Sinai in which a patient involved in a medical experiment you approved died."

Ronnie managed to control the wave of panic that rose in him. "I'll be happy to answer all your questions."

"Why did you approve a procedure that could endanger lives?" the detective fired at him, giving him a hostile look.

"Before the procedure you are referring to, eleven identical clinical trials had been conducted; they were all successful. The only difference between the last procedure and the ones that preceded it is that no company representatives participated in the surgery. Because the previous trials didn't call for the company representative's involvement, there wasn't any apparent reason not to approve the next set of clinical trials." Ronnie went silent.

"Apparently, there was a very good reason, seeing that the patients died."

"When the decision was made, we had no information that could even hint at a possible danger." Ronnie managed to maintain his calm.

"I've checked into the financial situation of your company. You ran out of money, and it seems like you couldn't afford to give up the operation. Was that the reason you approved it? Money?"

Bukowski leaned on his elbows. His jacket opened a bit, exposing a large handgun and armpit stains on a once white shirt.

"The company is indeed experiencing some cash flow issues. But that has nothing to do with me authorizing the trials. There's no way in hell I'd risk a man's life for money. I approved the experiment because all the information I had at the time supported this decision —"

"And then a father of five died," Bukowski cut him off.

"Which is truly tragic. I visited the family only yesterday, and my heart bled when I spoke with the widow and her children. But this still doesn't make my decision an erroneous one."

The agent kept quiet, continuing to closely examine Ronnie's face.

Ronnie was the first to break the silence, "Agent Bukowski, I don't know if you're aware of it, but another patient died in an operation conducted simultaneously in a Philadelphia hospital and using the same medicine. Unfortunately, in both cases, the families refused an autopsy, which could've shed some light on what happened and, to the best of my knowledge, clear our company of any suspicion. As I mentioned before, in both cases, our representatives weren't present in the operating room, so I don't have any information about what actually happened during surgery. We've invested a lot of effort in trying to understand what went wrong with the procedure from the doctors, but they were all instructed by the hospitals' legal advisors to keep quiet. As I said at the beginning of the conversation, I'm eager to help in any way I can, but I'm in the dark just as much as you are, and have no idea what could have gone wrong. Even though I can't ignore the horrible coincidence — two operations in which medicine developed by TDO was used, performed at the same time in locations about a hundred miles from one another, ended up with patients dying — I still can't see how the medicine could've been responsible for the deaths of the patients."

"I'm aware of the second death, and I have to admit I was positive you wouldn't be the one to bring up the subject." Bukowski's mouth stretched into a thin smile that didn't reach his eyes. "I think you're lucky the autopsies weren't allowed, otherwise we would be having this conversation in a jail cell." The agent stood and began to pace in the room, his hands clasped behind his back and his thumbs tightened.

"Forgive me for asking, but why is the FBI even investigating this matter? Were there any criminal accusations?"

"The FDA asked us to look into this case before they prosecute your company," Bukowski fired back.

"Even though the obvious assumption is that the company's responsible, there are too many suspicious things going on that can't be ignored," Ronnie erupted.

Bukowski stopped pacing, approached Ronnie, and bellowed, "If you have any information, now's the time to share it with me, because honestly, my patience is wearing thin."

Ronnie leaned back and said, "What I'll describe to you now is the result of some sniffing around my people have been doing at the hospital and my own conclusions about the findings. As you must know, I have neither the manpower nor the authority to investigate this case thoroughly, but—"

"Enough bullshit." A vein began to pulse in the agent's forehead. "I'm tired of all the wise guys sitting in front of me and trying to prove just how brilliant they are. Somehow, at the end of the day, they all end up in prison. There, they discover their brilliance to be absolutely useless."

"You may not believe me, but I want to find out the truth just as much as you do. I didn't come here with a lawyer, and I'm doing whatever I can to help. The threats you've been bombarding me with from the moment I entered the room are completely unnecessary."

"Talk," grumbled the detective and dropped into his chair.

"As mentioned, in the investigation I've conducted, two points arose which made me think we're not faced with a mere coincidence, but with a malicious act —"

"So why didn't you go to the police?" Bukowski interrupted him and straightened in his chair.

"Because I have no proof for anything I'm about to tell you now. Some of the pieces of the puzzle came together in my mind only while I was on my way here," Ronnie explained calmly. "In both cases, the families objected to a postmortem for religious reasons. Statistically speaking, that doesn't make sense. In my digging, I learned that the Philadelphia patient scheduled his operation two months ago, but the one in New York was scheduled shortly before the operation. In fact, there was another patient scheduled for that time, whose operation was cancelled and the appointment given to the deceased. The reason given to the patient originally scheduled for surgery proved to false." Ronnie went silent and looked at the detective.

"And the other thing?"

"The clerk who'd switched the dates of the operations suddenly decided to take a trip to Central America a day before the surgery."

"And what's so special about that? People take vacations, unless they work for the FBI, that is."

"It wasn't a vacation. Her work friends say there wasn't any indication that she'd been planning such a trip, and that she's not the type to just leave everything and go on a spur-of-the-moment adventure. She took care of her elderly grandmother, and her job was too important for her to just wake up one morning and tell her supervisors she was quitting. She could've at least tried to get an unpaid leave, couldn't she?"

"Who can figure out young people nowadays... what's her name?"

"Roselyn D'Angelo."

"All right, I'll check it out. But I have to tell you, I don't buy your story. You signed, people died, you're guilty. That's the way I see it. In my experience, the world is a simple place. Most people spend their entire lives thinking it's beyond their grasp. The rest of them spend their lives trying to make it complicated, but, after so many years in this business, *I know* the world is simple. And when we find out what happened in these two cases, we'll discover, one more time, that this was not about some crazy statistics or an unfortunate coincidence. Someone was responsible for this. If I have to guess, it is probably someone from your company." He got up from his seat. "Come, I'll walk you outside. Try not to disappear on me in the next few weeks. By the way, don't try to leave the United States with your Israeli passport, you'd be arrested as soon as you reached passport control."

They walked together toward the elevators, and when they reached the entryway, the agent pressed the call button. They both stood facing the elevator and keeping quiet. When the elevator arrived and the doors opened, Ronnie stepped inside but noticed Bukowski was preventing the doors from closing.

"What?"

"We haven't spoken about Christian Lumner yet, the company CEO who committed suicide. Do you consider that to be just another unlucky coincidence?" The agent released the doors and disappeared.

The subway ride to Presbyterian Hospital lasted an eternity. Ronnie ran from the station to the hospital. Liah gave him a faint smile when he finally reached her room.

"How are you?" she whispered.

"How I am is not very important right now. How are you feeling?"

"Weak, but the pain has subsided and the doctors told me if I'm able to inject myself with cortisone shots, as far as they're concerned, I can be discharged as early as tomorrow morning."

"Are you sure that's a good idea? Isn't it better for you to be here, so you'll be taken care of?"

"No, I'm not sure at all. Where've you been all this time? Is it so insanely busy at work?"

Ronnie debated whether he should tell her about the recent developments. He was afraid more stress would aggravate her medical condition.

Liah, who'd noticed his hesitation, gathered her strength, sat up in bed, and with a surprisingly steady voice, demanded, "Tell me everything, right now."

With a sigh of acceptance, Ronnie described to her what had happened from the moment he'd been notified about the death of the two patients. When he was finished, she smiled at him feebly, leaned back tiredly, and said, "The moment I leave you alone, you get into trouble. We'll talk about it later." Liah lay back in bed and was asleep in seconds, exhausted by the effort of following his story. Ronnie kissed her forehead and went out of the room quietly.

Half an hour later, he reached his apartment and was surprised to discover the front door ajar. He pushed it open slowly, preparing himself for the worst, and stepped carefully inside, his eyes scanning his surroundings. The house seemed quiet and it appeared nothing was missing. He locked the door behind him, and when he headed to the kitchen to grab a beer from the refrigerator he saw a piece of paper under Liah's favorite magnet: "A house without a dog is not a home." It was a printed note that said, "Stay away from the hospitals, and we'll stay away from you and your lady friend."

Chapter 27

Ronnie wasn't surprised to find Evelyn at her station, totally consumed in her work as if the workday had begun hours ago.

"He's in his office," she said without being asked.

David looked worried.

"There are two important points I'd like to bring you up to date on," Ronnie began.

"Please . . ." David sent him a forced smile, his hands moving restlessly.

"I've spoken with Robert and all the investors." Ronnie was careful to maintain a neutral and straightforward tone. "I'll try to close the deal this coming Friday."

"Can't you do it before that?"

"Friday was the earliest day Robert had available for the meeting."

"Excellent. What's the other thing?"

"You don't care about the terms of the purchase?"

"I'm already aware of them. Robert updated me right after your conversation. As I told you, we've been close friends for many years."

Perhaps too close, Ronnie thought.

"Well? What's the other thing?"

"Yesterday, I was summoned to the FBI office. They're investigating the deaths of the two patients. I believe the next time they call me down I'll need a criminal lawyer. Do you know any good ones?"

"Yes. Yes, of course." David wrung his hands. "I never thought it would come to this... I'll check with the fund's attorneys and send you their recommendation later on today. Will there be anything else?"

"No, thank you." Ronnie rose and went out of the room.

The corridors were silent as he returned to his office. It appeared only Ronnie, Evelyn and David were in this early. Ronnie closed the door behind him, sat down, tipped his chair back, rested his feet on the desk and analyzed all the facts that had turned his life into a miserable mess in just a single week: *I've been questioned by the FBI and the police, who won't let me off the hook even after the company's been sold. I've been unable to make even the slightest progress in understanding how the operation date switch was related to Christian's death, or understanding the connection between the operation's failure and what's been going on with the company or with me. Someone has broken into my house and left a clear threat, and all this time Henry and David have been working behind my back...* Ronnie allowed his fingers to dance across the touch screen of his phone.

"Yes, Ronnie." Apparently Jim recognized his number; he was glad to hear Jim's voice.

"Is there anything new I need to know about?" Ronnie took a shot in the dark.

"Sorry, but no. We've examined everything we could think of, and the conclusion is that all company procedures have been closely followed. If there's any relation between the deaths and the medicine, it can't possibly be the result of a malfunction on our end. The only thing I can think of is that the medicine was tampered with on the way from the factory to the hospital or while it was in the hospital."

Jim sounded certain of his conclusion, but that didn't cheer Ronnie up. "Please send me the list of procedures and the results of the investigation so I can go over them myself. Sometimes a fresh pair of eyes can discover something missed by someone too close to the subject."

"Gladly. I'll send you a link and a password so you'll be able to access the company's database. There, you'll find all the procedures, production reports and all the other information related to the medicine monitoring process."

"The procedures will be enough. It would be very helpful if you could place them in a single folder and email them to me." Ronnie decided not to let Jim know he'd gotten the password from Christian. "But that's not what I'm calling you for." He got back to the subject he'd originally called Jim to discuss. "We need to appoint a new CEO. I don't want to rush the appointment. It's no secret that Christian valued your work highly, and in the past few days I've come to realize why. Furthermore, I don't believe there's anyone who knows the organization better than you do. So, I'm hoping you will agree to temporarily serve as CEO, until I'm able to decide, along with the board of directors, who to recommend as permanent CEO."

"You don't think I can be the next CEO?" Jim sounded openly disappointed.

"Perhaps I didn't explain myself clearly enough. I don't know anyone who could do a better job than you would. But at the same time, I'm not willing to force a decision on the rest of the investors or future buyers, assuming there will be any. I need time, and I ask you to give me that time. You can count on my vote."

"Yes, of course." The usual appeasing tone returned to Jim's voice. "I'll do anything for this company to keep it operating at full steam until a CEO who's acceptable to everyone can be found."

"I'll issue an appropriate letter of appointment." Ronnie sighed with relief. "I won't be in New York tomorrow. Will you be able to come and meet with me on Monday afternoon, so we can decide on the next set of company goals?"

"No problem. I'll get there in the afternoon and buy a return ticket for eleven PM from LaGuardia. I believe that will give us enough time to discuss all the topics."

"Excellent. It'll be nice to finish the day with a good dinner. I'll make restaurant reservations. My treat, of course. I'll see you on Monday, then." For the first time since he'd woken up that morning, Ronnie felt things were starting to head in the right direction.

"So… eh… all right. See you."

"Did you want to say anything else, Jim?"

"There's something that's been bothering me for a few days, but I didn't want to involve you in it. Perhaps it's best if we discuss it face-to-face." Jim's voice was filled with hesitation.

"If something's bothering you, it's best that you get it out of your system as soon as possible. Do you want me to Skype you?"

"Good idea. I'm at the office. I'll be waiting for your call."

A few minutes later, Ronnie saw Jim's round, troubled face on his monitor.

"Ronnie, I'm sorry to involve you in personnel issues, but like I told you, in the comprehensive analyses we conducted, we weren't able to come up with even a theoretical way for someone to tamper with the medicine. Christian was the only one who had the key to the safe, and I can't believe he'd ever do something to hurt the company. The company was his entire life. The only other man who had access to the medicine is Brian, whom you met at Mount Sinai. The moment the medicine reached his hands, he was the one responsible for it. I've raised objections in the past about giving that playboy such a responsible job. He spends all his time flirting with anything wearing a skirt. More than once, he disappeared for hours without providing a reasonable explanation. I don't trust him, and I'd like to fire him or bring him back from the hospital to the company offices, where I'll be able to keep a close eye on him," Jim insisted with unexplained determination.

"Jim, you surprise me. You're the one who recommended I speak with Brian just a few days ago. He's been very helpful. What's happened since then?"

"I tried to put my personal feelings about him aside and concentrate on what's best for the company. But now that I'm convinced that if anything happened it took place after the medicine left the factory, suspicions are gnawing at me again. Maybe I'm wrong, but you can't be too careful." Jim's voice rose. "I'm telling you, Brian's dangerous."

"If you're right, perhaps it's better that he doesn't know we suspect him. I recommend that we keep him in the hospital for now. After all, he can't do any more damage. Right?"

"I want him next to me, Ronnie." There was disappointment mixed with anger in Jim's voice. "I don't know what damage he can or can't do. I don't trust him."

Ronnie was surprised by Jim's intensity of emotions. "Let me think about it over the weekend, and we'll reach a decision about it together on Monday." He tried to calm Jim down.

"So what you're saying is, even though I'm CEO now, I'll need your seal of approval for every decision I make?" Jim erupted.

"No. You brought up something, and I told you what I think about it. Let's talk some more about it on Monday. Have a good day and a relaxing weekend."

Ronnie ended the conversation and stared at his computer with a pensive look.

Could I have been so wrong about Brian? After all, he was the only one who provided me with some sort of breakthrough. On the other hand, perhaps he just did that to draw the fire away from him.

His cell phone announced a new incoming message. Stop all your investigations. If they find out something was wrong with the medicine, your signature approving the test trial will get you in trouble with the law.

Ronnie reread the message. Its tone was different than the other ones he'd received. This was the first time he felt the concern of the previous messages had changed into a threat. Has the sender changed his tune? Was it the same person who'd left the message on his refrigerator? And if so, where was he getting his information from?

Chapter 28

New York, October 24, 2013, 6:15 PM

"Hello, Robert." It was the familiar chilling voice on the other end of the line.

"I wired you the money, just like you asked," said Robert in a voice straining to sound determined. "From now on, we have nothing to do with each other. I don't want you to call me again."

"Robert, Robert…I don't understand why you're talking to me like that. I thought we were friends," said the speaker in a mock-friendly manner, then immediately changed his tone of voice. "Go down to the building entrance immediately. In five minutes, a limousine will come to pick you up for an appointment. I give you my word, no harm will come to you, and at the end of the meeting, which I hope will be a brief one, we'll take you back to your office. Five minutes. Get a move on."

"I'm busy at the moment and can't clear any time for appointments outside the building. Perhaps you could tell me what you'd like over the phone."

"Get down and be there in four and a half minutes, otherwise your son won't be coming back from baseball practice, which is about to end pretty soon. Perhaps your wife, who by the way, has already arrived to pick him up, might accidentally get hurt. And Robert, do us both a favor and don't call her. Now you've got three minutes and fifty-four seconds."

The call was disconnected. Robert slowly got up and opened the closet next to the office door. He took his coat from the hanger, inhaled deeply and went out of his office. "I'm going to run some errands for about an hour," he explained to his secretary and slowly moved toward the elevator, praying his feet wouldn't betray him.

"But you have an appointment with the attorneys about the TDO acquisition in fifteen minutes. What should I tell them?" Sinead was astounded.

"Just think of something. That's why I pay you so much," he answered angrily. Sinead's eyes followed his wide back, puzzled. He'd never spoken to her like that before.

When he reached the lobby, he could see the limousine already parked outside, its door open like a black monster's gaping maw. In a spur-of-the-moment decision, he approached the guard at the entrance.

"Yes, Mr. Brown, how can I help you?" The guard stepped over, waiting for his instructions.

"I—"

"There's no need, Mr. Brown. The car is already here." A hand grabbed him from behind and squeezed his left elbow. Robert tried to release himself from the grip but was unable to move his arm. "Your wife is waiting and we're already late." The man began to march forward, without easing his grip. Now Robert was able to see him. He was dressed in a casual black suit, wearing a flat cap and dark sunglasses, and motioning with his available hand toward the exit door.

"Mr. Brown...?" The guard was trying to decide what he should do.

"Everything is fine, Patrick," Robert muttered and walked outside.

When he sat in the car, the doors locked with a foreboding clunk. From that moment on, he was at the mercy of his escort. He wondered if he'd ever get to see the Loop skyscrapers again as the vehicle passed them, a heavy lump in his chest.

The limo turned from Michigan Boulevard onto Roosevelt Road, then continued toward Chinatown. A few minutes later, it slowed down next to an office building whose walls were covered with graffiti and slid down into an underground parking lot. The driver opened the limousine door and led Robert to an old elevator that creaked and groaned with effort before stopping at the fourth floor. The long corridor reminded him of two-star hotels in Shanghai. Worn-out carpets with curling, unglued edges, faded posters of banal paintings enclosed in dusty frames, and dozens of doors bearing signs in Chinese. The driver stopped next to one of the doors and opened it without knocking. At the center of an empty, dusty room stood a man with oriental features. Robert approached him hesitantly. The man put out a hand clad in a black leather glove and crushed Robert's with an intense handshake. His eyes were flat and emotionless. The eyes of a shark.

"We meet at last, Robert. I hope you'll forgive me for meeting you in such a graceless place, but this is the only office that was available at such a short notice. As soon as you get out of here and go back to your office, we'll disappear as well. I'm telling you all this just in case you were thinking you'd try to remember where you were taken. Would you like to sit down?" The man gestured theatrically to one of the two plastic chairs, the only furniture in the room, and sat in the other one, waiting.

"Before we begin to talk about the subject I've invited you to discuss, I wanted to calm you down and tell you your son and beautiful wife are safe and sound at home. Here's a picture to prove it." The man took out a smartphone and showed Robert a close-up image of his wife and son. "My men were very sorry this wasn't a summer mission. They thought seeing your wife sunbathing in her bikini by the poolside, or if they were lucky enough, fully nude, would have spiced up their assignment a bit." The Chinese man gave a hollow laugh without taking his dead eyes away from Robert, who felt like he was about to throw up.

"You must be asking yourself why you're here." The man turned serious abruptly. "My boss asked me to tell you it would be really nice of Mentor to forgo the TDO acquisition. I want you to promise me it's all right as far as you're concerned, and then my driver will take you back to the office and you'll never hear from me again."

"I don't understand," Robert stuttered.

"I apologize if my English is not clear enough, but I'm asking you to make an effort to understand, so I won't have to repeat everything I'm saying," the Chinese man hissed through clenched teeth. "I — want — you — to — assure — me — that — you'll — pull — out —of — the — acquisition — plans — for — TDO," he said, spacing out the words. "There, was that any clearer?"

"But all the paperwork's been drafted already, and tomorrow I'm supposed to close the deal. I can't just cancel without a reason." Robert mustered his courage.

"Tomorrow is a long time from now. You'll cancel the deal today."

"I can't do that. The board of directors will simply fire me and replace me with someone who will finish the deal. TDO is up for sale; if I don't buy it, somebody else will. I don't get it, what will you gain by this?"

"You're right. It's for sale, and we are the ones who will buy it. By the way, you won't have any problems with your board of directors because I promise you full cooperation between our companies. We intend to give you exclusive distribution rights for the product in return for your help in stabilizing the production line. I think not only won't the board of directors fire you, they'll even praise you for the wonderful deal you were able to close. Now—" the thug cracked his knuckles "—do we have an understanding, or do I need to move on to the next stage of our 'negotiations,' which, both of us know, I'll be the only one to enjoy?"

"Why are you so interested in a company that developed a deadly medicine? Do you own the knowledge that might fix the problem?"

"The medicine had no problem before we interfered." The man sent Robert a poisonous smile. "Perhaps now you understand why you should cooperate with us." He got up from his chair, lifted Robert to his feet without any visible effort and drew his face close to Brown's. "This conversation is starting to tire me," he whispered in his ear. "Do you agree to stay clear of this acquisition?"

Robert's head was spinning.

"So, what's your answer!?" his captor screamed in his ear.

Robert recoiled as if he'd just been slapped. "All right. All right," he whispered and dropped back in his chair.

The Chinese man took out a thin, black ring binder from a bag that rested near the wall at the edge of the balding carpet and handed it to Robert. "This is the cooperation agreement between our companies as drafted by our attorneys. You'll find that they've been very generous with your company. Please go over it with your advisors. If any questions arise, you'll be able to get back to our representatives. You have their names in the enclosed letter." The man extended his hand and pulled Robert from his chair. Then he wrapped his arm around Robert's shoulders and led him toward the door, where he said, "It's a pleasure doing business with you. Goodbye, Robert."

When he got in the limo, Robert asked the driver to stop at the nearest gas station. The latter obeyed his instruction without saying a word. Robert headed to the restroom and, after locking the door, washed his face then examined his clothes and carefully cleaned them. Finally, he fished out a comb and fixed his hair. Only when he was somewhat pleased by the image reflected in the mirror did he go out of the restroom and walk to the car.

When he got back to his office, a small army of lawyers was already waiting for him, with Sinead rushing among them, carrying a tray with coffee and refreshments.

"I'm sorry I'm late," Robert addressed them. "If you'll excuse me, I have one more telephone call to make before we get started." Without waiting for an answer, he dialed and said, as soon as his call was answered, "Mr. Saar, I'm sorry to be the bearer of bad news, but we've decided to cancel the deal. I wish you and TDO all the luck in the world. Goodbye." He hung up without waiting for an answer, raised his eyes and looked straight at the astonished attorneys.

"Sinead" — he took a CD out of the black ring binder he brought with him — "please print six copies of the document on this CD and give one to each attorney on his way out."

Once he'd handed off the CD, he turned his eyes back to the lawyers and said, "Gentlemen, the rules of the game have changed. I have information about another company that has entered the game and is interested in acquiring TDO. According to the information I have, they were about to offer a price that would make the deal unprofitable for us. I've spent the time you were waiting for me in the office to close a deal with them, defining the principles of the strategic cooperation between our companies. You'll get copies of the contract on your way out. Sinead will reserve a conference room for you to go over the material. We'll hold our meeting as soon as you're ready with your comments. The night's still young. Thank you."

He rose to his feet, signaling to them that the meeting was adjourned. Only after the last of the lawyers had closed the door behind him, did he allow himself to drop in his chair, ignoring the phone that wouldn't stop ringing.

Chapter 29

The telephone call he'd received from Robert had surprised Ronnie, and Brown's terse message didn't leave his mind for hours. He spent the night on the sofa, in front of the television. Even the last few drops of whiskey he'd found buried in the liquor cabinet couldn't help him fall asleep, and the light of dawn found him drained and despondent.

Liah threw a quick "Good morning" in his direction on her way to the kitchen.

Ronnie stood, stretched his aching limbs and followed her. "Liah, what are you doing? You were discharged from the hospital only yesterday. You need to rest. And besides, we need to talk about what stressed you out so much. If it was the wedding, I…" He sought her eyes with his own.

"Not now. I'm late for class." She rubbed herself against him in an official affectionate gesture on her way back to the bedroom.

"Liah!" he called after her. He waited a moment, and when no answer came, he left the apartment and slammed the door angrily behind him.

Wearing only a thin shirt, he was not prepared for the morning chill. He crossed the street running and rushed into the coffee shop on the other side. The warm coffee and the lively morning atmosphere helped him regain his spirits. He sat in front of the large store window and looked at the entrance to his building. A disheartening sense of loneliness engulfed him. Liah, the woman he loved, had become a stranger. Suddenly, he saw her emerging from the building, hurrying toward the subway station. *She didn't even try to look for me*, he noted sadly.

He left his coffee mug on the table and went back home. An hour later, he was at the office, shaved and showered. Evelyn wasn't at her station, and Ronnie went into David's office without knocking.

"Good thing I was supposed to be on the nine fifty-five PM Spirit flight from LaGuardia and didn't schedule an earlier flight," he said, eyes blazing. "Your son of a bitch friend didn't even ask me where I was when he cancelled the acquisition offer without offering any explanations."

"I really don't understand what happened," David admitted in a gloomy voice. "I've been trying since yesterday to get him to tell me what caused him to cancel the deal at the last moment, but the explanations he's been giving me sound far-fetched. They didn't contain even a hint about the new information that made him change his mind so drastically."

"At least he gave *you* the courtesy of answering. He's been avoiding my calls. The arrogant son of a bitch doesn't even have the decency to conduct a civilized conversation about the subject. Now, after wasting a few valuable days, I need to start looking for investors again. I hope that's acceptable to you and to the rest of the company investors you've convinced to vote for selling TDO at any cost."

"What's important now is saving the company. Do you have any ideas as to what we should do?" David lowered his voice in an attempt to calm things down.

"Same ideas I've always had. Ideas you and Henry constantly shot down. Before I get back to speaking with the funds about investment, I just wanted to know if you two will back me up and stop acting like Statler and Waldorf from the Muppet Show. Your demeaning remarks are of no help."

"I'm afraid sharp-eyed bankers will swoop down on the company like vultures," David remarked with an appeasing tone. "There are no secrets in the industry. As far as they're concerned, TDO is a wounded animal, so it's the right time to go for the kill. We can only hope we'll be able to create some competition among several potential buyers, so we're still able to get a reasonable price. I think we'll end up fondly reminiscing about the price Mentor Pharmaceuticals offered us. You can keep looking for investors. I don't want to discourage you, but I'm afraid the chances one of the funds will want to jump on the bandwagon now are close to zero. I wouldn't do it, and that's the answer I've been getting from friends in the industry I spoke with overnight."

Ronnie couldn't restrain his skepticism, "You've tried to convince funds to invest in TDO?"

"Tried and failed."

"I really appreciate it." Ronnie regretted his outburst. "Now, in another matter: I've appointed Jim to serve as temporary CEO and invited him for a meeting on Monday. I thought by then I'd be able to tell him about the acquisition of the company, but it appears I need him now more than ever. Regarding possible plans for saving the company, give me a few hours to think about it, and if I need your help, I won't hesitate to ask." Ronnie prepared to leave the room.

"Talk to Henry as well. He can help," David hurried to say.

Ronnie nodded and left.

Evelyn's desk was still empty, but Ronnie noticed a cup of coffee with a yellow sticky note on it saying: *Ronnie, you look like someone who desperately needs a strong cup of coffee*. He took the coffee to his office and sipped slowly, exhausted. The pieces of the puzzle refused to come together. He couldn't shake the ominous feeling that the path he'd been following was made of quicksand. He rested his head on the table and tried to relax. When he opened his eyes and glanced at his watch, he discovered he'd been sleeping for almost an hour. While stretching in a useless attempt to chase away the great tiredness nestling within him, he was surprised to see an email from an unknown sender on his screen. The subject line screamed with red bold letters: "Acquisition offer for TDO." Ronnie hurried to open the message and began to read:

"Dear Mr. Saar,

"Smith, Jones and Co. Investment Banking represents a large European customer who has shown an interest in acquiring TDO. The acquiring company began its due diligence checkup two months ago and is interested in proceeding with the process as quickly as possible. If you find this offer to be interesting, please contact Mr. Smith as soon as possible at the phone number at the bottom of this email."

Ronnie wasn't familiar with the name of the sender and neither with Smith, Jones and Co. He reread the email, trying to draw some more information from it but couldn't find any. A phone number was underneath the signature, but a physical or even a website address was noticeably missing. An investment banking company without a website? Without offices? What about the names? They sounded so overused and fictitious, as if they'd been taken out of a bad mystery book. Smith and Jones…

He pulled the phone over and dialed.

The phone rang for a long time, and seconds before Ronnie decided to hang up, a voice with an Oxford accent answered.

"Smith."

Ronnie decided to skip the pleasantries and get straight to the point. "This is Ronnie Saar. I read the intriguing email you sent me, and I'm interested in getting more details from you."

"I'm happy you got back to me so quickly. Sorry you had to wait on the line, but you've caught me in the middle of another meeting," the Englishman apologized. "I'd like to meet face-to-face, instead of wasting valuable time on the phone. I can assure you my client is serious and is willing to pay a fair price for the company you chair."

"I'd be delighted to meet you, of course. I'm available this afternoon and Monday." Ronnie managed to restrain his voice, but his heart was beating like a drum.

"If it's OK with you, my partner, Mr. Jones, and I would like to meet with you as early as today. Will two o'clock be convenient for you?"

His words were like celestial music to Ronnie's ears. "Two o'clock will be fine. Our offices are on—"

"I know where you are, Mr. Saar. And now, if you'll excuse me, I must get back to my meeting. Be seeing you." The call was disconnected.

Ronnie spent the next hour doing some in-depth searching on the internet and in various venture capital databases the firm subscribed to but was able to come up with only three references to the investment bankers' name. In all three references, they were presented as bankers who'd led acquisitions of American companies by nameless European purchasers. It was very noticeable that the sellers were quoted as praising the process that Smith and Jones had led and the decency of the purchasers, which made the absence of the identities of the acquiring parties all the stranger.

"David asked not to be disturbed," Evelyn scolded Ronnie, "he has a long list of telephone calls to make." When he got closer, she whispered, "Based on the sour look on his face, some of them are not going as well as he'd hoped."

"I'm sure he'll be glad to see me." Ronnie smiled. "I have some good news for a change."

Evelyn raised her eyebrows and gave Ronnie an inquisitive look. "Ray," she called him by the nickname she'd crowned him with, "if you were able to come up with some good news, you're a wizard..."

"I'm not a wizard. I think I just got lucky."

"Luck has a tendency to deceive desperate people. Don't trust anyone but yourself." Evelyn surprised him. "You can go into David's office, but it'll be on your head."

"Are you familiar with an investment banking company called Smith and Jones?" Ronnie asked while marching toward David's desk.

"What's this nonsense? I really don't have time for this now." David's face reddened.

"I just got an email stating an investment banking group that goes by that name is representing an organization that would like to acquire TDO," Ronnie continued. "I've no idea who this buyer is or who these bankers are. Either the heavens are smiling on us, or something fishy is going on. I think it's suspicious the offer was sent such a short time after I received the telephone call from Robert cancelling the deal. Anyway, they're scheduled to come to our offices at two o'clock to discuss the acquisition. I'd be happy if you could attend the meeting; I have a feeling I could use your experience."

"I was afraid this would happen; the vultures have come out of their nests," David mumbled, disheartened. "But I guess we'll have to settle for that. I'll clear some time and bring Henry with me as well."

"All right" — Ronnie hesitated — "as long as it's clear to Henry, *I'll* be the one leading the conversation. If the investment bankers think, even for a moment, that we don't speak with a single voice, they'll tear us apart."

"I'll talk to him. Goodbye." David cut off the conversation and began to go through his paperwork with exaggerated attention.

"David doesn't seem too happy. Neither do you, for that matter," Evelyn remarked as Ronnie left David's office, sunk in thought.

"Ye...s...s. In...teresting," Ronnie muttered to himself distractedly.

"Ronnie?" Her concern was evident.

"Everything's fine, Evelyn." Ronnie pulled himself together. "Two investment bankers will be coming in at two o'clock. David, Henry and I will be meeting with them. Please clear a conference room for us, and arrange some refreshments, if you would." He stopped in front of her desk. "And thanks for the morning coffee."

"For you — anything," she said with a joyless smile.

Chapter 30

At exactly two o'clock, the receptionist led two men, who looked like they'd stepped out of the pages of an Italian fashion magazine, into the conference room.

"Would you like something to drink?" she asked and felt a blush rising in her cheeks. The younger of the two was about thirty, tanned, blond, with turquoise eyes. He looked like a surfer who'd accidentally found himself in a three-piece Armani suit. The dimple that appeared in his right cheek when he flashed her an appreciative smile made her weak. His partner was about forty-five and bore a heart-stopping resemblance to George Clooney. She was rescued from her embarrassment when Ronnie entered the room. She apologized and hurried to get out and take care of their refreshments.

"Welcome." Ronnie shook their hands, trying to conceal the pressure he actually felt. "David and Henry, my two partners, will be joining us momentarily."

"My name is Smith," the George Clooney look-alike introduced himself, "and this is my partner, Mr. Jones, who's in charge of the deal."

Jones nodded in acknowledgment, opened his expensive-looking leather attaché case, took three thin ring binders out of it and placed them in front of him. "Should we wait for your partners, or can we begin?"

A hidden complaint seemed to be veiled behind his polished accent.

"We can begin," said Ronnie, his eyes following David and Henry, who were approaching the conference room.

"Perhaps we should start by telling you a bit more about our company..." Jones' eyes tracked David and Henry resentfully as they entered the room silently and sat beside Ronnie. "As shown in the binders in front of you, we're a boutique investment bank that mainly represents buyers who'd like to keep their anonymity. Our field of expertise is arranging the acquisition of promising American companies for well-established European organizations. I assume you've searched for our website and were surprised to discover it doesn't exist. The reason is simple: We don't need a website. All our clients come through word of mouth from satisfied customers. I hope at the end of the process, you'll join this exclusive group."

"We share your hope," Ronnie answered with marked iciness. "With your permission" — he gestured with his hand toward his partners — "allow me to introduce David, the managing partner of the fund, and Henry, a general partner in the fund and, till recently, TDO's chairman."

Smith and Jones greeted them with nods. "Now, unless you have any more questions about our company," Jones began as they fished out their business cards and threw them on the table as if they were experienced card players, "with your permission, we'll move on to discussing the deal. As my colleague has already told you, Mr. Saar, the buyers are familiar with TDO and believe its acquisition is in line with their long-term expansion strategy." Jones' gaze focused on Ronnie, ignoring the two other partners in the room. "In the material I'll hand out in a moment, you'll find the details of the Luxembourg-based company who'll be the acquiring party, as well as the details of the transaction. In order to not waste valuable time in useless negotiations, we've decided to present you with our best and fairest offer right from the start. I hope you won't see it as a sign of weakness and be tempted to do some horse-trading. You can take the offer as is or reject it. The option of discussing the price — or any of the other basic terms — is not on the table."

Jones went quiet, waiting for a sign from Ronnie that he approved the rules that were presented. Ronnie sought cracks in the investment bankers' confidence. "Before we talk about money, I'd like to understand the reasons behind concealing the identity of the acquiring party behind a Luxembourg straw company. I also want some assurances the IRS won't be coming in tomorrow to charge me with assisting in money laundering."

"Fair enough," Jones' words were laced with frost, "at least as to your first concern. In any event, I'll speak to the second issue first. As stated, you'll be able to find all the purchaser's constitutional documents in the file you are about to receive. I'm confident your accountants and attorneys will find the company to be spotless. I don't want the tax authorities to come knocking on my door any more than you do. To address your more serious point" — Jones stopped for a moment, making sure his criticism did not escape the ears of anyone present in the room — "the company that conducted the due diligence investigation believes TDO's product represents a major breakthrough and could prove to be a great asset in the future. Nevertheless, I hope you won't be offended if I tell you my client is very concerned by the possibility that in spite of all the effort and funds he's willing to invest in the company, the drug will not be approved and the investment will end up as a complete waste. This is why it's important for us to completely separate TDO and the acquiring company, in order to prevent possible damage to the company's stock value and reputation. This is why we intend to run TDO as an independent organization for the first two years following the acquisition, to see if it's able to stabilize the medicine and receive the FDA's approval to put it on the market. If you'd like, you can regard us as a buyout fund[4] that would like to purchase a hundred percent of the company shares."

---

[4] A buyout fund is a fund that acquires all or most of a "mature" company's shares. This way, it establishes complete control over the acquired company. The fund invests in the company and improves it, in order to raise its value, then either sells it or takes it public for a much higher amount than the one it was originally acquired for.

"If that's the case, why don't you wait for the investigation regarding the two patient deaths to end? What's the urgency in closing the deal?" Ronnie kept pressuring, ignoring David's and Henry's disapproving glances.

"That was our recommendation," Smith joined the conversation, "but our client decided he prefers to gamble and acquire the company now, instead of paying three times as much or even more, in the event the medicine is approved by the FDA. We've tried to dissuade him from making this, if I may say so, erroneous decision. But at the end of the day, that was his choice and that's why we're here." He glared at Jones, silently instructing him to take the reins once more.

"Shall we continue?" The turquoise eyes stared at Ronnie.

Ronnie kept quiet. He was bothered by the obvious belligerence underlying the logical explanations. This wasn't the usual aggressiveness that typified investment bankers but a sense of superiority based on the certain knowledge Ronnie had no choice but to accept the offered deal.

"Of course," Henry interrupted, "we'd love to hear the offer."

"Before we get to the offer, a few more clarifications, with your permission," Jones continued to address Ronnie alone. "The offer which will soon be presented to you, is valid for a single business week only, meaning the contract will need to be signed by next Friday. I hope we'll all be wise enough to make use of the time we have left to finalize all the small details which remain to be discussed. We intentionally chose to use a standard contract we've used on more than one occasion in the past. I believe you'll find it fair and clear. The only changes we'll agree to will be the ones specifically related to the aspects that distinguish TDO. Mr. Smith and I also serve as the acquiring company's solicitors, so we'll handle all the negotiations. We'll be at your service twenty-four hours a day and promise to quickly respond to any question. We'll be heading back to Europe next Saturday to handle our next acquisition. Since we guarantee all our clients that we won't handle two deals simultaneously, the acquisition offer will be off the table exactly one week from today." Jones pushed additional three binders to the center of the table, expecting Ronnie and his partners to collect them. "And of course, the most important thing of all: The price we're offering for the company is three hundred and fifty million dollars in cash, to be wired to your account on the day of signing."

"This is indeed a fair offer," Henry hurried to approve, extending his hand toward one of the ring binders.

Ronnie threw him a mocking glance, collected the two remaining binders and handed one to David. He left the one in front of him closed and turned to Jones. "As you suggested in the introduction to your short speech, we promise that we'll carefully review the proposal and get back to you with a definite answer. I accept your position that the amount is non-negotiable, and I'll take that into consideration while weighing our answer. I thank you for your faith in TDO — if you're in New York this evening, I'd like to invite you both to dinner."

"We appreciate the invitation, but we have a previous commitment. We'll be happy to dine with you once the deal is signed. Have a pleasant weekend." They rose simultaneously, collected their attaché cases and following a brief handshake left the conference room.

"Why were you so cold to them?" Henry erupted as soon as the two investment bankers were out of sight.

Ronnie got up slowly, took his binder and turned to leave the conference room.

"Ronnie, come back please," David spoke for the first time since he'd entered the room, "now's not the time to be arguing amongst ourselves."

"I agree with you, David, and that's why I'm leaving the room. Ever since I got this job, Henry's been criticizing me and putting spokes in my wheel. Perhaps you have enough patience for him, I don't. So, with your permission, I'll go and carefully study the offer in my office."

He left the room, still able to hear Henry erupting before closing the door behind him.

In his office, he gave the offer a cursory glance. It seemed too good to be true. It appeared as if the buyer wanted to neutralize any possible excuse for rejecting the deal. He wondered what the buyers had found in their due diligence that had made the company, with all its current difficulties, so attractive in their eyes. He would have been less suspicious of the offer had it been a hundred million dollars lower. He had no doubt that the paperwork of the Luxembourg-based acquirer would be faultless. Even so, he felt as if he'd just spent an hour with a couple of venomous snakes.

He needed to know more about Smith and Jones' investment banking company, and so he dialed Gadi. The Spanish voicemail message made Ronnie redial to make sure he'd called the right number. *What's he up to now?* he mused. The phone buzzed in his hand. The incoming message was in Hebrew this time: Waiting for you at home. Love you. Liah.

Love you too, thought Ronnie. *In a parallel world, in a different time.*

Chapter 31

He wasn't used to things not immediately going his way. Ever since he was a child, he'd recognized that his cruelty could make any person do his bidding, no matter how odd his demands were. The update he'd just received from Smith, or perhaps it was Jones — he couldn't always tell the difference between the two, and in all honesty didn't especially care to — had caused a rage-filled wave to bubble up inside him. It was difficult for him to decide what had upset him more, the condescending tone, or the message that had been relayed to him. As far as he was concerned, they were lackeys running errands as he and his boss directed. Without him, they would be two more miserable lawyers rotting away in a large law firm. The authority they emanated derived from his power, not theirs. He knew they charged their customers huge sums, but as long as they delivered the goods, he wasn't bothered by questions regarding their income. Money had never been a problem for the organization he belonged to. Professional honor was much more important, and the knowledge that the Israeli was still undecided and his two partners were allowing him to hinder the process was more than he was willing to bear. Smith recommended that he wait until Monday. "Wait" was a word he deeply despised.

The Chinese man picked up the receiver and dialed.

"Now listen to me, and listen well," he screeched. "I thought I made it perfectly clear — you are responsible for finalizing the TDO acquisition as quickly as possible. Now, I get an update that you've suddenly mustered some courage, God only knows from where, and asked for some time to consider whether or not you should accept our offer. I've already explained to you, you don't have the luxury of being uncertain. Only I do. Last night, for example, I went into your bedroom and looked at your beautiful wife. I was uncertain whether I should get into bed and have a little fun with her, until I finally decided it was enough to give you a subtle message by placing your wristwatch on the bathroom sink. What did you think? That you left it there by mistake? Next time, I'll drop it in the toilet bowl, with your hand still attached to it… I want to hear the deal is closed very soon," he snarled furiously and slammed down the phone.

He picked up the receiver again and dialed. "I'm moving on to phase two. By the end of next weekend, the company will be ours."

Ronnie Saar, he thought, *I think it's high time we meet.*

Chapter 32

"Can you send me a thousand dollars to Bedford, Massachusetts?" Ronnie heard Gadi's voice on the other end of the line.

He hesitated for a moment, then decided not to ask too many questions. "I can use Western Union. I'll get down to one of their branches right away and transfer you a thousand dollars in cash to—" the list of company branches in the Bedford area was already on his computer screen "—the Stop and Shop at 337 Great Road. I'll text you with the tracking number. They close at eight PM. I suggest you get there right away."

"Send it under the name of Ramon Garcia."

Ronnie wasn't able to contain himself this time. "Who's Ramon Garcia?"

"I am. As soon as I have the money, I'll be able to come back to New York, then I will update you. There're a lot of things you need to know, as soon as possible. See you."

Ronnie grabbed the folder Jones had given him and left the office running. Forty-five minutes later, he received confirmation that the money had been transferred. He texted Gadi the tracking number and decided to head home on foot.

The casual walk soothed him, and the chilly air helped him to organize his thoughts. The atmosphere of the coming weekend could already be felt in the crowded streets. The usual energetic march of suit-and-tie-wearing businessmen, so typical of Manhattan, gradually dwindled and was replaced by leisurely tourists walking with their heads turned toward the skyline and New Yorkers scouring the store windows to find the next sale or discount.

Ronnie's thoughts wandered to Liah. He simply had to understand what'd been bothering her. Lately, her behavior had become strange, indecipherable. The outbreak of her disease, after years of a threatening silence, proved that his suspicions were justified. In his eyes, she was the one and only. If she wasn't ready to get married yet, he simply needed to make it clear he was willing to wait for as long as it takes to make her feel confident enough in their relationship. He thought about the morning's events and decided he'd never allow work-related grievances to hurt their relationship again.

Suddenly, he felt a hard blow to the shoulder that knocked him down to the sidewalk. A man wearing running clothes stood above him, as if he were deciding whether he should help Ronnie get up. Before Ronnie was able to support his body with his hand and rise, the man stepped on his knee, sent him a frigid smile and drew his hand across his throat in a threatening gesture. "You should have paid more attention to the warning we left on your refrigerator door," he whispered. People began to gather around him. An intense pain overwhelmed him. *That was intentional*, he thought, before losing consciousness.

He woke to the sound of ambulance sirens. "Where are you taking me?" he asked the paramedic who was busy trying to insert an infusion needle into his vein.

"Presbyterian Hospital Emergency Medicine, Columbia University."

Ronnie tried to take the phone out of his pocket, but the paramedic gave him a disapproving look. "Please let me do my work, sir. We need to inject you with morphine. Looks like you've suffered some severe damage to your knee."

"Please help me get my phone. My wife is a doctor at Presbyterian and I'd like her to be there when we arrive."

It seemed that the words "wife" and "doctor" had the desired effect, and the paramedic helped Ronnie take out his iPhone. Then he dialed the number Ronnie dictated to him and brought the phone next to his ear while getting back to handling the infusion.

Hearing Liah's voice on the answering machine calmed him a bit. "Liah, everything is fine," he said in a steady voice, "but I'm on my way to your hospital. I think I broke my knee or severely sprained it. I'll explain it when I see you. Thanks for the message you texted me. I love you." The morphine shot began to cloud his thoughts and he sank into a dreamless sleep

When he woke up, he found Liah by his side wearing a white lab coat bearing a "Dr. Sheinbaum" name tag and holding a sheaf of X-rays. A doctor wearing a yarmulke on his head explained in a serious tone, "The knee wasn't fractured, but the X-rays show tears in the meniscus and a severe sprain to the ligaments. We need to immobilize the leg for three weeks and then, based on the progress of recuperation, consider an operation. If there's someone who can help you at home, you can get discharged right after we put your leg in a cast."

"He's got his own private doctor," said Liah and sent Ronnie a reassuring smile. But when the doctor had left the room, she turned serious at once. "I've seen leg injuries before; this is not an accident or a case of bad luck. Tell me how it happened."

"Funny, just a few days ago you were lying here in bed and I was the visitor. Looks like the tables have turned."

"Don't try to avoid my question," she scolded him.

"I bumped into someone who was running up the street —" Ronnie began to explain.

"Stop treating me like I was a child. Tell me the truth or I'm leaving. I'm your wife, goddamn it!"

Ronnie was filled with joy. The word "wife" combined with the morphine still flowing in his veins made him feel he was floating on air. He looked at her lovingly, when suddenly, her expression changed.

"Tell me, the man who ran into you, was he a broad-shouldered Chinese guy?"

"Chinese?" Ronnie tried to buy himself some time.

"Everything's clear now." Liah sat on the edge of the bed.

"What is clear?"

"When I got your message, I ran out of the house and stopped a taxi. Before I got inside, a handsome Chinese man came over and said he'd flagged the taxi first. I explained to him I was hurrying to the hospital and asked him to let me take the taxi. He smiled politely, turned to the driver and asked him to take me as quickly as possible to Presbyterian Hospital. Until now, I hadn't given any thought to the question of how he knew which hospital I was going to. Ronnie, what have we gotten ourselves involved in?"

Before he was able to reply, the phone on the nearby chest began to vibrate.

"Where are you?" Gadi's voice rumbled. "We were supposed to meet at your place, weren't we?"

"I'm in the hospital. Here, take Liah, she'll explain everything to you." He handed the phone to Liah and was surprised when she silently shook her head and refused to speak with Gadi. "The easiest thing to do," he spoke with Gadi again, "would be for you to wait for us at home. Liah is checking with the doctor in charge to see how long I need to stay here. I'll give you all the details when we meet."

"Do I need to worry about you, Ronnie?" There was apprehension in Gadi's voice.

"Yes, just a little. We'll talk about it soon. I see Liah coming back. Bye." Ronnie hung up and turned to Liah. "What was that all about?"

"I had a fight with Gadi, and I don't feel like talking to him. Tell me what happened and don't try to change the subject."

"When exactly did you manage to have a fight with Gadi?"

"Tell me what happened or I'm leaving. As far as I'm concerned, they can keep you here overnight. I'm not a baby, and I'm tired of you trying to protect me all the time. I'm listening." She gave him a sharp look, while pinching her lower lip with two fingers.

"All right," Ronnie conceded. "I'm pretty sure whoever hit me did it on purpose. And yes, he was Chinese. I don't know why, but I suspect it has something to do with the attractive offer we received for TDO today."

"I don't understand how the two are related. And why do you believe it was intentional?" Her voice became harsh. "What are you hiding from me, Ronnie?"

"Nothing. I just can't shake the feeling that this is all somehow related to the patient deaths, but I can't see how. Furthermore, we got a pretty attractive acquisition offer today, perhaps too attractive. I asked for time to think about it. I've never liked deals that seem too good to be true. A few hours later, someone bumped into me on the street. I don't think this is a coincidence."

"Bumped into you? He ruined your knee! With a bit less luck, you would be limping for the rest of your life. How do you know he intentionally hit you?"

"He stopped, looked at me, and when I thought he wanted to help me get up — forcefully and cold-bloodedly stepped on my knee." Ronnie chose to omit the part about the cutthroat gesture that'd accompanied the deed. And the note he'd found on the refrigerator door. Now, he realized, Liah wasn't safe either, even in her own home.

Even the little he'd told her shocked Liah. "You need to tell the police."

"And what will I tell them? Someone I may or may not be able to identify tried to hurt me? I prefer to have the hitter think I was intimidated and from now on intend to do whatever he wants me to. Perhaps that's what I'll actually do. After all, the offer's good and all the investors want to sell. I'm just waiting for the lawyers' opinion on a few legal points. If the buyer represents a legal organization and our attorneys can guarantee I'm not about to be involved in a possible future money laundering investigation, taking the current offer might just be the best way to get out of this nightmare."

Pain returned to sting and burn in Ronnie's knee. He caressed Liah's hand, but she gave him a dispirited look and asked, "Why don't I believe you?"

Chapter 33

Ronnie woke up in front of his bedroom window overlooking the sunlit Manhattan skyline. Liah sat next to him with her legs crossed, reading from the binder he'd gotten from Smith — or was it Jones? She wore a pink tracksuit that complemented her complexion and held a cup of coffee in her hand. Ronnie tried to move, and the anguished groan he emitted caused her to set down her cup and ask with concern, "Would you like another painkiller?"

"I want the medicine we developed at TDO — one that can make the pain go away, but allow me to keep a clear head." Ronnie forced a smile. "And if that's impossible, I guess a strong cup of coffee will have to serve as a substitute. By the way, where's Gadi? Did I even talk to him last night?"

"The tranquilizers made you fall asleep. When we got here from the hospital, Gadi helped me put you in bed and insisted he stay and sleep on the couch. When I woke up this morning, he wasn't here, but he'd left a note asking us to wait for him for lunch."

Liah headed to the kitchen. A few minutes later, Ronnie heard the whistle of the kettle from afar. He stared at his plastered leg, and for the first time since yesterday, actually felt fear in his heart. He recognized the attacker as the same Chinese man they'd met in the Sunnyvale hotel elevator, the one who wore a Phi Beta

238   Avi Domoshevizki

Kappa ring. Now he was convinced his presence was proof Christian's death was not a simple case of suicide. *Am I next?* he wondered. The assault was still fresh in his mind. It was executed by a professional who got the exact result he'd wanted, but based on the smile that had washed across his face as he'd looked at Ronnie before crushing his knee, he undoubtedly also took sadistic *pleasure* from his deed.

Ronnie recreated the event in his mind. The assailant pushed him at the exact point that would make him lose his balance and fall onto his side, while exposing the knee for the painful blow. Any bully would've taken advantage of the situation to kick his head or his stomach in order to cause pain. His assailant didn't care about hurting him. All he wanted was to give him a clear and intimidating message, and he did that with terrifying cold-bloodedness.

"Come, I'll help you to sit." Liah interrupted his thoughts and placed the coffee cup on the chest beside him.

"I'll manage. I need to clean up." Ronnie leaned on his hands and shifted himself to a sitting position with the aid of his healthy leg. The mission proved to be more difficult and more painful than he'd anticipated, but he didn't want to increase Liah's concern and somehow managed not to wince. When he was finally able to reach the bathroom, his phone rang. "Should I answer?" Liah asked.

Ronnie nodded. Liah went to answer the call and immediately came back and reported, "It's Henry."

"I'll get back to him in twenty minutes. I want to enjoy my morning coffee, before he ruins my day."

"He's waiting for a call back. Says it's important."

"With Henry and David, everything's important." Ronnie tottered back from the bathroom and sat on his bed, taking the coffee cup in his hands. "The last quiet moments of the day," he said with a sigh.

"You want us to go jogging?" Liah retreated to her usual sarcasm.

"Afraid I'll grow a potbelly?" Ronnie teased her back and immediately added, "Sweetheart, I promise I'll take what happened very seriously and won't try to play the hero. If I could, I'd transfer all the responsibility to David, but I think the message the attacker tried to relate to me was 'Close the deal, and be quick about it.' And that's what I'll do. You're welcome to listen to my conversation with Henry and see for yourself how serious my intentions are."

On the other hand, the message could have been, "Don't you dare close a deal with those investment bankers." Who knows…? he pondered in frustration, deciding not to share the eerie thought with Liah.

He kissed her and immediately dialed. "Yes, Henry?"

"David and I would like to know: Have you reached any conclusions regarding the acquisition?"

"Truth is, I haven't had a chance to go over the material yet," Ronnie tried to sound matter-of-fact, "but assuming the Luxembourg entity is legit, I recommend we go for it and close the deal."

"I'm happy to hear that's what you think. I'm also happy that you've taken a little time off this weekend and managed to restrain yourself from diving into the paperwork the two lawyers left us. I don't possess your kind of wisdom and patience, so I've read it all. I also sent a copy to the fund's attorneys. I assume you've transmitted a copy to TDO's lawyers. This morning, I received an email from our attorneys saying that the contract, other than some minor points, seems to be completely fair. 'Too good to be true' was the actual expression they used."

"Excellent. I'm happy to hear that, Henry. Thanks for your help. I'll see you on Monday." Ronnie hung up and looked at Liah with his hands spread, awaiting applause.

"I hope Henry bought your answer. I didn't. I know you too well to believe you're going to give up just because someone has physically hurt you." She drew nearer and rested her head on his chest. "Just promise me you'll be more careful now. It would be pathetic if after all the covert operations you did for the army, you get killed by some local bully only because you wouldn't sell some company…"

"I promise," he whispered in her ear.

"Ronnie, get dressed! Liah, feel free to take your time." They were startled to hear Gadi's voice coming from the hall.

"I didn't know he had a key to our apartment." Liah was clearly annoyed.

"I allowed myself to take Ronnie's key this morning," Gadi answered from the threshold of their bedroom. "I didn't think he'd need it today. Anyway, it seemed like a good idea to make a copy for myself. I promise to knock before I let myself in."

Gadi returned the key to Liah, and Ronnie tiredly leaned back. "Tell us what you were able to find out," he demanded.

Gadi looked at Liah, and when he realized she wasn't about to leave the room, began, "Allow me to start with everything that has happened in the last two days…" He took off his shoes and propped his feet on their bed, ignoring Liah's disapproving glance. "This whole story about the late night telephone call between Lumner and his wife didn't smell right to me from the moment I heard it. I decided to fly to Boston and from there to drive to Bedford, where the Lumner family lives, to check out this whole power outage story Christian's wife had described. When I reached the Direct Energy local office, I was welcomed by one Sarah Goldenberg, apparently Jewish, cute as a button, well, at least that's what I first thought, who offered her help. I explained to her that I work for a consulting firm that checks customer satisfaction with various electricity providers and I needed to know what time Mrs. Lumner's complaint was received and how long it took to send her a repair crew. She insisted that she couldn't provide me with information that was not about my account. I used all my charming tricks" — Gadi winked at Liah, who kept giving him angry looks

— "but to no avail. The girl was immune. She just wouldn't give me the information. I asked her to just tell me what time the call had been received, but that Goldenberg wouldn't budge. She said she didn't believe me and that I should leave. When I asked her why she didn't believe me, she hurled at me, 'Because we don't send people to make repairs in the middle of the night, unless it's a matter of life and death.' Gadi turned silent, allowing his words to sink in.

"So who was at Mrs. Lumner's?" Ronnie looked at him with confusion.

"That's exactly what I've been asking myself." Gadi smiled mysteriously. "I asked her again to only check when the call had been received, but she refused again. I noticed that both times I asked her for information, her eyes rested for a moment on a ledger in front of her. I snatched it, and while she was screaming, went over all the calls that'd been received between the night of October 16th and the morning of the 17th. I couldn't find any reference to a call received from the Lumner family. A minute later, two security men came in with a police officer and arrested me. They took me to the local police station, where they held me in custody without allowing me any contact with the outside world. Not everything you see in the movies works in real life. I screamed, 'I have my rights, you know!' until my throat got sore, but it seemed they weren't familiar with the concept."

"So what's the story with Garcia?" Ronnie asked.

Gadi lowered his eyes, just like he had all those years ago, when they'd first met in Lod. "When we met more than a week ago in Sunnyvale, I searched the staff locker room and found the driver's license of a certain Ramon Garcia. Looking at the license photo, you'd think he's my long lost twin brother. Well, actually he's not as handsome as I am, but pretty close. I had a feeling his identity might come in handy in the future."

Liah shook her head in disbelief.

Gadi offered her a devilish smile in return. "When I'd reached Bedford, I rented a car under that name and that's how I identified myself at the electric company and the police station. My real ID was carefully hidden beneath the seat upholstery of the rented car. A day later, they let me know I could be released for a bail of five thousand dollars. I only had five hundred. I sat in the cell and thought, 'Who's going to give a miserable Latino such as myself another forty-five hundred dollars?' But then one of the cops, who, lucky for me, was also Hispanic, a real one for a change, told me there was actually someone who might. He was a tough bail-bond agent that could serve as my guarantor. He said he expected me to pay him seven hundred dollars and took care to warn me if I tried to run he'd find me and break every bone in my body. I guess he'll be looking for Ramon Garcia for many years to come. I destroyed all the paperwork and shaved the beard I'd grown during my time in jail. I think I should be pretty safe for the next hundred years or so."

"Did they take your fingerprints?" Ronnie asked.

"Yes, but who'll compare the fingerprints taken in a small town in—"

"There's a federal FBI database," Ronnie insisted.

Gadi simply shrugged.

"You're nuts," Liah whispered.

"Nuts about you and Ronnie." Gadi flashed two rows of brilliant white teeth.

"Cut it out, you two." Ronnie stopped the budding argument. "About Christian Lumner, are you thinking what I'm thinking?"

"Yes," answered Gadi gravely, "and I really don't like it."

Chapter 34

Roselyn D'Angelo sat curled up on the floor in a small hotel room off the Las Vegas strip, her entire body shivering. She knew the car that'd almost hit her just an hour ago had intentionally attempted to harm her. *Did they somehow find out I'd called my grandmother?* She tried to rise, but her feet betrayed her and her body collapsed back to the floor. *He was so polite at first,* she remembered, *how could I've known a monster was hidden behind that pleasant appearance?*

He'd made their meeting appear like a coincidence. She was late leaving her station behind the orthopedics department desk, on her way home and running through the hallway toward the elevator. He held the door for her and gave her a warm smile that gave her shivers. They began to talk, and he told her about a hospitalized relative and how pleased he was with the excellent treatment he and his family members had been receiving from the staff. When he asked her what her job was in the hospital, she exaggerated and told him she was in charge of scheduling operations for the orthopedics department. He laughed at her heartily, gently held her arm and told her, "Thank you."

"What are you thanking me for?" She was surprised.

The man smiled again and said, "For giving me a chance to make the acquaintance of another wonderful staff member." This time, they both laughed. When they went out of the elevator, he invited her for coffee and said he'd like to get to know her better. When she answered that she needed to get back home urgently, without mentioning the embarrassing fact she didn't really have a home to go back to, just a small bedroom in a small apartment where her disabled grandmother lived, he promised he was asking for just a few short minutes of her time.

"I've had a terrible day," he said pleadingly. "I'd be so happy if you could spread some light on it."

What a fool I've been. What was I thinking? I couldn't even get a date for the high school prom and had to go by myself. I'm the only one in the orthopedics department who never got any dirty offers. Why would such a handsome man hit on me?

He wasn't only handsome, but also had a tongue as smooth as silk. His oriental features were soft and caring when he listened to her, and pretty soon, he'd invited her to spend the evening together. Her heart was fluttering with excitement as she accepted and said she'd love to go out with him.

Her grandmother was delighted to hear her beloved granddaughter was finally going out instead of spending another evening with her on the sofa watching reruns. He arrived at exactly eight o'clock, dressed in a yellow jacket and a blue t-shirt that complemented his muscular body. His green eyes, which she would later discover were the product of colored contact lenses, hypnotized her. They never made it to the restaurant. The sex, even though it took place in a run-down motel room, was amazing. The best she'd ever experienced in her almost nonexistent sex life. He told her how beautiful she was and insisted on taking pictures of her. She felt lucky, perhaps even in love.

The night flew by quickly, and they arranged to meet again the next evening at the same place. She couldn't pay attention to her work the entire day and needed to use all her self-control not to get to the motel room too early. The sex was just as amazing as it'd been on the previous night, but as soon as they were done something in his mood changed. "I need to ask you for a favor," he said, then pleasantly added, "and I'm willing to generously reward you for it." For the first time, she felt something rough and unpleasant in him, but it quickly disappeared again behind the mask of pleasantries.

She said that, of course, she'd love to help him and tried to get back into his arms, but he moved away from her and with an icy voice instructed her to get dressed. She gathered her clothes from the floor and could hardly believe the man sitting on the bed now, following her every movement, was the same pleasant and soft-spoken man she'd just finished making love to. When she turned to leave, barely able to contain her tears, he grabbed her hand with an iron grip and demanded that she copy for him the list of all scheduled operations for the next two months. In return, he would be willing to pay her a handsome amount. When she refused and explained such an act could make her lose her job, he just tightened his grip and smiled.

When she'd returned home, she was happy to discover her grandmother already sleeping. She couldn't fall asleep all night. The insult stung her even more than the fear, as she realized she'd gotten herself in trouble.

To her surprise, the following day passed by uneventfully. She was hoping the man had just given up and even started to think perhaps she'd imagined the entire affair. On her way back home, she'd already suppressed the events of the previous two days and was completely at ease when she entered the little apartment she and her grandmother shared. They ate dinner together, chatting about this and that, then they sat together to watch their favorite shows.

The telephone call startled her. She rose from the sofa and hesitantly went to answer. When she picked up the receiver, she heard his cold voice asking, "Did you have time to think about my request?"

All the tension that had accumulated within her throughout the day burst out as she yelled at him to leave her alone and slammed down the phone. A few seconds later, the telephone rang again. She decided not to pick up. The phone rang for a long time, until her grandmother moved to answer it. Roselyn, who was afraid of what that terrible man might say to her grandmother, sat her back down gently and asked her to ignore the phone. That was also the moment the blood froze in her veins. A red laser sniper dot darted on her grandmother's chest. The phone stopped ringing and she jumped up. The laser dot didn't budge. She tried to help her grandmother to her feet, and the dot travelled to her forehead. She felt she was about to faint and crawled back, falling on the nearby sofa. The phone rang for the third time. With a hesitant step she went to answer. "Let me explain to you again. You're going to do what I've asked you to, because you're afraid, and you should be, that I'll kill your grandmother, or because seventy thousand dollars might just buy you the life you've always dreamed about. Tomorrow morning, at exactly ten o'clock, you'll come with the orthopedics department's surgery schedule to the coffee shop where we first met. Don't say anything to anyone, especially not to the police. We're following your every move."

She remained standing, staring at the silent receiver. Her grandmother gave her a questioning look, and she hurried to apologize for having to go back into her room to work. Deep down, she'd already accepted the fact she had no choice but to agree to the man's demands and hope he'd then leave her alone.

The following morning, she arrived at the office very early and managed to print the schedule and place the copy into her bag before any of her coworkers arrived. The next few hours passed by in a haze. Twenty minutes before the designated time, she approached her manager and told her she wasn't feeling well and needed to go back home and rest. She politely rejected the offer to be examined by a doctor and left the place on trembling feet.

"You're two minutes late," the man welcomed her with an emotionless expression.

The coffee and cake she'd ordered on their previous meeting were already waiting on the table. She sat in front of them and silently handed him the papers. He copied a few names to his phone and texted them to an unknown recipient. "I'm happy you've decided to help me. I wouldn't want to hurt you or your family. If you do exactly as I ask, I promise to disappear from your life for good." The same warm smile that had conquered her heart the day they'd met appeared on his face, but his eyes were hidden behind a pair of fashionable sunglasses.

An incoming message vibrated his phone. He carefully read it, then returned to examine the list in front of him. When he was finished, he raised his face to hers and pleasantly explained she should reschedule an operation for one Abraham Berkowitz to an earlier date. He continued to give her precise details specially emphasizing the date and exact time of the operation.

She couldn't understand the relationship between the Chinese man sitting in front of her and the Jewish person he wanted to help so much, but she was afraid to ask. The man took out a thick envelope from his pocket and said, "There's seventy thousand dollars here, a little gift for your help. Take it. I trust you to do what I've asked. And I have another little request. Quit your job and go on a long trip. South or Central America, Las Vegas, Europe, wherever you want. You can't be in New York on the day of the operation. You've got enough money in the envelope to help your grandmother as well as to travel without worrying about any financial difficulties. You'll also find a passport and a driver's license there, both under a different name. Use only them. Don't worry, they're very high quality and you look very happy in the photos. If you decide not to go because of your grandmother, I'll see to it that the reason for your refusal to leave will be eliminated." He removed his sunglasses and looked at her. This time, his eyes, no longer green, appeared completely dead to her, and an uncontrollable shiver run down her spine. He dictated an email address to her, asked her to send a confirmation to it that the dates and exact time had been changed, and added that from the moment she left New York, she mustn't tell anyone about what'd happened and under no circumstances was she allowed to contact anyone. Without adding a word, he left the table, leaving her by herself with the thick envelope.

The following two days were the most difficult of her life. She changed the operation dates and bought an airline ticket to Las Vegas under her new name. The city had always fired up her imagination. The thought of the warm weather and the distance from New York appealed to her. She explained to her grandmother she was going with her new sweetheart to Central

America. The happy news caused her grandmother great joy, which helped balance her discomfort with the nursing student who'd rented Roselyn's room in return for taking care of her.

Her resignation had left her coworkers shocked. "I owe myself a trip like this. I've spent my entire life doing what other people expect me to. Now, I've decided that's it, I deserve to add some spice to my boring life." She'd practiced this little speech dozens of times, until she felt she'd be able to say it to her coworkers without bursting into tears. A bitter sadness overwhelmed her when she saw the envy in their eyes. She promised to post photos on Facebook, so they would be able to share all the wonderful travelling experiences with her.

In Las Vegas, she rented a room in a small, clean hotel that cost thirty-eight dollars and ninety-nine cents per night, including breakfast. It was located away from the hustle and bustle of the casinos and everything that went with them, and pretty soon she realized, that with proper planning, she'd be able to live off the money she had for a long time. In the first few days, she explored the city and was surprised to discover the casino restaurants were fairly inexpensive and that one could even watch free shows there, all in order to lure stray tourists into the gambling halls.

She decided to try and forget the circumstances that had brought her there and enjoy her new life. Yet, the growing concern for the only person on earth she cared for refused to leave her. The call from the hotel lobby pay phone was brief. She was happy to hear her grandmother was feeling well, and that the student who'd rented the room was taking good care of her. When she'd finished, she decided to walk to the nearest casino for an early dinner. A few minutes later, a black SUV with dark windows appeared suddenly and drove up on the sidewalk in front of her. She froze. The driver had turned the wheel at the last moment, got off the sidewalk and disappeared.

The message was clear, just like the realization she was the only witness to whatever it was they'd done, and even if she keep quiet, sooner or later, there was a good chance they'd decide to get rid of her.

Chapter 35

The moment he stepped into the darkened restaurant, he realized something was wrong. He quickly glanced at his watch and relaxed a bit when he saw he wasn't late for the appointment. The one time he'd arrived two minutes late for an appointment with the head of the family, he'd found himself with a loaded gun against his temple. "Germans, even though I despise them, have some good qualities," the boss had explained to him in a heavy, venomous accent. "Punctuality is the most important of them. Being late for an appointment is unprofessional, and the last thing I need is an employee who is unprofessional." He'd breathed onto his face, before slowly uncocking the gun.

The bodyguard who blocked his way wouldn't have been able to stop him even if he wanted to. None of the people in the room could. But the Chinese man knew there were enough weapons in the room to arm a small country. He stopped in his tracks and waited. Behind the back of the fat Italian who was blocking his way, he could see the boss sitting at the head of the table, a plate of gnocchi and a glass of 2009 Lamoresca Rosso in front of him. The boss imported dozens of cases of the wine and during each meal took care to tell everyone a man is measured by the quality of the wine he drinks, and there's good wine only in Sicily.

As if they'd been given a sign, all the people in the room stopped talking and looked at him. Even though he was careful to maintain a relaxed appearance, his eyes, hidden behind his sunglasses as usual, searched the room, while in his mind he was already planning his next move. He'd been working for the boss for over ten years and the latter had never barred his way before. The message was clear — they were not pleased with his performance.

The bodyguard, encouraged by the hostile atmosphere, extended his hands to search for concealed weapons on the Chinese man's body. That proved to be a grave mistake. Before the former could realize what was happening, his wrist was twisted with a painful screech, followed by his obese body, which was hurled toward the floor where his nose met the guest's knee, already moving up with lightning speed. The encounter was devastating. Before anyone could react, the bodyguard lay unconscious, blood pooling on the floor around him.

The Chinese man remained standing erect, ready for any development. The silence was broken by the boss who, with an indifferent flick of his hand, ordered the unconscious man to be removed from the room and the floor to be cleaned. He raised his glass toward the assassin and instructed him to come closer. The Chinese man reached the table, lowered his head and waited for an invitation to sit down. The invitation never arrived.

"Why did you attack the Israeli?" The question was hurled in his face. "Now he must be convinced that the family or a similar organization is behind the recent moves. When will you start using your brains, or perhaps Chinese people are brainless?" The boss drew a gun and pointed it at the Asian's head.

The killer didn't blink. "I received information that the Israeli objects to the acquisition. I thought that if we continued in the same way, he would eventually block the deal and decided to let him know there's a lot more at stake here than he knows."

"And since when are you the one calling the shots here?" The gun barrel remained directed at his face.

"You've promoted me in the organization because I get results. I have every intention to get them for you this time as well."

"The results you'll get will have the FBI opening an investigation that may endanger many similar deals we've made in the past. When will you learn to see the bigger picture and stop thinking with your muscles?"

The Chinese man remained erect, removed his sunglasses and directed a venomous look toward the diners, before answering, evidently unconcerned, "He won't complain. He's got no proof he could take to the police."

"My lawyers—" the boss tipped his chin toward Smith and Jones, who were sitting beside him "—tell me that your move puts the entire deal at risk. They're asking me to restrain you. What do you I suggest I do?"

The Asian turned his head slowly toward the two lawyers, who shrank in their chairs. He turned his face back to the boss and smiled. "Then why don't you ask them why they called me to complain about the Israeli? What did they think? That I'd send him some chocolates to mellow him out?"

The bullet that was fired passed next to the assassin head. He didn't move a muscle and continued to smile. He knew the boss was unpredictable and that human lives had no value in his eyes. He'd witnessed that himself on numerous occasions and even more times executed the killing himself. And yet, he was gambling that the boss wouldn't want to harm such a valuable asset as himself. "I won't suffer any disrespect. Without respect, our organization loses its ability to operate. If you value your miserable life, see to it that the deal is closed this week without the police or the FBI getting into the picture." The boss lowered his gun and the Chinese man turned to leave. The boss' voice stopped him. "What's going on with that nice girl in Las Vegas? I heard even she's making problems. Do I understand there's another loose end you're unable to tie up?"

The Asian turned around slowly. "If my memory doesn't deceive me, you're the one who instructed me not to kill her so as not to draw any attention to the patients whose operation dates were switched. Right now, she has only forged documents on her. We can kill her. By the time the authorities find out who she is, assuming they even find her body, it will be almost impossible to connect the stories. All you need to do is change your previous instruction." The assassin turned his eyes to the two lawyers and an icy smile spread on his face. The fact that they'd dared to complain about him would cost them dearly one day in the future, but it was important for him that they realize it right now.

"Do what you need to do. You're dismissed. Don't get us into any more trouble, for your own good," the boss whispered and took another sip of his wine.

Even before he reached restaurant door, the Chinese man was already busy trying to remember the name of the Las Vegas hotel where Roselyn D'Angelo was staying.

Chapter 36

Ronnie spent Saturday and the morning hours of Sunday in restless sleep. The medication eased the pain in his leg but also fogged his mind. The pain returned and woke him up around noon. He stretched his hand toward the pill bottle but stopped midway. He couldn't afford to sink into a chemical fog again. He clenched his lips, drew his body up and sat with his back against the bed pillows. The effort left him exhausted. He looked around and saw two notes resting on the chest. The first one was in Liah's handwriting.

Out to study with a friend. Will be back home late. I've got an exam tomorrow and I can't study with Gadi around. I'm sure he'll keep you safe. Love, Liah.

Ronnie reread the note. The rift between Liah and Gadi was getting wider by the day. What could have caused them to dislike one another so much they couldn't even bear to be in the same room anymore? He picked up the second note and read.

Liah can't endure my presence. I've decided to leave. Don't worry, I'm keeping you safe. You need to stop popping pills and start thinking. You're pretty useless as a zombie. I left some food on the floor next to your bed. Eat!!! I sent Liah a message to let her know I've left. I hope she'll come back soon. Bye.

At the foot of the bed rested a tray with some pita bread, hummus and chicken kebabs, a bottle of Coke and some salad. Ronnie lifted the tray with effort and discovered the food was still warm. *If only I'd woken up a few moments earlier, I could have put an end to their misunderstanding*, he thought with frustration. The smell of the chicken kebabs reminded him he hadn't eaten for more than twenty-four hours. He gorged on the food and ten minutes later put the empty tray back on the floor. *I need to get back to myself*, he decided through the veil of pain and stretched his hand toward the crutches leaning against the wall behind him. With an aching limp, he reached the bathroom and looked at his miserable image reflected in the mirror. He shaved and put on his tattered "Sussita 12 — The Best Station Wagon Ever" t-shirt he liked to wear on the weekends. Then he collected the ring binder the investment bankers had given him what now seemed like ages ago, and inched his way back to bed.

Liah, sweetheart, I feel much better. Gadi left me some food. Stay and study for as long as you need. See you soon. He texted the message and began working. He spent the next few hours reading the share purchase agreement the Luxembourg solicitors had presented to TDO. When he was finished, he stacked the papers on the bed, filled with confusion. *This is one of the fairest acquisition offers I've seen in my life, so why are they rushing me to close the deal within a week? Why can't I shake the feeling hurting me was part of this persuasion campaign? Was I the only target, or were Henry and David hit as well?*

He glanced at his watch. It was eight o'clock.

"Yes, Ronnie, how can I help you?" David's voice was hesitant.

"I was attacked on my way home from work yesterday. Right now, I'm lying at home with my leg in a cast. Even though I can't prove it yet, I believe this has something to do with the TDO acquisition offer."

David breathed heavily on the other end of the line. "Wh-what do you mean you were attacked?"

"The details are unimportant at the moment. I wanted to know if you've been pressured to take the deal as well."

"N-n-no, not really," came David's instant yet shocked reply.

"David, if not for my sake then for yours, be honest with me. Were you under any pressure to sell the company?"

"Ronnie, let me repeat myself — I wasn't!!" David suddenly sounded determined. "If I felt someone was pressuring me, I'd turn to the police right away. I suggest that you do the same."

"I don't have any evidence at the moment to tie the two incidents together and no information that might help the police locate the suspect." He decided to conceal the truth and added, "Unfortunately, I wasn't able to get a good look at him."

"Then what do you suggest we do?"

"I've read the contract and it seems fair, even excellent in light of our current circumstances. I intend to sit down with the company lawyers tomorrow; if they approve the deal, I'll sign it. Henry told me he'd already checked with the attorneys representing the fund and they also think the contract is drafted well and fairly."

"Henry has already spoken with our lawyers?" A hint of doubt could be heard in David's voice. "When did he manage to do that?"

"I have no idea, but that's what he told me."

"What did Henry say when you told him about the attack?"

"I didn't. I'm not sure he's not involved in it." Ronnie considered telling David about Henry's gambling habit but decided against it.

"Henry can get on one's nerves," David admitted, "but he's a straight arrow. I'm willing to personally vouch for him."

"Fine, I'll call him," Ronnie conceded.

The call with Henry was very similar. No, he hadn't been pressured, he said and sounded shocked when he learned Ronnie had been attacked, and insisted he should turn to the police. When they finished speaking, Ronnie was worn-out. The pain, reading the contracts, and the telephone calls had exhausted him. He turned off the lamp next to his bed and closed his eyes, trying to fall asleep. *Someone's lying*, was the last thought that passed through his mind.

Chapter 37

New York, October 28, 2013, 7:45 AM

"Good morning, this is Special Agent Archibald Bukowski speaking."

"Good morning. To what do I owe the pleasure?" Ronnie answered in an assured voice, trying to conceal his fear.

"We started our first meeting on the wrong foot. I'm convinced it would be worth our while to meet again. I believe I have some information that you might find interesting, and my instincts tell me you have a lot to tell me as well. I'd like it if you could drop by my office this morning."

"I'd be delighted to meet you, but I'd really appreciate it if you could come to my office this time. I was assaulted yesterday; someone broke my leg. It is reasonable to assume that the attack is somehow related to the subject we discussed."

For a few long seconds, only silence could be heard on the other end of the line, then it was broken by a sigh. "OK. I'll be there around eleven.

"Thanks. I appreciate it."

"Who was that? Your breakfast is ready. Kumar sends his regards. I'm running to my exam. Bye." Liah threw him a kiss and left without waiting for an answer.

Ronnie knew that as long as he was on crutches, any New Yorker would beat him to a taxi, so he ordered a town car and gave the driver his office address.

"What the hell happened?" Evelyn's eyes widened when she saw Ronnie hopping on his crutches, dressed in a tracksuit and wearing sneakers.

"Apparently, sports are not always good for you." Ronnie waved off her concern with a smile. "Is David in the office?"

"No, David and Henry are not here yet." Evelyn continued to stare at him with worry-filled eyes.

"Jim's coming in to see me today, could you see that he's let into the office without me having to run and welcome him?" Ronnie tried to calm her down, without much success. "Also, there's an Archibald Bukowski about to arrive as well, please escort him to my office the moment he shows up."

Evelyn rose from her seat and accompanied Ronnie to his office. She waited until he sat down, following his eyes, which narrowed with pain, with a concerned look. "Who's Bukowski?" she asked. "I've never heard his name."

Ronnie was quiet for a moment, trying to find a position that would ease the pain in his leg. "An FBI agent," he answered dryly.

Evelyn sank into the visitor's chair. "I don't know what's going on here, but do me a favor and stop whatever you've gotten yourself involved with right this moment. Now the FBI is involved! Ray, nothing is worth this. What exactly are you trying to prove?"

Ronnie couldn't ignore the concern in her voice. "I promise to be careful." He tried vainly to shake off the subject.

The concern in Evelyn's eyes transformed to anger. "Your macho games are not going to end well. Just cut it out." She got up and stormed out of the room. Ronnie was stunned. He'd never seen Evelyn so emotionally involved. Finally, he shook off his surprise, turned on the computer and connected the portable drive he'd received from the buyers' representatives. He sent all the material to TDO's attorneys, asking to receive their expert opinion that same day, as well as all the information they were able to come up with about the acquiring company and the investment bankers who represent it. "I authorize the use of as much manpower as you deem necessary, as long as I get the answers as soon as possible," he finished the email and signed as company chairman.

The door opened and Evelyn invited Jim to come in. She stole another glance at Ronnie and left without saying a word.

"Please excuse me for not standing up to greet you" — Ronnie extended his hand, still seated — "but I broke my leg two days ago and each movement hurts like hell."

"I'm sorry to hear that. Evelyn told me you were injured doing some sporting activity. That's exactly the reason I try to stay clear of sports — nobody has ever been injured watching TV," Jim recreated a lame joke. Evelyn came into the room holding a cup of coffee. She left it in front of Jim and left the room. Jim followed her with his eyes, sending Ronnie a questioning gaze.

"We received an offer for TDO on Friday," Ronnie began, ignoring Jim's inquisitive look. "The buyers are represented by a pair of investment bankers. They submitted an offer on behalf of a Luxembourg company that's acting as a buffer between TDO and the real buyer. They intend to keep running TDO as an independent company for at least two years and then decide about its future. I have to admit that based on our financial situation, as well as the results of the last two trials, I find the offer to be exceptionally good. I wanted to hear your opinion."

"What was the price they offered?" asked Jim, maintaining a matter-of-fact expression.

"Three hundred and fifty million dollars."

"Normally, I'd recommend rejecting the offer. I think the company could be worth five times as much, or even more, within a couple of years. On the other hand, we need money in order to survive this year…what do you suggest we do?"

"I'll be honest with you: I'm in the minority here. The rest of the investors are interested in selling and not trying to exhaust bank loans or perhaps even raise some money based on a low company valuation. I passed the material to the company lawyers, and I hope we'll hear from them soon. If I had to gamble, I'd bet the company will have a new owner by next Friday."

"That fast?"

"That was the buyer's only condition. The offer will expire on Friday. Because it's the only offer we currently have, I'm focusing on doing some background checks on the buyers and their representatives. If they come up clean, I'm afraid I'll have no choice but to sell the company. I intend to recommend the buyers that they appoint you as permanent CEO, if that's all right with you."

"Thanks. I really appreciate it."

There was a knock at the door, followed by Bukowski's gray-haired head leaning in. "May I?"

"Please." Ronnie motioned with his hand. "Jim, could you wait outside for me, please? Ask Evelyn to set you up with a free room. Check if the lawyers are already working on the contract and feel free to act as a slave driver. You'll find a copy of the email I sent them in your email. Thanks."

Jim rose from his seat, curiously examined Bukowski, and then slowly left the room. A moment later, Evelyn came in with a cup of coffee, set it down next to the detective and left the room.

"It's never a good idea to irritate a secretary." Archibald sighed and sank into the chair Jim had just vacated.

"Tell me about it." Ronnie chuckled in agreement.

"So, how'd you break your leg?" Bukowski asked conversationally while sipping his coffee.

Ronnie took a deep breath and began to describe what'd happened, not omitting any of the details.

"You say you recognized your attacker?" Bukowski cut him off. "Why didn't you report this to the police?"

"I can't identify him. I only know I saw him at the Sheraton Sunnyvale the day after the TDO CEO had been found dead there."

"How do you know it was him? Did you manage to notice any distinguishing features?"

"He looked like many other Asian men, black hair and black eyes. He was around five foot eight or nine." Ronnie paused for a moment. "But in both instances, the person I saw was wearing a Phi Beta Kappa ring. The odds that we're talking about two different people are close to zero."

The detective took another sip, leaving the cup close to his mouth, sunk in thought. "We'll get back to what you've just told me," he suddenly said. "Before that, I'd like to update you on Ms. D'Angelo. It looks like she did switch the dates of the operations and disappeared right after that. I was even more surprised that I wasn't able to find any record of her flight to Central America. No one by that name has left the country or even boarded a domestic flight. She seems to have disappeared into thin air. I've spoken with her grandmother, a very nice woman. She told me Roselyn's trip is documented on Facebook, and she's following it with pleasure, delighted her granddaughter is having such a good time. Something here doesn't smell right. I hope she's still alive. This thing's a challenge for me now. I must find her. The problem is, my superiors instructed me to shut down the investigation because there's no evidence of criminal actions. I don't know what you're doing in the background, and I'm not really sure I want to know, but if and when you find something out, please update me. If you think I can help, please don't hesitate to ask. No one will be happier than me to reopen the case and bring the guilty parties to justice. And by the way, you can relax. I've been convinced for a long time that you're not guilty."

Ronnie thought the agent seemed like a much nicer person when he was smiling. "And the Chinese guy with the ring?"

"I'll check in our databases, but I wouldn't get my hopes up. Take care of yourself. You're a civilian. It's not your job to solve murders." Bukowski winked at him and left the room without saying goodbye.

Ronnie's cell phone vibrated indicating an incoming message. Don't be stubborn. Nothing could be worth the consequences.

Ronnie, frustrated that he was unable to determine if the message was a threat or an expression of concern, turned off the screen and asked Evelyn to send Jim back in. While waiting, the same questions kept gnawing at him: *Why was the mysterious informer insisting on anonymity? Does he truly have my best interests in mind? Perhaps he's trying to trick me?*

When he'd woken from his thoughts, he found Jim standing in front of him, looking at him curiously.

"The painkillers are making me fuzzy," Ronnie justified himself. "What were we talking about?"

"The acquisition, the low price…"

"Yes, the price," said Ronnie. "If not for those two deaths, we'd be on top of the world right now."

Jim nodded in agreement. "As I've said more than once, I think it's a case of sabotage that was performed outside the factory premises."

"Exactly what I wanted to talk to you about. Two days ago, you sent me the company's security measures. I've read them carefully, and I tend to agree with you that if someone sabotaged the medication, it was done only after it had left the company premises. On the other hand, the medicine was sent in a sealed container, and any attempt to open it would've instantly been revealed. Which leaves us with the question — Is it possible the medication was indeed defective in the first place, and all the events which followed, including the ones we've been undergoing in the last few days, were merely a coincidence?"

"That's a possibility, but I don't think it's a particularly reasonable one. As I've explained to you, and as the records clearly demonstrate, this is the same medicine we used in the previous operations." An expression of uncertainty settled on Jim's face.

"And…?" Ronnie encouraged him.

"Brian is in charge of the medicine from the moment it arrives at the hospital. Like I've told you, I don't trust him. He's slippery and unreliable, and also—"

"Even if everything you say about Brian is true, this doesn't explain the second death case, as it took place in another hospital. Do you really think both crimes were committed simultaneously by Brian and an unknown partner in Philadelphia?"

"As I tried to say before you cut me off," Jim's voice became impatient, almost hostile, making it clear to Ronnie his respect for someone who would no longer be the company chairman in just a few days was diminishing by the moment, "I've discovered that from time to time, Christian would give Brian the keys to the safe and ask him to take the medicine to the hospital himself. We have at least two such cases on record. Who knows how many more are not even recorded?"

Ronnie was surprised by Jim's consistent and determined dislike of Brian but held off that thought to ponder something else: He couldn't ignore this newest piece of information Jim had given him, nor the fact he hadn't told him anything about it until now. He needed to make a quick decision. He picked up his cell phone and dialed.

"Brian, please come to my office, immediately. I need your help again." Ronnie listened to the answer, then turned to Jim. "Brian is at Thomas Jefferson University Hospital in Philadelphia for two days."

"That's where the second death took place. He's stirring the pot again?" Jim turned red. "You still think I'm harassing Brian for no good reason?"

Chapter 38

Ronnie spread out the marked contracts he'd received from the attorneys and read the remarks. He was surprised at how few there were. For a moment, he felt as if the errors had been purposely inserted to allow the seller's attorneys the illusion the contract needed some minor work. The buyer even took it upon himself to handle any possible future prosecutions. It was all too good to be legal, he thought, but at the same time realized he couldn't possible use that as an acceptable excuse to stop the acquisition process. He felt defeated, without really knowing why. The contract was good, he'd been cleared of all suspicions in the patient deaths, the company would sell that very week at a profit, he'd be able to spend some time with Liah… The door opened and David came in and sat down in front of him.

"I understand you've been looking for me this morning. I was in the middle of a series of appointments regarding the next fund. How can I help you?"

"I was worried about you. When we spoke on the phone, you sounded more stressed than usual. I guess I was wrong. I'm happy to see life goes on and you're already head over heels busy with fund-raising."

David lowered his head. "Thanks for your concern, Ronnie. You're right. I'm under a lot of pressure as well. Your assault really shook me up."

Ronnie found it hard to believe the event had indeed influenced David that much and preferred to get the conversation back on a more formal track. "I received the TDO lawyers' legal opinion, and I'm about to send it to the investment bankers. I believe we'll be able to sign the acquisition forms tomorrow or the following day. By the end of the week, this will all be behind us."

"Wonderful" — David leaned over the table and patted Ronnie's shoulder affectionately — "wonderful. There are deals you should just grab right away, even if you think there's theoretically more to be gained. Some companies just have 'bad luck' written all over them. I'm so happy we insisted you continue to lead the deal." David rose to leave. When he was by the door, he turned around and said enthusiastically, "Thank you, Ronnie. Thank you," and left.

Twenty minutes later, Ronnie finished writing the email to the investment bankers, lingered for a brief moment, and then, before he could change his mind, clicked the send button. The mail was on its way. The acquisition process had started to roll.

He reached out and grabbed one of the leftover sandwiches from his lunch with Jim. Then he opened an Israeli news site and began to read. He didn't see anything too interesting. He moved on to the gossip section and read: "Bill Gates Celebrating 57th

Birthday, Mahmoud Ahmadinejad Celebrating 56th
Birthday, Hemi Rudner Celebrating 49th Birthday,
Julia Roberts Also Celebrating Today, but Nobody's
asking how old she is…"

What is Roselyn D'Angelo doing today? The
question suddenly struck him.

He logged in to his Facebook account and typed
Roselyn's name in the search box. To his surprise, he
discovered there were only a few women with that
name in the social network. From there, it was very
easy to recognize her. He leaned back and began to
read all the posts she'd published for the past year. If
there was such a thing as "an average person" then
Roselyn fit the definition exactly. Most of the posts
she'd published were about cake recipes, photos from
social get-togethers with friends or with her
grandmother. A boring and bored girl, the thought
passed through his mind, not one to just leave
everything and run off to Central America following a
spontaneous, last-minute decision. Definitely not
someone who'd be able to cover her tracks so well the
FBI couldn't trace her.

Then, about a week ago, her Facebook page had
drastically changed. Magnificent landscape photos
from Guatemala were posted daily, along with detailed
and joy-filled descriptions of all the experiences she'd
been enjoying. From the reactions of her girlfriends,
one could see how envious they were of the courage
that'd driven Roselyn to simply leave everything and
go on her dream trip. *Perhaps I need to take Liah on*

such a trip. Ronnie smiled sadly while gazing appreciatively at sunset photos taken from the heights of the Tikal Pyramids. The photos were remarkable, and the stories that accompanied them were no less impressive. It seemed as if Roselyn had dedicated a lot of time to their writing. The style was different from the posts she'd written before her disappearance. Was it possible she wasn't the one who'd been writing them? Ronnie grew suspicious — could someone be posting for her, just so the world would think she's still alive? He moved on to the New York White Pages website, and searched for Roselyn's number. He got lucky this time as well, and there were few listings. After ruling out addresses in expensive areas, he was left with only three numbers. He dialed the first.

"Hello, may I speak with Roselyn?"

"Who wants her?" an angry man's voice barked at him.

"Is this Roselyn Romero's house?" he asked. The call was hung up abruptly. He dialed the second number and repeated his request.

"Roselyn's in Guatemala, on a trip," explained a tired voice. "Who's asking for her?"

"My mother was admitted in the orthopedics department. I went there today to thank Roselyn on her behalf, for the wonderful treatment, and I was disappointed to find out she's no longer working there. Could you give her my thanks next time you talk to her?"

"She doesn't call much. Yesterday she suddenly called, but only for a minute or so. You know, calls from abroad cost a lot of money," the old woman answered with a sad voice.

"I understand. Have a good night."

"What's your name? Just in case she calls."

"It doesn't matter. I wouldn't want you to waste one of the rare telephone conversations you have in talking about me."

"It was nice talking to you, sir. Good night."

At least I know she's alive, he thought while flipping through the pictures again. Suddenly, he stopped, returned to the beginning of the Guatemala album and went over all the photos one more time. Roselyn didn't appear in any of them.

Ronnie rubbed his face with his hands, trying to maintain his concentration. *How come I didn't notice that before? The photos are amazing. So amazing, they look like Guatemala tourist office brochures. And the descriptions? It seemed Roselyn had plenty of time for writing — too much time for someone who's travelling...* He opened a Google search page and typed "Tikal." The screen was flooded with links to dozens of websites describing the ruins. Ronnie began to go through the various websites, when suddenly a photo of a beautiful sunset caught his eye. The same photo that appeared on Roselyn's Facebook page. Ronnie felt the adrenaline level in his blood rising. He dialed the young woman who sat at the building's reception area in the evening.

"Do you have a Facebook account?" he surprised her by asking.

"Yeeess, why?" wondered the young woman.

"How can I communicate with someone on Facebook without anyone else seeing it?" He sounded old and out of touch to his own ears.

"In a message," she sounded confused. "If you send someone a private message, she or he would be the only one who could see it."

"Thanks. You've been very helpful." He disconnected the call and began to write a message to Roselyn:

"My name is Ronnie Saar. I know you're hiding. I also know you switched the dates of the operations because you were threatened and perhaps also because you received some money. You can't continue to hide. They'll find you in the end. Your life is in danger. I can help you. Open a new Gmail account under a random name and send me an email at RSDtogether@gmail.com. Please do that quickly and make sure you're not being followed. If you Google me, you'll find out I can be a wonderful ally. Awaiting your reply, Ronnie. P.S. Please delete this message the moment you read it. You can never be too careful."

Ronnie sent the message, created the Gmail account to receive her email and turned off the computer.

Now all that was left was to hope she made the right decision.

Chapter 39

It was way past midnight, but Ronnie was unable to sleep. He stared at the list he'd just finished writing. *I'm missing something*, he thought, *but what exactly?* During the late evening hours, he'd spoken with the TDO lawyers. "Tell me again what were your findings regarding the Luxembourg company," he opened with a determined tone that was the exact opposite of the helplessness he felt.

"Like we told Jim, we didn't have enough time to—"

"No need to cover your ass with legal niceties. Just tell me what you think," Ronnie snapped.

"O-K," the lawyer said, drawing out the word slowly. "OK, let's see now. The company is beyond reproach. It has never been prosecuted, its articles of association seem organized and legit, and in a conversation I had with a man I know and trust who works with tax authorities, I've been told its managers file their reports regularly, pay their taxes on time…in short, everything's flawless."

"But?"

"Who said there's a 'but'?"

"Don't…" Ronnie restrained himself from bursting out again. "Sorry, but I feel there's a 'but.' I'm certain there must be a 'but.' All I ask you to do is share your gut feeling about this one. Off the record, if that'll make you more comfortable."

The silence that followed stretched Ronnie's nerves to the edge of pain.

"Off the record?" The lawyer made sure.

"Off the record."

"Even though everything's legal, the ownership structure is very complicated for a company whose sole purpose, to sum up its definition in the articles of association, is 'the buying and selling of promising hi-tech companies.' The ownership structure of the company is more complex than the NSA org chart. I tried to dig all the way to the bottom, but each time I managed to scratch one layer, it only revealed another layer of ownership. After three layers, I just stopped digging. It's completely legal, but at the same time, very strange." The lawyer stopped talking.

"So what you're saying is that someone put a lot of effort into hiding the real identity of the owners?"

"Yes, that's the idea."

"The investment bankers we met with claimed the purpose of the acquiring company is to serve as a buffer that will prevent the final buyer's name from getting into the deal, in order to protect the purchasing company's stock value. This could explain the secrecy, couldn't it?" Ronnie spurred on the lawyer.

"Maybe, although I can't really see the logic. The moment the buyer is not holding, if I'm not mistaken, more than fifteen percent of the Luxembourg company stock capital, it is not financially connected to it and does not need to report it to the authorities. On the other hand, if it holds more, no matter how many levels separate them it has to report it. Even if we assume the real buyers want to be extra careful, the number of ownership layers is bordering on paranoia." The lawyer chuckled.

"Thanks," said Ronnie, then promised, "Don't worry. This conversation will remain between the two of us."

The lawyer's words strengthened Ronnie's suspicions, but he also recalled David's and Liah's pleading that he drop the subject. He knew they were right, but he also knew he wouldn't be able to stop digging before he fully understood what had happened in the last two weeks. He took a blank piece of paper from the printer and wrote down all the subjects that bothered him. Then he stared at the list and read it again and again.

Who is the mysterious buyer and why is he hiding?

Why did he present us with such a generous offer?

Why did they physically intimidate me and not rely only on the generous offer?

Who helped Roselyn disappear and will I be able to make her come out of her hiding place? Am I risking her life just to satisfy my curiosity?

Is my curiosity endangering Liah as well?

Can I trust David? Henry? Jim? Brian?

Why is Evelyn so concerned/angry?

What is Brian doing in Philadelphia?

How could a medicine that underwent so many test trials be the cause of the death of two patients?

Why did Mentor rescind their offer?

Why is everyone who has invested in TDO — and should understand the potential inherent in it — so determined to sell it at any cost?

What happened to Christian? Was it truly a simple case of suicide? Was someone really following him in Waltham?

Why doesn't the Bedford electric company have records verifying Christian's wife's call?

Why does Jim loathe Brian so much? Perhaps he's right and I refuse to see the uncomfortable truth only because Brian helped me?

Are Henry's gambling habits related to the subject? Were the problems caused by his financial difficulties? Perhaps they even got confused and meant to break Henry's knee?

Where did Gadi disappear to for three days?

Who is the Chinese guy with the Phi Beta Kappa ring who attacked me? Was it the same man I saw at the hotel where Christian was found dead? Was it the same man who followed us in Waltham?

How did my name appear in the directors registry before I'd signed the paperwork? Over-efficiency of someone in the fund? Who? Why? Does it have anything to do with this entire disaster?

Can I trust Archibald Bukowski? Is it possible that the moment I expose my suspicions to him, he'll drag me right back into the swamp as the main suspect?

Why did the investment bankers give us such a tight deadline? What or who are they afraid of?

Who is sending me text messages? Are his intentions positive? Or is he merely trying to prevent me from seeing the real picture? Where is he drawing his information from? Why does the tone of the messages keep changing?

Was the process of safeguarding the medicine properly followed, as it was explained to me? Perhaps someone found a breach in the process and was able to use it? What was that breach?"

Finally, why is all this happening to me? Bad luck? A conspiracy?

Ronnie was too tired to think clearly, and the pain in his leg didn't help any, either.

He swallowed another pill and slowly returned to bed, careful not to wake Liah.

So many unanswered questions, he thought, *and I haven't even touched the biggest one of all: What's bothering you, Liah?*

Chapter 40

An uncomfortable silence lay in the kitchen. Ronnie stole a glance beyond the coffee mug he held in front of his mouth. Liah aimlessly dug at the bottom of her fruit bowl, her eyes lowered, avoiding his gaze. He stretched his hand toward her and shuddered when she recoiled from his touch. Her eyes didn't leave the bowl in front of her, and her movements became even more nervous.

"If you're angry about—" Ronnie tried to break the aching silence.

"I'm not angry with you," she cut him off in a hoarse voice.

"Then what is bothering you? Ever since we came back from Sunnyvale, you've been avoiding me. I didn't pressure you, because I hoped you'd find the right moment to explain to me what you're going through. I think I have the right to know, Liah." He reached out his hand again and placed it on her arm. Liah tried to pull back but stopped herself and remained motionless.

"I love you, you're my best friend, I trust you with my life. That's the reason I've chosen to spend the rest of my life with you. I'm asking you to please tell me what's been bothering you."

Liah slowly raised her head. Ronnie's breath was stolen away from him at the sight of the deep despair reflected in her eyes. She slowly rose from the table, poured herself a glass of water and sipped from it with her back turned. Suddenly, she seemed so small and vulnerable to him. He felt all his strength draining away.

"There's something I must tell you" — her back was still turned to him, but her voice was surprisingly steady — "but I want you to promise not to cut me off. I've been trying to have this conversation from the moment you proposed to me, but I could never find the courage to do it." She turned around and sent him a pleading look. Her drooping shoulders projected defeat.

Ronnie yearned to go to her, take her in his arms and tell her to never mind. No need for her to say whatever it was she found so difficult to reveal. But he didn't move and simply nodded. "I promise."

"I wanted to reveal this secret to you long ago but was afraid you'd leave me the moment the truth came out." Liah took a deep breath, closed her eyes and quickly uttered, "I'm married."

Ronnie turned pale.

Liah continued, "When I was twenty, I fell in love with a thirty-two-year-old lawyer. He charmed me with his wisdom and experience and spoiled me in every possible way. It was love at first sight. My parents strongly opposed our relationship, but the more they objected, the stronger my love grew. After six exciting months, we got married in the rabbinate. We didn't invite anyone. It was just the two of us, the rabbi, and two incidental witnesses. I thought if I forced my parents to face the fact we were married, they'd learn to accept my husband and see what I'd seen in him when we fell in love. At first, they did try to be nice to him, but it was clear they were doing it only because they were afraid to lose me. Very quickly, family gatherings became uncomfortable and I found myself drawing further and further away from them. The idyllic relationship between me and my husband lasted a little less than six months. The first crisis took place when I found out he was up to his neck in debt. He'd gambled on failing real estate projects, lost everything he had, and owed everything he didn't. Apparently, he'd sold, without my knowledge of course, the apartment my parents had bought for me before I got married. But even that didn't help him get back on his feet, and pretty soon he went bankrupt. I tried to support him as much as I could. I gave up studying medicine at Tel Aviv University and started working odd jobs. But nothing helped. My husband began to suffer from melancholy and for a long time refused to even leave the house. All our conversations began and ended with him pressuring me to take money from my parents to cover what he referred to as 'our debts.' Our married life continued to deteriorate, and my husband, in an attempt to find answers to his troubles, discovered God and became very religious, a baal teshuva who turned to orthodoxy as a way to repent."

She rinsed her mug in the sink and sat down. "My life became unbearable, but I kept on believing we got married for good or ill and that if we only wanted to badly enough, we'd manage to survive this rough patch of our lives together. The straw that broke the camel's back was his religious fanaticism and the violent tantrums he'd throw every time I would refuse to go bathe in the mikveh or to study the sacred laws of halakha with the rabbi's wife. I finally gave up and asked him to let me go and give me a divorce. He agreed right away, but conditioned it on my parents covering his debts. Two and a half million dollars. When I told him my parents didn't have anywhere near that amount, he told me I'm their only daughter, and he was convinced they'd agree to sell all their assets in order to offer me a better life. I went to the rabbinate, but I didn't stand a chance against the rabbinical student who only sought reconciliation. Finally, as a desperate measure, I applied for a scholarship in the United States and ran away to study medicine in New York."

"How…" Ronnie began, but went quiet when she raised her hand, begging him to stop.

"I don't know exactly how, but Gadi discovered this secret, and a few days ago he confronted me and demanded that I tell you everything. I swore to him I'd do that, and before he left he promised to help me solve the problem. I was very scared. I know what Gadi is capable of doing to protect your interests. I begged him to stay out of this. He wouldn't agree to anything and demanded over and over that I speak with you and that we try and solve this problem together."

Liah leaned her elbows on the table and rested her head in her hands.

"When you read out loud a short news item about the death of a Shlomo Klein who'd been murdered in Bnei Brak, probably at the hands of a robber, I felt as though my world had just come to an end. Shlomo Klein was my husband. The first thought that came to me was that Gadi was somehow behind it. I tried to talk to him, but he wasn't available for three days. I didn't know what to think. I still can't shake the feeling Gadi decided to take the law into his own hands and release us both from my recalcitrant husband."

"How could you keep something like this from me for so long?" Ronnie erupted. "What else are you hiding?" He got up and hurled his mug at the kitchen wall, trailing coffee across the room and down the bright yellow paint.

"That's the reason I didn't tell you anything. When you told me about your girlfriend, who cheated on you with her ex-boyfriend, I realized I couldn't possibly bring myself to hurt you with a similar admission."

"So you decided to cheat on me in another way? By hiding your marriage? You didn't believe my love for you was strong enough to fight for it with you? Only when Gadi discovered your secret did you realize you had no choice but to share it with me? And when were you going to tell me? Right after the bigamist wedding you planned for us?"

Liah bit her lower lip, trying hard not to burst into tears. "Ronnie, enough, I love you, you're my whole life."

"I'm not sure that's enough." Ronnie got up and silently limped to the bedroom, leaving Liah depressed and despondent. After what seemed to her like an eternity, he came out, holding a crutch and a suitcase. "I'm moving to a hotel. You can stay in the apartment for as long as you'd like." He walked past her and left.

"Ronnie!" Liah shouted and ran after him. "Come back, please. I promise we'll solve this. Please. Without you, I'll go back to Israel."

Ronnie turned around and gave her a hard look. "You do what you want. But personally, I suggest you take your last exam before you go. You've already ruined my life, no need to ruin yours as well."

The elevator arrived and he hobbled inside. He kept his back turned to her until he heard the doors sliding shut behind him.

Chapter 41

New York, October 29, 2013, 10:02 AM

Ronnie lay in bed and stared at the ceiling of his room in the Hyatt Times Square. Just fifteen days ago, he was on top of the world. He was promoted to partner much sooner than he'd anticipated, was awarded chairmanship of one of the most promising companies in the fund and, most importantly, Liah said yes to his marriage proposal. Today, he was lying by himself in a lonely hotel room after leaving Liah and the apartment he'd bought. His relationship with the two managing partners in the fund had hit rock bottom, and the pain in his leg reminded him just how deeply he'd complicated his life in his attempt to rescue TDO.

On the pillow beside him lay a letter that had been pushed beneath his hotel room door that morning. Although he knew it by heart he picked it up and read again:

Ronnie my love,

Sadly, I've realized it's too late and the damage I've caused is irreversible. Nevertheless, I feel the need to tell you that yesterday afternoon I received a letter from the rabbinical court releasing me from my marriage after my ex-husband received my compromise offer. The letter arrived by regular mail. It had been sent on — believe it or not — October 13th, the day before you proposed to me. I've been waiting for this letter for so long so I could show it to you while telling you the truth, and now, it turns out my ex-husband and his friends in the rabbinate managed to give me the final, and cruelest, blow when they decided to save on the postal fees and send this crucially important letter via regular mail.

I can't stop thinking about the danger you're in because of your insistence on "rescuing" JDO. The more I think about what happened in the operations, the more convinced I am someone sabotaged the medicine before it was sent. There is no chemical way to cause the same reactions with two different patients by using human interference during the operation. Therefore, I suggest you check the numerator. I think this is where you might find the answer.

Love you, but also understand and ache over your disappointment in me.

You'll always be the man of my dreams,
Liah

He wanted to scream until his lungs were bereft of air but knew by doing so all he'd achieve would be to bring the hotel's security personnel into the room, not Liah. He felt defeated. Beaten. His phone vibrated for the tenth time. He gave it a quick glance. Ronnie, answer me please, said the message that appeared on the screen. He shut his eyes tightly, clenching his fists until he felt his nails puncturing the skin of his palms. He opened his eyes, took a deep breath, picked up the phone and dialed.

"What are you doing at the Hyatt Hotel?" Gadi answered, as usual, after the first ring.

Ronnie didn't bother to ask how his friend knew where he was staying. "It's because of you," he yelled angrily. "Tell me, did you murder Liah's husband?"

"Tell me you're not asking this seriously," Gadi's voice turned dark and solemn at once.

"I'm very serious. Where did you disappear to for three days? Were you in Israel? You know, with my connections I can check it in less than a minute."

"So check, you idiot."

"Where have you been?"

"That's none of your fucking business." Gadi hung up the call.

Ronnie remained seated, panting with frustration. *Now I've accused my best friend of murder and ruined the last good thing I had in my life.* He dialed Gadi again. The phone rang for a long time before Gadi finally answered.

"I'm sorry," Ronnie blurted in a weak voice. "Everything's falling apart around me, and I need you as the last anchor of sanity I have left in the world. I never thought I'd say something like this, but I really don't know who to trust anymore. Hold on a moment, someone's knocking on the door." Ronnie got up with great effort and walked clumsily to the door. Through the peephole, Gadi's face smiled back at him. Ronnie opened the door and embraced him tightly.

"Would you like a kiss as well?" Gadi gently pushed Ronnie into the room. Ronnie let go and measured him with a careful look. Finally, he blurted, "I'm sorry."

It was hard for Gadi to see Ronnie so broken up. "How can I help you?" he asked, changing the topic of conversation.

Ronnie sighed and sat on the bed, trying to organize his thoughts. "How did you know I was staying at the Hyatt?" he asked. "Are you following me?"

"Yes. I don't believe whoever attacked you will stop there. Only this time, I plan to be ready for him." Gadi pushed aside his coat and exposed a gun that was shoved in his waistband. "Good thing they don't check your bags or have security checkpoints everywhere like they do in Israel," he said, chuckling.

"Where did you get the gun? What will you do if you get arrested?"

"Why would the police arrest me?" Gadi chose to reply only to the second question. "Now that Liah is out of the way, tell me all the little details about the assault."

In the following minutes, Ronnie described carefully everything that'd happened from the moment he'd left the office on his way home. Gadi listened to him attentively.

"The kick that the bastard sent to my knee was of surgical precision. He's a professional and undoubtedly a martial arts expert. His cold-bloodedness was sadistic, and he ignored all the people around us on the street. I don't think he's afraid of anything. The man is very dangerous."

"Is there a way to recognize him?"

Ronnie described the honor society ring to Gadi and also showed him a photo of one he'd found on the web. Once he was finished, he added, "In spite of everything that happened, I don't believe the guy will attack me again. If he does, I'll be ready. I think even on one foot I still have a trick or two up my sleeve that might just surprise him. Otherwise, everything I learned during all my military service was a big waste of time."

"Still, I prefer to stick around."

"No. I need your help elsewhere."

"OK, whatever you say." Gadi realized no argument could make Ronnie change his mind. Even so, he was glad to discover Ronnie had gradually recovered during the conversation and returned to the self-possessed man he remembered and admired.

"Brian, the man who represents TDO at Mount Sinai Hospital, helped me above and beyond in trying to understand what went wrong with the operation during which the Jewish man from Brooklyn died. For reasons not entirely clear to me, Jim, the company's new CEO, is convinced Brian is unreliable and that it'd be a mistake to rely on him. Jim even hinted he suspects Brian is involved in criminal activities. When I told him I find that hard to believe, our conversation deteriorated into an uncomfortable confrontation. According to Jim, Brian had access to the locked safe in the company office. He claimed that Christian, who'd fallen under Brian's charms, used to give him the keys and allowed him to take out the medicine without any supervision. According to him, Brian was responsible for keeping the medicine safely locked up until the moment of the operation—"

"So you're saying he switched the medicines before they were sent?" Gadi thought out loud. "That would explain how the damaged medicine reached Philadelphia as well."

"Up till now, I also thought that was the only explanation, but last night I found out Brian went to Jefferson University Hospital in Philadelphia of his own accord. He refused to explain to me what he was looking for down there. I need you to go to the hospital and try to find out what Brian is up to. Wait a minute…" Ronnie went through his wallet until he found a note with a long list of letters and numbers. He typed them on his computer and accessed the TDO server. From there, he made his way quickly into the personnel department's records. Seconds later, Brian's photo appeared on the screen.

"This is Brian. I'm sending you an email with his photo." Ronnie continued to work without waiting for an answer.

"A handsome devil," Gadi muttered to himself.

"Yes. And he knows how to use it pretty well. All the female nurses and doctors in the New York hospital were dazzled by him. That's how you'll find him. I'm sure he'll use the same tricks in Philadelphia.

On second thought, I'll send you Moses' photo as well; he's the TDO representative in the Philadelphia hospital."

"What do you think Brian's doing at Jefferson?"

"I have no idea, but if he's really involved in the tragedies of the final trials, as Jim believes him to be, I wouldn't be surprised if he were there to conceal evidence related to his criminal actions."

"If he has bad intentions, why would he expose himself and tell you he's in Philadelphia?"

"I've been bothered by the same question. The only explanation I'm able to come up with is that Moses accidentally crossed paths with him, and the moment his hospital visit was revealed, Brian realized any attempt to hide it would simply confirm the suspicions against him."

"OK. I'll be on the first train to Philadelphia. I'll update you the moment I have any relevant information. Keep yourself safe." Gadi turned to leave, but when he reached the door, he turned around and said, "And answer Liah. You have to find a way to forgive her."

"Before you leave, please take this thumb drive. It contains all the material I've gathered about the company from the moment I was appointed as chairman. Take a look at it with your detective's eyes. Perhaps you'll be able to find something. I can't shake the feeling I'm missing something here."

Gadi took the drive and left the room without adding a word.

When he was by himself again, Ronnie looked at his cell phone once more, then finally deleted all the messages from Liah. He returned to his computer and checked the new Gmail account he'd created. Unfortunately, there wasn't any reply from Roselyn. He checked his regular mailbox and found an email from the investment bankers:

"We've accepted all the changes your lawyers requested. Attached, please find a clean copy of the contract, signed by us. We await a summary session, in which you will sign the contract. Once that happens we will transfer the funds to your designated bank account.

"Sincerely yours,

"Jones."

This is it. The sand in the hourglass has stopped trickling and started to pour, Ronnie thought. *Gadi's the only one who may still be able to stop it.*

Chapter 42

New York, October 29, 2013, 10:12 AM

The Chinese man listened to the voice on the other end of the line. When he hung up, he already knew precisely what he should do. Someone by the name of Brian, apparently a TDO employee, had become a walking menace. If he finds out the local medical examiner with the backing of the police objects to the family's wishes, and refuses to release the body for burial in the hope they'd give in and agree to an autopsy, things might just get out of hand. He'd never been involved in a job that kept on getting tangled up as much as this one. What does this Brian have to look for in Philadelphia? Out of all the cops in Philadelphia, why did the case have to fall into the hands of the only detective who insists on getting to the bottom of things, and not one that simply wants to close another case?

He knew the next few days were critical. The contract would be signed this very week, then this entire TDO business would not involve him anymore. The big boss would never forgive him if the deal fell through for some reason. If he valued his life, he needed to go out to Philadelphia and eliminate the problem before it got out of hand. Roselyn's elimination would simply need to be postponed. The assassin checked his suitcase and made sure that the gun with the silencer, the sniper rifle, the passports and the counterfeit driver's licenses, as well as the twenty thousand dollars' worth of used fifty-dollar bills, were all in place. He covered the suitcase's contents with two ironed white shirts, closed the suitcase and headed out of his apartment toward the nearest subway station, while checking his smartphone for the next train leaving for Philadelphia.

Chapter 43

Roselyn opened her eyes and sat down. She hadn't showered for a day, and the wrinkled, unwashed clothes she was wearing emitted a sour smell. She couldn't recall when during the night fatigue had finally beaten fear and pushed her over the edge into a dreamless sleep.

The message she'd received from Ronnie Saar had shaken her deeply. Why did he think her life was in danger? Suddenly, she realized chances were she would pay a high price for what she'd done. Ever since she had run away to Las Vegas, she had avoided reading the news. She wanted to maintain the illusion that her only crime had been rescheduling an operation for someone who really needed it. After all, the scary man had promised her that in a few months she would be able to return home and continue with her life. After she'd almost been run over, and especially after receiving that message from Ronnie Saar, she had realized she must be involved in a much bigger affair. She opened her laptop and Googled "Mount Sinai, Abraham Berkowitz." The short item that appeared on her computer screen left her in a state of shock. "It is with great sorrow that we announce the untimely death of our dear husband, father and brother, Abraham. May his soul rest in peace. The Berkowitz family." She stared at the obituary for a few long minutes then began to type on the keyboard furiously, praying she would find additional information proving the relationship between the two names was merely coincidental. "Our reporter learned that yesterday, at noontime, Mr. Abraham Berkowitz, a father of five from Brooklyn, died on the operating table at Mount Sinai Hospital. Mr. Berkowitz was undergoing a standard orthopedic operation, and there is suspicion that his death resulted from the use of a medicine that was still in the experimental stage. The hospital's response to this death could not be obtained, and it is still unknown whether Mr. Berkowitz had been warned the experimental medicine would be used during the operation."

A father of five!!! What have I done? She shuddered uncontrollably. She left the bed and began to pack her suitcase. Suddenly, she stopped and slowly slid down until she sat on the floor, knees bent, back against the wall. *Who am I kidding? I can't go back. I can't even get out of the hotel with a suitcase. I'm being followed. He'll kill my grandmother. Maybe he'll kill me first.* She sat in front of the computer. Ronnie's Facebook page wasn't very impressive. It included a little bit of background information, a few photos, in which the same gorgeous woman always appeared by his side, and many greetings for Jewish holidays and Israel's Independence Day. *He's Israeli, then. What did he have to do with this entire business?* She quickly typed his name in the search engine. The dozens of articles that filled the screen left her thrilled.

She began to read with interest and when she was done she remained seated, allowing the new information to sink in.

It appeared she had no choice but to trust him. *I don't know anyone else who'd be willing to help me, and he's also wealthy and connected enough to manage it. The big question is how can I get out of here without being caught? And what's to guarantee I won't get arrested the moment I show up in New York? And how will I make sure no harm will come to my grandmother?* The questions kept running around in her head along with the realization she mustn't act hastily. She took off her clothes, stood beneath the spray of hot water in the shower, and scrubbed off the malodorous scents of yesterday. When she was done, she dressed and went down to the fast-food place across the street. Perhaps because it was already late in the morning, or because of the overwhelming smell of grease, the place was completely empty. She sat in a corner booth, her back to the wall, her eyes returning to the entrance door with apprehension. Then she opened her laptop and, as usual, searched for new tourist information websites about Guatemala. She selected an article that appeared in the forty-fifth place of the search results, copied a selection and published it as a personal post on her Facebook page. *I need to maintain my daily routine, just in case I am being followed*, she thought, as a waitress with blond hair and dark roots placed a plate before her with a two-egg omelet and a pile of greasy potatoes. Roselyn attacked the food and five minutes later found herself hungrily examining an empty plate. She signaled the waitress she was interested in a cup of coffee and an additional bread basket. Meanwhile, she went to the Gmail website and opened a new account under the name gphm@gmail.com — the name she'd found to be most appropriate for the purpose for which she'd opened the account. The second cup of coffee was quickly drained, and the waitress slowly wandered over to pour her another one. Roselyn began to write the email to Ronnie. She deleted and revised the message again and again until she was pleased with the result. Finally, she read the email for the last time, closed her eyes as if waiting for a sign, and clicked the cursor that lay waiting on the oblong "send" button, hoping she wasn't signing her own death warrant. When she received confirmation the message had been sent, she deleted all traces of the activities she'd performed in the past two hours and turned off the computer. She stood up, waited for a long minute, then walked on trembling legs toward the cash register and paid for the meal. On her way out she threw a weak smile toward the waitress and stuffed a fifty-dollar bill in her hand. As the door was closing behind her, she heard the surprised waitress shout, "Thanks, sweetheart!"

I hope the money will help you. Looks like pretty soon it won't do me any good, she thought as she headed out to aimlessly wander in the clothing stores.

Chapter 44

As soon as he neared the orthopedics department's reception desk, Gadi recognized Moses from the photo Ronnie had sent him just a few hours ago. The man stood in the corridor speaking with one of the doctors. Brian was nowhere to be seen. Gadi decided to explore the rooms, when suddenly the door of the laundry storage room to his left opened and a nurse carrying a large pile of clean sheets emerged from it. He smiled and hurried to hold the door for her. She offered him an appreciative smile and briskly marched down the corridor. Gadi quickly slipped into the storage room. Among syringes, sheets and adult diapers lay a pile of folded orderly uniforms. He hurried to put a pale-blue uniform gown on over his clothes and slipped back out of the storage room. His new attire and Hispanic features had immediately made him invisible.

After despairing of finding Brian in the patient rooms, he took a chance and pushed his head through the open door of the doctors' on-call room. Moses was sitting there, continuing his conversation with the same doctor, but there was still no trace of Brian. The hands of the giant wall clock in front of the nurses station showed the time to be one fifteen. He only had one last place to check: the cafeteria. He took the elevator down to the ground floor and followed his nose to the cafeteria. *Bingo!* Brian was sitting at the far end of the hall, speaking intimately with one of the female doctors. Gadi sat at a nearby table and followed their conversation, which was interrupted, from time to time, by her shy bursts of laughter. The phone buzzed in Gadi's pocket. He pulled it out and read the message from his American partner: Brian Campbell is staying at the Independent Hotel room 205. 1234 Locust Street, about a quarter of a mile from the hospital. A short time later, Brian finished his date and accompanied the doctor on her way back to the department. Gadi followed them into the elevator. To his surprise, they pushed the basement-level button. Gadi crossed his hands behind his back, as if he intended to go there as well. The two gave him a quick look and he lowered his eyes. The elevator reached the basement, and Gadi got out after them and turned in the opposite direction.

"Can I help you?" the doctor addressed him in an authoritative voice.

The doors closed and the elevator began its trip back up. Gadi looked at the doctor with a bewildered glance and quickly said, "I'm sorry, I guess I got confused. I didn't see the elevator was going down," and pressed the call button.

"I guess you couldn't possibly have come to pick up any patients from here…" The doctor gave a critical look at Gadi's orderly uniform. Then she turned around and marched on, holding Brian's hand, toward metal doors on which the word "Morgue" was displayed.

Gadi remained standing in the elevator niche, following Brian and the doctor with his eyes. The doctor punched the entry code, but when the morgue doors opened, she stopped Brian with an open palm, preventing him from coming inside with her. It was apparent that Brian was disappointed. He tried to convince her to allow him to join her, but all his attempts were in vain and encountered a stubborn refusal.

The elevator arrived. Gadi gave the two another glance, and when he saw they were still busy arguing, he returned to the alcove, reached into the elevator, pressed the second floor button and went back out into the hall, sending the elevator up without him.

From his hiding place, he could see that the argument had settled down in the meantime. Brian had given up. He wrote something on a piece of paper as the doctor dictated then leaned toward her and kissed her briefly on her cheek. When the automatic doors of the morgue reopened, he patted her arm goodbye and turned toward the elevator.

"Still here?" he asked with wonder when he saw Gadi standing there, waiting. Gadi shrugged submissively and looked at the elevator door that had just opened. He moved aside a bit, clearing the way for Brian, then followed him inside. When they reached the lobby, they both stepped out of the elevator, and Brian turned toward the hospital exit. Gadi waited for a few people to walk between them before following him. Outside the hospital premises, he removed the orderly's gown, folded it and slung it carelessly over his shoulder. It appeared that Brian was walking to the parking lot. Gadi crossed the street and went down the stairs toward his car. He paid the outrageous parking fee and hurried to drive toward the exit. A minute later, he saw Brian driving out of the parking lot as well. He let Brian pass then followed him. After less than a mile, Brian signaled and turned into a hotel parking lot. They were at the Independent, which Gadi had learned about in the text message. Gadi waited in his vehicle for a while then entered the hotel lobby. He managed to see Brian stepping into the elevator as he turned to the reception desk.

"A room for the night, second floor, please."

"Room 203 is available. Enjoy your stay, Mr. Abutbul." The efficient desk clerk swiped Gadi's credit card and handed him a magnetic key-card.

"Thanks," Gadi muttered when out of the corner of his eye, he saw a figure hiding in the corner of the lobby.

The man with the oriental features was dressed in a long coat; a pair of jeans poked out from beneath. What had drawn Gadi's eye was the slight sparkle that twinkled on the ring on his right hand. He ignored the man's presence and walked slowly, looking at the phone in his hand. With relaxed movements, he sat on an available sofa in the lobby and sent Ronnie a message:

I found Brian. The Chinese dude is also here.

Where are you? Are they together?

At the hotel where Brian is staying. I don't think they're together. The scumbag is stalking him in the lobby.

What do you intend to do?

I want you to call Brian. I'm sending you the hotel telephone number. He's in room 207. Don't tell him what this is about but convince him to open the door for me.

Done.

Gadi pretended to still be exchanging text messages, writing and deleting imaginary messages, until a real one from Ronnie came in:

He doesn't understand what's going on. I think he suspects me of something. Be gentle with him.

"Gentleness is my middle name..." Gadi muttered to himself, rose, took out the key-card to his room and walked toward the elevators. The Chinese man didn't move.

He gently knocked on Brian's door. The security chain rattled, the door opened a tiny crack and Brian's head peeked out.

"Are you?...the orderly?" Brian gave him a confused look.

"I'm not an orderly. I'm a friend of Ronnie's. Please open the door, before someone sees us together."

The confusion on Brian's face transformed into fear. He continued to stare at Gadi, until finally he closed the door, released the chain and opened it with renewed apprehension. He stepped aside for Gadi, who walked toward the large bed that filled almost the entire room and sat on it.

"I don't know if I speak the Boston dialect, so I'll try to explain myself as quickly and clearly as possible. I assume you're confused and don't know who you can really trust. The good news is, that if I were one of the bad guys, you'd probably be dead by now." Brian's face went pale. "But I'm one of the good guys. Ronnie thinks you're one of us too. But he's basically the only one. Other people believe you've done some horrible things...Now tell me, what are you doing here, and why did you try to get into the morgue?"

"Who are you?"

An impatient look flashed across Gadi's face. "My name's Gadi. Ronnie sent me to help you. I don't intend to say it again. Now tell me what you're looking for."

Brian shrunk a bit and sank into the only armchair in the room. After some hesitation, he leaned forward and began to speak. "I believe both deaths were murder. I don't have any other way to explain what happened." He looked at Gadi, who gazed at him indifferently. "I happened to learn from Moses that contrary to what we'd thought until today, a persistent coroner is still trying to convince the family of the deceased to allow an autopsy and, therefore, refuses to release the body for burial. I decided this is my chance to prove all my claims. I intend to try and draw some fluids from the body and prove the presence of toxins in the tissue. I contacted a pathologist and hoped she'd allow me to go into the morgue with her..." Brian took out a large syringe from his pocket and waved it around, as if to prove he'd spoken the truth.

"That's your brilliant plan? And what would you do with those fluids?" Gadi scorched him with his look.

Brian ignored his skeptical tone. It seemed that speaking about his plan had infused him with strength. The color returned to his face and his voice became more assured. "I found a private laboratory that agreed to provide initial test results within twenty-four hours. They promised to maintain complete secrecy, no matter what the results were. I intend to try and get in the morgue overnight. I memorized the access code the pathologist punched in. She also gave me her telephone number, so if I fail tonight, I could still try something out with her tomorrow."

Gadi sent him an appreciative smile. *Not only is he a handsome devil, he's pretty brave and smart to boot. Should I tell him about the killer lurking for him outside, or will he be paralyzed by the revelation?*

"OK. This sounds like a solid foundation for a plan. But God is in the details. So is the devil, by the way. Assuming you're right, and we're dealing with murder here, we need to assume other people are involved, and we have no idea who they are or whether they've already found out what you're up to. I'm here to guarantee your safety. In my day-to-day life, I manage a VIP security company; I'm considered one of the best in the world," lied Gadi, sending Brian a reassuring look. "In order for me to ensure no harm comes to you, you need to do exactly what I tell you to. And when I say exactly, I mean exactly. Not almost or approximately. If you stick to what I tell you to do, you'll be safer than the president of your country. Agreed?"

Brian nodded in agreement, and it appeared to Gadi he was beginning to trust him.

"Now let's move to my room — they won't be able to find you there — before we head out this evening to perform your 'vampire mission.'" Gadi opened the door carefully and peeked outside. "Come on," he said and pulled Brian after him. They crossed the corridor quickly and less than a minute later were in Gadi's room.

When the door closed behind them, Gadi sat Brian down and began to describe the plan that'd begun to form in his mind. When he finished, he forced Brian to repeat and memorize all the little details, and once he was satisfied with the results, he lay back on the sofa and said, "I haven't slept for two days. Wake me up at eight. Till then, don't leave the room. You can turn up the television as loud as you like; nothing disturbs my sleep." Then he closed his eyes and fell asleep immediately.

It was seven fifty when Gadi opened his eyes. He went into the bathroom, took a quick shower, put on dark clothes and came out. "Are you ready?" he asked Brian.

Brian nodded, finding it difficult to conceal the doubts that had trickled into his mind with every hour that'd passed.

"Wonderful!" Gadi clapped him on the back with exaggerated force, startling him into action. "I'm going downstairs. As soon as I make sure everything is all right, I'll text you a message, and from there you know exactly what to do. Ready?"

Brian gave him a forced smile. "Ready."

Gadi headed down to the hotel lobby and stood in front of the reception desk to return his key-card, while his eyes quickly scanned the area. The thug was standing close to the place he'd seen him last time. *A real professional with endless patience*, thought Gadi, *our plan had better be successful, otherwise...* While walking toward the parking lot, he sent Brian a message to come out of the room. He started his car and left the door open with his left foot dangling out. Brian was on his way to his own car when the Chinese man emerged from the hotel entrance, threw a quick look at Brian and hurried to get into a gray Ford Focus. Out on the road, Gadi's car passed Brian, who was purposely driving slowly. The next stage was the most dangerous, the only moment in which Brian would be alone and unprotected. It was a gamble, but a calculated one. Gadi stopped at the hospital entrance and ran inside wearing the pale-blue orderly's uniform. Over his shoulder, he was pleased to see Brian parking his vehicle in front of a fire hydrant and hurrying into the building as well. The Focus driver, who arrived just a few seconds after him, deliberated for a moment before leaving his vehicle in a no-parking zone and hastening toward the entrance Gadi had gone in.

By the time Brian's tail entered the hospital, Gadi and Brian were already on their way to the elevator. Gadi stood in the open elevator door keeping the door open, delaying Brian's entry. When he was certain the pursuer had noticed Brian, they both stepped into the elevator, which began to descend. He knew as soon as it stopped, the Chinese man would read the floor number Brian had headed to and would rush after him.

The elevator doors opened and they went out into the corridor.

"It's dark as death here." Brian chuckled in a desperate attempt to ease his fears. His eyes scoured the area with apprehension. Only the light of a red bulb, hanging above the morgue door, hinted the way to his destination. The rest of the corridor was shrouded in utter darkness.

"Get going. Remember, I'm right behind you, even if you can't see me." Gadi took off the uniform and stuffed it into the nearest trash can. Then he turned in the opposite direction and whispered, "Good luck." Brian looked back, but Gadi had already been absorbed by the darkness.

Brian walked toward the morgue door, repeating the secret entry code in his mind again and again. When he reached the heavy doors, he pressed his ear against them and waited. *Not a living soul inside*, he thought, enjoying his clever choice of words. A moment later, he began to punch in the entry code. The elevator door opened behind him, and the assassin silently emerged from within, a gun in his hand. The morgue's electric doors began to move slowly, the sound of the hinges blocking the almost inaudible "poof" the silencer produced as the deadly bullet was fired.

Chapter 45

New York, October 30, 2013, 8:30 AM

When Ronnie entered the conference room, Henry, David and Jim were already waiting for him. He apologized for the slight delay and placed the three copies of the acquisition contract on the table, ready for signing. Satisfied grins appeared on everyone's faces, and the atmosphere at once turned relaxed and congenial. Ronnie began, "As you know, yesterday we were able to iron out the final details of the TDO acquisition agreement and I have in my possession a signature sheet with the names of all the other investors in the company, authorizing the four of us to sign the contract on their behalf. I've scheduled an afternoon appointment with the investment bankers, and once we deliver them the signed documents, they will transfer the payment to our escrow account."

Ronnie made a slight pause, drank from the water glass in front of him and ignored the expectant looks of all present.

"Before we sign, I'd like to say a few words. I wouldn't be telling you anything new, if I told you we wouldn't be sitting here if not for the two tragic events that we experienced during the final two operations — incidents that pulled the rug out from under our feet and blackened TDO's reputation, turning it into a company that didn't stand a chance to raise money from venture capital funds. Throughout the process,

I've felt the sour taste of disappointment, which I know you've all felt as well. I know I've lost my temper more than once and insulted some of you. I'd like to ask for your forgiveness." Ronnie smiled toward Henry and David, who returned conciliatory nods. "But what I'd like to stress the most is that we wouldn't have reached this happy day without Jim's active involvement."

Henry gave Jim a pat on the back in appreciation, as the latter couldn't conceal his pride.

"In a consultation with the fund's attorneys, they pointed out that even though the contract we'll soon be signing has a clause that releases the investors and the company from any future claims, this clause is not legally binding unless it is signed in good faith. Therefore, they've recommended we formally discuss the subject before signing and create an ordered protocol to properly protect ourselves. I suggest we have this discussion now, and I'll distribute the protocol at a later time. It won't take long, but it's an important step—"

"Ronnie, we all agree the company didn't commit any crimes. I suggest we postpone this discussion, sign now and prepare the protocol later," Henry cut him off and looked around the table, as if seeking everyone else's approval.

"Of course, I agree with you regarding the innocence of the company, but I ask you to give me five minutes of your time, if only so we can provide honest testimony, if this ever reaches a court of law. Is that too much to ask, Henry?"

"All right. Just keep it brief, please."

"Thanks, Henry. I don't know why Christian killed himself and probably never will. The subject of the patients who died remains shrouded in mystery as well. True, we've discovered one of them had had his surgery rescheduled at the last minute, but the clerk who scheduled the surgery, switching it with another patient's, disappeared without a trace. Why were the dates switched? I can only assume that as one of the patients was a member of the Amish community, which opposes postmortem operations, there was a need for another patient whose family would object to an autopsy as well—"

"Ronnie," Henry cut him off again, "in the type of discussion you'd like us to have here, it's important to try and avoid guesses and theories and stick to the facts. Let's finish up quickly, sign the contracts, and then you can tell whoever's interested everything that's preying on you." The rest of the people in the conference room nodded their approval.

"You're right, Henry," Ronnie answered. "So let's talk about what I do know. Someone broke my leg on purpose. The man was Chinese. I saw him at the hotel where Christian died as well. Yesterday, I came across the following item which appeared in some of the Philadelphia newspapers." Ronnie took copies he'd printed off the internet and handed them to his colleagues in the room.

"The body of a Chinese male, about forty-five, has been found dead at the Thomas Jefferson University Hospital morgue in Philadelphia. The cause of death was determined to be a gunshot to the back of the neck. The hospital has no explanation as to how the body reached that location. Anyone who's able to identify the deceased is urged to contact the police." At the bottom of the message was a photo that had obviously been retouched to make it appropriate for publication.

"This is the Chinese man who broke my leg. What was he doing in the Philadelphia hospital? Perhaps one of you might know?" Ronnie gave Henry an inquisitive stare.

"Are you out of your mind? Your racist insinuation that because we're both of Chinese descent I had anything to do with this and sent someone to break your leg is infuriating and inappropriate." Henry turned red, snatched the folders and began to flip through them nervously. "Just tell me where to sign and let us be finished with this sad joke."

"The other question that bothered me was how could someone have managed to sabotage the medicine and who would have the knowledge to do so?" Ronnie ignored Henry.

"Enough," Henry shouted and pointed a warning finger at Ronnie. "I don't understand your outrageous behavior, Ronnie."

The door opened and Gadi entered the room. "Good morning," he addressed the group; they just stared at him in confusion.

"Who are you and how'd you get in here?" Henry shouted. "Someone please call the police."

"What makes you think the police are not already here?" asked Ronnie in a calm voice. Utter silence fell on the room. Henry and David sat stone-like in their places, expressionless.

"May I continue?" Ronnie's eyes wandered over the attendees. "As mentioned, the question that kept eating at me was who would be able to exchange the medicine, and who would have the know-how and the opportunity to do so. I must admit, I was convinced, more than once, that Christian was the one behind the sabotage. I thought that once he'd realized the severity of his actions and that there was no way for him to correct his error, he decided to commit suicide. Nevertheless, another question has been gnawing at me: What could have been Christian's motive to ruin the company he'd built with his own hands? Does anyone have any ideas?"

The room remained silent.

"Then, Jim opened my eyes," Ronnie continued, giving Jim a reassuring smile. "Christian was not the only person who had access to the medicine or the knowledge to change it. Jim, would you tell everyone your theory?"

Jim shifted in his chair uncomfortably. "It's just a theory. I don't want to defame a man without proof. I'd rather not talk about it."

"I'd rather you *do* talk about it. We're all family here. You didn't have a problem sharing your suspicions with me, why would you feel uncomfortable telling them to Henry and David..."

Jim turned his head toward Gadi.

Gadi smiled. "That's all right, I'm one of the good guys."

Jim shifted in his chair uncomfortably and began to speak, "The medicine's quality control process requires each handling to be done in the presence of at least two people. I've recently discovered that Christian used to give Brian, the man appointed to supervise the Mount Sinai clinical trial, the keys to the safe, so he'd take the medicine out by himself. Brian had also been responsible for the medicine from the moment it left our laboratory until the medicine vials were opened in the operating rooms. This gave Brian countless opportunities to 'take care' of the medicine—"

"And why would he do something like that?" Henry interrupted.

"I suppose someone had paid him a lot of money," Jim hurried to answer.

"Who?"

"I don't know. Perhaps a competitor..." Jim squirmed. "It's just a theory."

"So you're claiming he damaged the medicine while it was still in the company laboratories?" Ronnie persisted.

"Maybe, or maybe just in the hospital. After all, the doctors had no way of knowing whether he'd already treated the medicine. They let the fox guard the henhouse."

"And how was he able to do this simultaneously in New York and Philadelphia?" Ronnie asked, wide-eyed.

"Perhaps he had a partner. I don't know. All I know is that without telling anyone, Brian has been in Philadelphia for the past two days, roaming around in the hospital. If I had to guess what he was doing there, I'd say he's trying to hide evidence." Jim turned toward Gadi. "And perhaps the police should really handle this."

"Thank you, Jim." Ronnie moved the conversation forward. "Does anyone have any more questions for Jim?"

"Where's this Brian now?" David asked quietly.

Gadi went to the door and opened it. Brian entered the room and sat down.

"Everyone, this is Brian," said Ronnie. "The distinguished gentleman who opened the door for him found him in the hospital and arranged for his arrival. But let's continue. Brian, some of the people present in the room suspect that you're the one who caused the deaths of the two patients. Would you like to respond to that?"

Brian looked around him, considering his words. "I'm very relieved that you've finally realized this is about murder—"

"How dare you speak that way?" Henry screamed. "There isn't a single piece of evidence to support what you say. There were no autopsies; the two patients were buried. I suggest you don't throw around accusations of murder, unless you also intend to confess to your crimes."

Brian searched his bag, took out a three-page document and placed it by his side. "I broke the law. I admit it. And I know I'll pay for it. But I had no choice."

"Why did you murder them, and how can you be so indifferent while admitting to it?" asked David, his face pale and his hands trembling.

"I never said I murdered anyone." Brian narrowed his eyes at him. "Contrary to what you were all thinking, only one of the victims has been buried. Samuel Yoder, the patient who died at Jefferson University Hospital, is still in the morgue. The local police are trying to convince the family to agree to a postmortem. I decided on my own to break into that morgue and take a tissue sample from the body. I don't exactly know how to pronounce all the exact terminology, but this document is a report produced by a private laboratory confirming that the sample I gave them contains a toxic substance known to be slow acting. That would explain why the operations had been underway almost an hour before the patients died."

"You're claiming someone injected the patients with a toxic material during the operation?" Jim wasn't able to hide the ridicule in his voice. "In two separate hospitals at the same time? Well, come on…"

"That isn't what I'm claiming. I agree with you, Jim, that the only way to pull this off would have been to insert the poison in the medicine before it left the company grounds."

"It's impossible to add any substances to the medicine" — Jim scornfully waved off Brian's explanation — "unless you did it after the medicine left the—"

"Why do you think it's impossible?" Ronnie interrupted.

"Because before we package the medicine, we weigh it and recheck it. From that moment on, the medicine is in the safe. Before we send it to the hospital, we weigh it again. No one would be able to add even a drop into the vial without it being discovered. In addition, any attempt to tamper with the vial covers would've been discovered because the covers are breakable and wrapped with a sensitive material bearing Christian's or my signature. I personally checked the vials before they left the company offices. I even took photos of them, as the protocol requires, and I'm willing to swear they were both intact."

"But just a few minutes ago, you explained to us that it had to have been Brian who sabotaged the medicine because he had access to the safe."

Fear and embarrassment mixed on Jim's face.

"Brian, I understand you took a photo of the medicine vial before it was taken into the operating room. Would you please show us the photo?" Ronnie continued, without waiting for Jim's reaction.

Brian took his cell phone from his pocket, brought up the photo of the vial on the screen and handed it to Ronnie.

Ronnie passed the photo among all the people present in the conference room and finally handed it to Jim. "Jim, would you please explain to us the nature of the defenses preventing the forgery of the vial?" he asked in a low voice.

Jim turned the screen toward those present, and said with evident reluctance, "As you can see, the vial is covered by a delicate material bearing my signature. Any attempt to mishandle the cover would blow the casing like a popped balloon. This prevents anyone from injecting materials into the vial or secretly drawing some medicine from it," Jim finished his explanation.

"Impressive," said Ronnie. "I assume there are more safety measures on the vial. Would you show them to us again? Unlike Henry, I've never had the chance to see them."

"There aren't many. The main mechanism to prevent forgery is the sticker, which is also below the casing. The sticker provides the vial its identity. For example, here you can read the number describing the batch and the specific vial number. But why are you asking me all this?"

"Because you're the CEO and CTO of the company and the only one in this room who truly understands the details. Would you please read the number and explain what it represents?"

Gadi got closer and looked at the vial from up close as well. Jim shot him a hostile look and continued with evident contempt, "The first six digits — 070613 — describe the production date, which is also the last date on which we produced the medicine. The next two digits represent the batch. In this case, the number is 01 because in this lot we produced only a single batch."

Ronnie raised the bottle and looked at it with indifference. "And what does the serial number signify, and why is it so long?"

"Ah" — Jim waved off the question — "it's just a random number provided for each bottle by a computerized system, called a numerator. This is common practice among pharmaceutical manufacturers. The number is long and meaningless. You know, no company would want its competitors to know the exact number of units it manufactures."

"So how do you know how many vials were produced in each batch? I suppose it's an important number, at least for organizational purposes, financial reports and so on?"

"The numerator itself does the counting. According to the production and the batch date, it adds up the total production numbers and sends the information to the company's enterprise resource planning — ERP — and accounting systems. Everything is done automatically."

"Thank you, Jim. I see that your signature is on the sticker as well. Why is that?"

"It is part of the company's strict procedure. Once the medicine was checked and before it was packaged, I signed to confirm the quality assurance tests had been properly conducted."

"So it seems there was no way to tamper with the medicine in the factory," Ronnie summed up, and everyone emitted a sigh of relief and reached their hands toward the binders in order to sign the contract.

"Before we sign, just one last little thing," Ronnie added, much to the dissatisfaction of Jim, Henry and David. "I've been bothered by two things ever since the surgical deaths. The first is how, from an eight-unit batch, only two vials were involved in death cases—"

"We've decided they were not implicated in the deaths." He was interrupted as they all started to lose their patience.

"That's right," answered Ronnie evenly, "but two days ago, I logged in to the company's ERP system and found out the numerator had reported the production of ten units in the batch we're examining. But Christian reported to me in our last meeting that only eight had been produced. Jim had also reported to me that no medicine vials remained in the safe, other than the six empty vials from previous trials. To prove his claim, he'd also sent me a photo of the bottles in the safe. So why did the numerator report ten units? There was another thing that subconsciously kept bothering me, but I wasn't quite able to grasp, until yesterday, when I suddenly realized what I'd found so disturbing. It happened when my friend Gadi, the man standing in front of you here, enlarged the photo Jim had so generously sent me, and turned my attention to the fact that on each of the stickers both Christian's and Jim's signatures appear, and only the vial photographed by Brian at Mount Sinai bears a single signature, Jim's. From there, the road leading to the realization Jim had created two poisoned vials, while destroying the originals, was a short one—"

"Nonsense. And you don't represent any law enforcement agency!" Jim tried to rise from his chair, but Gadi forcefully shoved him back down.

"Perhaps he doesn't, but I sure as hell do." Bukowski entered the room. "Jim Belafonte, you're under arrest for the murders of Samuel Yoder and Abraham Berkowitz. You have the right to remain silent. Anything you say can and will be used against you in a court of law."

Epilogue

Newark, November 8, 2013, 8:30 PM

Ronnie and Gadi were sprawled on spacious sofas in the United Airlines business class lounge. Three glasses of beer and a bowl of peanuts were on the table in front of them. They were on their way to Israel and waiting for a flight leaving at ten forty PM. Gadi's available arm was around the shoulders of a beautiful dark-skinned woman he wouldn't stop kissing, ignoring all the other passengers in the lounge. Even the casual onlooker could have no doubt he was in love. Ronnie looked at them and smiled.

"What are you smiling about, dumbass?" Gadi pretended to be upset.

"I never thought you'd be in love enough to buy a girl a business class ticket." Ronnie tried to maintain a serious expression.

"Never gonna happen. I bought *both* my tickets with your credit card. I thought you owed me at least that. Don't even think about complaining, because I couldn't care less what you think. By the way, I bought a third ticket for her." Gadi waved toward Liah, who was walking toward them. "I told her *you* asked her to join us. Of course, you can always tell her I lied. On the other hand, this could be a pretty good opportunity for you to grow up and admit how desperately you've missed her." He rose and embraced Liah, kissing both her cheeks noisily. "Liah, I'd like you to meet Juanita. Juanita, sweetheart, this is Liah, the love of Ronnie's life," Gadi introduced the two women to each other, a sly, satisfied smile on his face.

Liah took a quick look around, and when she saw the only available seat was next to Ronnie, she sat beside him carefully, making sure she wasn't touching him.

"Come, let's grab us something a little stronger than beer," Gadi said to his new girlfriend in Spanish, lifting her from her seat while hugging her hips, and dragging her after him to the lounge bar.

Ronnie and Liah remained seated, avoiding each other's eyes. After a long and embarrassing moment, Ronnie turned to her and quietly said, "I'm glad you're joining us. How are you feeling?"

"Sad. Very sad. Sad for the misery that I've caused you. Sad for the way I've messed up my life again. Sad for the fact I'm going back to Israel for good, without the man I hoped would one day be my husband."

"What do you mean going back to Israel for good?"

"I finished my studies. I've been approved for an internship in Israel and accepted at Kaplan Hospital. I'm starting next week. I'm going to spend the next year in Israel, then, God only knows."

"And you never thought..." Ronnie stopped and grew silent.

"No, Ronnie, I never thought of asking you. I didn't want to add to your misery. I realized I needed to respect your decision to sever all contact."

Ronnie allowed his hand to search for hers until he finally found it. She raised her head and met his eyes. They both froze for a moment, then she drew nearer and rested her head on his chest.

"Good thing I'm heading back to Israel myself. We'll have all the time in the world to examine our relationship," he whispered in her ear, feeling her palms tightening.

Liah drew away from him, questioning him with her eyes. "What about your job? After all you've been through, you're just going to walk away?"

"I already have. The same day word of my resignation spread, I received four tempting job offers, including one from Accord, but I rejected them all. At the moment, I feel like I need time to reorganize the priorities in my life. For starters, I bought a villa in my kibbutz's expansion area. Perhaps I paid a bit above the market value, but it was important for me to go back and live among the people I love most."

"But why? You've never been one to give up so easily, especially after what I heard from Gadi about the TDO affair ending so well."

"You don't know all the details. It turns out, the Chinese guy who broke my leg, the same one who so generously let you take the cab, had also threatened the life of David's wife. David was the one who'd been pressuring the investors to sell their holdings contrary to reason. He was also the one who'd systematically pitted Henry against me, under various obscure pretenses. After everything blew up in his face, David broke down, admitted his actions and resigned from managing the fund. Henry was elected by the other partners to take his place. As you know, Henry and I don't really get along. He asked me to stay, but I refused."

"You don't need to love someone in order to work with him."

"True, but you need to respect him. And I can't respect a man who conceals information from company reports, not to mention that he's a compulsive gambler. He confessed to the other partners and swore never to repeat his foolish behavior. They've all chosen to believe him, perhaps because they realized they wouldn't be able to raise money for another fund without him and a failure would cost them a lot of money. Money, as I've learned the hard way, has a tendency to bend a lot of people's principles. Not for me. To their credit, they were decent enough to leave me with my shares in the fund. I didn't say no to that. Even my principles have their limits." A tiny smile sprouted on his lips.

At the other end of the room, three young men began to cheer together about something. One of them read something off his laptop to his friends, and the three reacted with rowdy joy. Their happiness was natural and enviable. Liah sighed and turned back to look at Ronnie.

"When they offered you the chairmanship of TDO, did they know it was about to collapse?"

"They didn't. That was just a coincidence. I really matched David's vision of the buildup of the fund. He knew Henry was very attached to TDO and was afraid he'd change his mind and decide not to transfer the company to me at the last moment. That's why he forged my signature on the paperwork. After he had sent the paperwork, he informed Henry that I was already listed as chairman in the company's directors registry and claimed that if we changed it again, it might hurt the company's reputation."

"What are you two so serious about?" Gadi cut off their conversation. "Well, at least you're talking. What are you having? The barman will do anything for Juanita."

"Well, I do feel like having a gin and tonic. Get Liah…" Ronnie turned his gaze to her.

"Plain tonic water," said Liah and got back to Ronnie.

"And what was the turning point that helped you to understand what'd happened in the hospitals?"

"It wasn't just one point, but rather several things that I was finally able to piece together to form a clear picture. The first was the letter you left in my room, which made me realize for the first time that whoever treated the medicine needed to have in-depth knowledge about its chemistry. Only Christian and Jim had that kind of knowledge. Your hint about the numerator sank in only later. To be honest, I didn't even know what a numerator was. But when I happened to run across the word in one of the company reports, it set my warning bells off, and when I delved into it, I discovered more vials had been produced than were listed on the clinical trial reports. Furthermore, throughout that period, I'd been receiving confusing text messages. Only when I realized the anonymous sender was trying to protect the fund and its employees did I recognize that one of the messages had been different and was probably sent by someone else. That somebody, so I started to suspect — was Jim.

"The breakthrough took place after Gadi found out the signatures on the older vials were different from the ones on the last two. When I learned that, I realized Jim was behind it all. My only problem was proving a motive. The motive was revealed when I managed to contact Roselyn, the clerk who'd switched the operations at Mount Sinai. Only after Bukowski, the FBI agent, promised her immunity — and, if need be, joining a witness protection program — did she agree to come back to New York, accompanied by agents. The testimony she provided cleared both me and the company of all suspicions. Furthermore, based on the extortion methods applied to pressure Roselyn, the FBI has no doubt a criminal organization was behind the entire plot. An organization that was probably interested in using TDO for money laundering then selling the company at a profit. In a conversation the FBI had with Mentor's CEO, he broke down and admitted he'd been pressured too and was forced to back out of the deal. He gave them a description of the person who'd threatened his life, an exact match to the one Roselyn and I gave them, a description of the Chinese man. It was clear to me that I couldn't possibly sell the company, but I needed to put on a show, pretending I was about to sign the contract, in order to make Jim confess he was the one who'd switched the medicine. It turns out the mob had promised him ten million dollars and an equal amount in company shares. The FBI found some of the money in a bank account Jim had opened solely for that purpose. Jim was a number two kind of employee throughout his professional career. He knew they'd never let him run such a company for long. This was a chance for him to prove to the world he was capable of being a good CEO who could lead a company from a crisis to success. When he broke down, he dragged the two investment bankers down with him. According to his testimony, they were the ones who'd given him his instructions all along. The FBI is still looking for them, but it looks like they've disappeared, or were made to disappear, off the face of the earth."

"And what happened to the Chinese man? Are you sure he won't come after you to make you pay for ruining his deal?"

"I'm sure. They found his body, with a little extra lead in the skull, next to the Jefferson University Hospital morgue. No one has a clue how it got there."

"Dead?"

"As dead as it gets."

"How did that happen?"

"I asked Bukowski the same question. He claims it was the work of a professional, nice and clean. No traces of what had happened were found. The FBI's working premise is that someone followed the Chinese guy in order to eliminate him and took advantage of the fact he followed Brian to a dark place. Because they have no leads to follow, the police and FBI decided to close the case."

"Gadi?"

"Gadi's a lot of things, but he's not a killer. He's also a pretty messy guy. He didn't murder the Chinese guy, just like he didn't kill your husband."

"What about Gadi? Again you're talking about me behind my back?" Gadi placed the drinks on the table in front of them.

"Did you hear they caught the drug addict who murdered my husband?" asked Liah, ignoring Gadi's remark.

"Of course I did," Ronnie and Gadi answered together.

"I need to ask for your forgiveness, Gadi. I'm sorry I suspected you."

"There's no need. I forgave you long ago. Ronnie, on the other hand, will keep paying for suspecting me for a long, long time."

"Gadi, would you excuse us for a minute, I need to discuss a few private matters with Ronnie," Liah said.

"And why would you..." Gadi began but then saw her expression. "The bar is a much happier place to be," he told Juanita, and they both left for the bar laughing.

"I also should have asked for your forgiveness long ago." Liah's voice cracked as she said it.

"Forget it. It doesn't matter. What's important is that we're together again."

"One evening, I missed you so much that I went to the hotel you were staying at. I stood outside for an hour before mustering enough courage to go inside. I saw you sitting in the lobby with a young man, Hispanic. You were both talking excitedly. You seemed so happy and relaxed, it took the wind out of my sails... I just turned around and ran away, praying you wouldn't see me."

"That was Javier Rodriguez, the son of the woman who told us about the suspicious changes in the operation dates. Thanks to her, we were able to find Roselyn. He's brilliant, her son, and I've decided to help him."

"All right. Yes. Maybe. But forget about that. There's one thing I can't figure out. Why did Christian kill himself?"

"He believed he had no choice. That was also one of Gadi's discoveries: The Chinese guy's men were the ones who'd caused the power outage at Christian's house. When his wife called to report it, she was actually speaking to his men. They'd managed to connect to her telephone line and impersonated the electric company's employees. I assume the Chinese man told Christian about it and threatened to kill his wife and twins unless he cooperated. When Christian found out, while speaking with his wife, that the thugs were at his house that very same moment, he realized he had no choice but to swallow the pills the Chinese guy had given him. We'll never know if he hoped he'd somehow manage to call for help, after his assassin left his room, or if he simply sacrificed his own life to save his family, whom he loved so dearly."

"It's frightening," Liah's voice turned hoarse, "just thinking we were in the same elevator with that cold-blooded monster! And that he attacked you, and was so close to me when I flagged the taxi..."

"It is really scary, but it's also behind us." Ronnie caressed her arm, enjoying the sensation of touching her skin again.

"So what happened with TDO in the end?"

"After it turned out, beyond any shadow of a doubt, that the company was not responsible for the tragedy of the final two operations, I went back to Accord and convinced them to invest in the company. Of course, they tried to take advantage of the situation and had a lot of special conditions, but following a brief negotiation process we signed the investment deal. Yesterday, we received the FDA's approval to continue with the clinical trials, and right after that the money was wired to the company's bank account. This morning, while preparing for this trip, I got an interesting call from Mentor's CEO, asking if we'd be willing to sell the company for one point two billion dollars. I must admit, I felt a primitive sense of satisfaction when I rejected his offer."

Liah caressed the back of Ronnie's neck, familiarizing herself anew with the rough bristles she'd always liked so much. "And who's the Latin beauty Gadi's running around with? Am I wrong, or is Gadi really in love?"

Liah's touch sent a pleasant shiver through Ronnie. "Do you remember when Gadi disappeared on us for three days? Turns out, he spent them in her bed. Wondrous are the ways of chemistry. And yes, it looks like they're head over heels in love."

"Like us?" asked Liah.

"Like we used to be. Like I hope we'll be again." Ronnie kissed her, and for the first time in a month, felt whole again.

Two hours later, as the airplane began to speed down the runway, Evelyn sat in her apartment rearranging the huge bouquet of orchids in their vase, and for the umpteenth time, rereading the note attached to it:

Thanks for all your help and the anonymous messages. Love you forever, Ray.

Acknowledgments

I would like to thank Amnon Jackont, a wonderful editor and a charming man. Each moment of our mutual work has been one of sheer pleasure.

A huge thanks to Dvora, Tal, Eilam, Liat and Or, my wonderful family members, who had to bravely suffer my ceaseless chattering about the book and were still able to find the strength to share insights and constructive revelations.

Thanks to Betty Ben Bassat, Beni Kopelovitz, Pinni Haviv, Gilad Rosenzweig, Tomer Belkind, Nurit Weis, Israel Hoyda and Pazit Amado for their willingness to serve as the first draft's "guinea pigs" and for their important contributions to the final product.

Thanks to Yaron Regev for translating my book into English and special thanks to Julie MacKenzie of Free Range Editorial, the amazing creative editor who taught me so much during our work together.

And how could I not thank my parents, Moses and Judith, of blessed memory, for planting the love of the written word within me. This book wouldn't have been written without them.

Made in the USA
Lexington, KY
10 July 2018